NOTHING TO YOU

SCARLETT FINN

Also by Scarlett Finn

GO NOVELS
GO WITH IT
GO IT ALONE
GO ALL OUT
GO ALL IN
GO FULL CIRCLE

EXILE
HIDE & SEEK
KISS CHASE

WRECK & RUIN
RUIN ME
RUIN HIM

**THE BRANDED
SERIES**
BRANDED
SCARRED
MARKED

**FORBIDDEN
PREQUEL DUET**
ALL. ONLY.
ONLY YOURS

THE FORBIDDEN NOVELS
FORBIDDEN DESIRE
FORBIDDEN WANT
FORBIDDEN WISH
FORBIDDEN NEED
FORBIDDEN BOND

**BOMBSHELLS & BILLIONAIRES
(ROXIVERSE)**
NOTHING TO HIDE
NOTHING TO LOSE
NOTHING IN BETWEEN: ONE
NOTHING TO DECLARE
NOTHING TO US
NOTHING IN BETWEEN: TWO
NOTHING TO SAY
NOTHING TO GAIN
NOTHING IN BETWEEN: THREE
NOTHING TO YOU
NOTHING TO THIS PREQUEL: ONE WILD NIGHT
NOTHING TO THIS
NOTHING IN BETWEEN: FOUR
NOTHING TO DO
NOTHING TO NO ONE
NOTHING TO FEAR
NOTHING TO DENY
NOTHING TO BEAT
NOTHING TO THE WEDDING
NOTHING TO TELL
NOTHING TO IT
NOTHING TO SEE
NOTHING TO WIN
NOTHING TO OFFER
NOTHING TO PROVE

**LOVE AGAINST THE ODDS
STANDALONE COLLECTION**
SWEET SEAS
HEIR'S AFFAIR
RESCUED
MAESTRO'S MUSE
GETTING TRICKY
THIRTEEN
REMEMBER WHEN...
RELUCTANT SUSPICION
XY FACTOR

KINDRED SERIES
RAVEN
SWALLOW
CUCKOO
SWIFT
FALCON
FINCH

MISTAKE DUET
MISTAKE ME NOT
SLEIGHT MISTAKE

LOST & FOUND
LOST
FOUND

**THE EXPLICIT
SERIES**
EXPLICIT INSTRUCTION
EXPLICIT DETAIL
EXPLICIT MEMORY

TO DIE FOR...
TO DIE FOR TRUTH
TO DIE FOR HONOR
TO DIE FOR VIRTUE
TO DIE FOR DUTY
TO DIE FOR LOVE

**RISQUÉ & HARROW
INTERTWINED**
TAKE A RISK
FIGHTING FATE
RISK IT ALL
FIGHTING BACK
GAME OF RISK

ONE

"OH MY GOD, do you even know what you're talking about?" Roux Radley asked.

Wearing a wireless headset, she strolled back and forth in front of her home desk, running a pencil through her fingers over and over.

"Do I know what I'm talking about?" his deep voice came through her earpiece.

"The whole point of this group is to debate different points of view…" another voice, the moderator, said. "Respectfully."

"Ha!" Hotshot got in before she could respond. Damn him. "Firefly doesn't do respectfully. She's loud and obnoxious—"

"And right every time," she said, triumphant.

Hotshot snatched the victory. "Thus, I rest my case."

"No," she said, shaking her head, her speed increasing. "Thus nothing. You don't. If I'm loud and obnoxious, you're brash and arrogant. You never rest your case—you go on and on and—"

"Please," the moderator cut in. "Huddle rules are specific. There can be no name calling or bullying."

"He started it."

"I'm afraid I'll have to finish it by ejecting both of you from the group."

"But I—"

Dead silence betrayed it was done. No arguments allowed. It wasn't the first time. On a sigh, she tossed her pencil to the desk and went into the kitchen to retrieve fruit from the freezer. Definitely time for a treat.

Huddle was a sort of social media site. Sort of because it was like all of them and none of them. Profile pages didn't exist. You were your handle on Huddle. Your handle and your level. Nothing else. No one came from anywhere or had any family… that the group at large knew.

The network consisted of temporary booths. Each one had a tier number, a color, and a topic. The tier and color of the limited time booths were determined by algorithms and employees based on their divisiveness. Users could pop in, join the conversation, and zip out whenever they wanted.

Booths were rooms, groups, where people got together to voice chat. No one had a face. No video allowed. Audio only. A user leveled up depending on their platform history. The higher their level, the higher tier booth they could participate in.

An actual human approved and monitored every member. They limited new admittance each week so the humans at the Huddle end could keep an eye on their charges.

Being disruptive or bullying at a lower level would get a member banned, which meant they never got a chance at the higher, more contentious, levels.

At level one, you got to join the most benign chambers. Like "Who doesn't like puppies?" And "Air is good." That last one quickly got boosted to a higher tier after the debates on climate change took over. Talk about a raucous.

Being ejected from a chat could get someone dropped a level, but the human involvement at Huddle kept a close check on users. Spot checks happened regularly. Twenty-four, seven. Huddle employees could be listening at any time. She should know. She was one.

Cutting up strawberries, she tossed them into the blender, popping the odd half between her lips.

A Huddle ring came through her headphone.

"Huddle, answer," she said into the microphone.

"Been a while since that happened."

She smiled. "It was your fault."

"Want to find another fight?"

"Not tonight," she said. "How'd the date with Red Shoes go?"

"Wasn't a date," he said. "How's Darts Man doing? Break his heart yet?"

"They all have their hearts broken eventually."

"Did you bring him home?"

"I never bring men home."

"Distance from the crime scene. Smart."

"Crime scene?"

"Your kind rips a guy's head off after sex. Don't worry, I won't turn you in. You're way too entertaining."

She sucked the juice from her fingers. "Are you asking me for personal information, Hotshot?"

He groaned. "You're making daiquiris."

Sometimes his perceptiveness freaked her out. "How do you know that?"

She hadn't started the blender yet.

"The strawberry juice on your fingers."

"Sometimes I think you're a stalker."

But her blinds were shut and the desk on the wall by her bedroom door faced out into the room. No cameras on her.

"To stalk you, I'd have to know your name, or what country you live in."

"It's against Huddle rules to pressure a user for personal information."

"Who's pressuring?" he asked and exhaled. "There's a high chance I'll have to have sex this weekend."

"Don't pretend you're not a player," she said, collecting the rest of her ingredients. "You always do this, pretend you're not smooth as silk or like dating is a chore. You're gun-shy and I get why."

"Can we not talk about Diva tonight?"

"You haven't talked about her for a while. You know how I feel about you repressing stuff."

"I told you months ago, Diva's out of my life."

"The break-up took its toll. And your feelings—"

"Babe, enough. Mix your daiquiri. Get some alcohol flowing through those veins."

She put the lid on and did as he said.

When it was done, she retrieved a glass. "It messes with my head."

"Relationships? I know. Don't worry, you have to find me before you can jump me."

"In your dreams," she said, pouring her drink. "I can't believe you got anyone to sleep with you. Was she drunk? Like just completely shit-faced? Did you blackmail her into bed?"

He laughed. "If she was drunk, I'd have made a sharp exit before we got to the bed… If I'd known what was good for me."

"Men usually don't when it comes to hot women and sex," she said, taking her drink to the couch. "You don't regret the entire relationship."

"Put the lid back on and put the rest in the

fridge."

Rolling her eyes, she set the glass on the coffee table and went back to do just that. "You didn't hear me licking my fingers that time."

"No, but how many times have I heard you complain about losing another daiquiri or two because you didn't refrigerate?"

"You know you don't have to remember everything ever."

Smug satisfaction bled from his words. "You're lucky to have me as a friend."

"Talking to you is part of my private research into the less fortunate," she said because teasing was their way. "Are you on tomorrow?"

"Same time every day. You're away this weekend?"

"Well remembered," she said, because her work weekend hadn't come up for like a month. "Thursday through Tuesday, but I'll try to be on at our usual time."

"You could stay home."

She smiled. "Could I?"

After talking to each other basically every day for over a year, the missed days were significant. Neither of them would admit it, but without their daily vent, their playtime, other areas of their lives suffered.

"Stay home and we'll moderate: do snitches really get stitches?"

"Not bad," she said, returning to her couch and the drink. "You know when we moderate no one gets a word in."

"You haven't noticed no one gets a word in anyway? No one else worth listening to."

"Who are you kidding? You don't listen to anyone. Haven't you noticed you're always the one in the wrong?"

"Oh, am I?"

"Yes," she asserted, her lips curling again. "You're a chauvinistic bigot."

"You're a dandelion snowflake."

"You don't know how to be in the world."

"My world's just fine, sweetheart. Yours is the one with the problem."

"Only when men like you open their mouths."

"You're too sensitive, Babycakes. You need a man looking after you. A real man."

Gritting her teeth, she didn't know whether to laugh or throttle him. "So not you then."

"Baby, there are not enough hours in the day for me to treat you like you deserve."

Ah, triumph. "Couldn't have said it better."

"Didn't mean that as a compliment," he said.

"You never do, Hotshot. God forbid you say something nice."

"I like you better when you're drinking."

"I know you do," she said, picking up the TV remote control. "Want to watch a movie?"

After a user reached level twenty, Huddle allowed one-on-one chat. Even then, the line would drop out after an hour. They knew to wait the required seven minutes, then whoever didn't make the first call would call the other back.

"Something gory?" he asked.

"You hate horror movies."

"Yeah, but I like it when you get scared. You know, weak and in need of my protection."

"If I was being chased by a homicidal maniac, you'd be more likely to trip me than help me." She smiled while scrolling through the options. "What about something romantic?"

"You hate chick flicks."

"You know we'll go back and forth and wind up on action. Just pick something so I can start it and get off this call faster. And don't say *Die Hard*. We've watched it like fifteen times this month."

"It's a classic."

"So is *Snow White* and you never choose that."

"She lives with seven men. It's pornography in disguise. The animators were a step away from drawing pedophilia in action."

"Shh!" she said, stretching her legs along the couch. "How many times have I told you to avoid using keywords?"

"This would be a lot easier if you'd just give me your number… and send me a picture. You don't even have to get dressed, I'm low maintenance, I'll take just your boobs."

"And now if our Huddle monitors are listening, they know you're pressuring me."

"No pressure," Hotshot said to any ears that may be listening.

"I know you're joking. They don't. One or both of us gets kicked, that's it. Bye-bye, double act." She sipped her daiquiri and selected *Die Hard* on mute. "I'll give you one trivial, if you hurry up and pick the movie."

"One trivial? Is it my birthday?"

"Tick tock, Hotshot."

"What are you wearing?"

Seriously? That was his question? Again?

She groaned. "That's always your first trivial question. You should learn to mix it up. Shorts and a tank."

"And you should try harder to tantalize me. Either it's hot where you are or it's night. Is it dark outside?"

"That's not trivial. What's the movie?"

"*Die Hard,*" he said.

"Oh, wow, what a surprise," she said, unmuting the TV. "Are you going to quote the whole thing again?"

"Until you learn it word for word, yes."

"Ready?"

"You know I don't have to be watching it, I can just play it in my head."

"If you're not watching, I'm hanging up."

"I'm watching. I'm watching, geez, Firefly. Thought your period didn't start until next week."

Hilarious? Nope, but she'd rise above it. Hotshot needed to work on his act.

Anonymity was their shield. They knew so many intimate details of each other and so few big things. They'd never exchanged names, numbers, addresses, yet she knew he wore silk boxers and drank his coffee black. Even their respective time zones were a mystery.

How had it started? Completely by accident. After facing off with him in half a dozen booths, Roux hosted her own, and, of course, he crashed. It wasn't really crashing, anyone could join, but whatever.

By the end of that session, they were the only two left. From then on, they met every day, sometimes for a few minutes, sometimes the whole night. They always met at the same time her booth had started that fateful night. They'd met by accident. Though, if she believed in it, fate could've been at play.

"Shut up," she said. "The movie's about to—"

But he was already quoting the lines as the characters delivered them on the TV. Voices and everything. Yep, he was that guy. What a goof. Whoever he was, he'd made her life better. How had she survived without him?

TWO

"EVERYONE TAKE A pack, take a pen." Helena went down the line, handing the compiled dossier to each member of their team. "This is it. Everyone's chance at a big break. We only get one opportunity to pitch this, people. One and done."

Maybe, but they also weren't the only ones pitching.

The Huddle Conference was the highlight of their corporate calendar. It was a chance to exchange ideas. Talk of advancements. Learn about the future.

This year was special. Very special. Huddle was owned by a larger firm. As was, let's face it, just about every company these days.

Their parent corporation, Mosaic, wanted something new from Huddle. A side mission or greater purpose for the brand. Hoping for an innovative new perspective, they'd thrown open the doors to their employees. "*You know it best, be inspired*," kind of thing. They dubbed it the See It Through campaign. Not only were they accepting ideas from employees, but Huddle would also set those responsible for the chosen idea up in Mosaic's California base to see the proposal through to fruition and beyond.

If it bombed, they'd be there to see it too. Which wouldn't be so good. High stakes, high rewards.

At least sixty different groups were pitching through the weekend. Their spot happened to be on the Thursday, the first official day of the Huddle Conference. The pitches had begun the previous day and would keep on going until the end of the event on Tuesday.

Top candidates would be whittled down to a short list and undergo private interviews at the infamous Mosaic HQ in California until one group came out on top. They'd then be invited to nurture, develop, and build their idea into a reality, basing themselves in MHQ.

She had faith in their idea. A lot of faith. Did that mean they'd emerge the victors? No, it didn't. Success hinged on the panel getting the concept and being ready to take a risk. A big risk.

Still, as her teammates went to their corners to review the presentation again, she was optimistic.

"Roux," Helena said, approaching before she could go anywhere.

Having read their pitch fifty thousand times and being instrumental in its creation, she didn't need to go over it again. What did Helena want?

Didn't take long for the woman to get to the point.

"Don't get argumentative," Helena said, touching the diamond on her necklace. "If you feel the urge to butt in or disagree, contain it. Resist. Smile."

Their two colleagues, supposed to be reading the pitch, would no doubt be eavesdropping. Some people loved the drama.

"Are you giving this advice to everyone?" Roux

asked, aware of the answer.

Helena folded her arms. "You know you can be a hothead."

Affront opened her mouth. "Excuse me?"

"You can't be argumentative today. This is our one chance. Our only chance. Don't mess this up for the whole team."

Anyone from the Huddle hierarchy could form a group and pitch an idea. Nothing was too whacky. Nothing off the table. Theirs would be one of the riskiest ventures. That might disqualify them immediately. Did the Mosaic higher-ups have the balls to gamble on Huddle Hope?

Maybe not. If the panel, whoever they were, had questions or talked out of their asses, she'd put them straight. Yes, it was a hazardous area, but it would be worth it for those helped in the long run. Their concept was about more than money or commercial success, it was about social care and corporate responsibility.

"I wouldn't be here if I didn't want this to work out for us," she said, offended and pissed off in equal measure.

Helena thought if they screwed up their pitch, it would be on her?

"We'll be dealing with serious people. This isn't like talking back to Mr. Terence."

She scowled. "I don't talk back to…" It didn't take more than a head tilt for her to concede. "Okay, but I judge people. Like not in a bad way, I take them in, judge their character, and get a feel for their limits."

"By pushing the boundaries," Helena said. "You push people."

"If I'm so volatile, why did you want me on the team?"

Helena glanced at each of the guys.

Franco answered. "It was your idea."

"And you can talk to people," Helena said. "You're articulate."

"Yeah, you're bold," Myles said, eyes wide. "You're like…"

"I'm like what?" she asked, her fist rising to her hip as she swayed a quarter turn to take in her cohorts. "Is this a coup?" Okay, so it wasn't like she was in charge. "Or an intervention?"

Maybe both.

"And…" Franco paused, then exhaled. "No one thought he would be here."

Helena raised a hand. "It's an unsubstantiated rumor."

"Wow, unsubstantiated rumor. Juicy. Share."

"No, it's… it's not important."

"Xavien Rourke is here," Myles said, somehow sounding both thrilled and terrified simultaneously.

Mosaic bigwig. The guy in charge behind the curtain, conjuring his spells of success. He'd likely be too busy with some strategy to increase his fortune to even know the Huddle Conference was on.

She could've laughed. "Xavien Rourke is not here. He doesn't give a shit about Huddle."

"He's a hardass. No room for error. No sense of humor."

"Guess that's how you become a billionaire," she said. "You're afraid I'm going to piss this guy off?"

"If he is here, there's no indication he'll be in the pitch meeting," Helena said. "He's a busy man who wouldn't have time to—"

The door opened, a long-legged blonde came in.

"Team Hope. You're up."

THREE

SO THE UNSUBSTANTIATED rumor? Totally true. When they shuffled into the presentation room, four stony faces behind a long table awaited them. They weren't the only ones.

In the background, near a door at the rear of the room, someone stood next to the tall window that would overlook the exterior courtyard. She couldn't see out, just knew the layout of the building.

His height. Shit, he had to be six four. The certainty of his stance, broad, proud, entitled… it added up. All of them hesitated at the sight of him. Damn. Maybe she would fuck this up.

With his hands clasped at his back, he turned, slow, yet there was something severe in the action. Even laid-back he looked mean, unimpressed, eager to throw them off their game.

But, seriously, forgetting the hardass stuff and the asshole reputation, the man was hot. Seriously hot. Way hotter in real life than on the internet.

Most billionaires weren't necessarily celebrities,

and he was no exception. The concession that meant his picture was much more available online? His relationships with the world's sexiest supermodels. Damn lucky women. Somewhere at some time, she'd read he only dated models. Exclusively. If they hadn't walked in Paris or graced the pages of *Vogue Italia*, he couldn't even get a semi. Okay, so she added that last detail. Maybe he could get hard for lowly, regular women, but why bother with the exertion when the alternative with sex on legs, little conversation required.

They got set up, as fast as they could, in case the time ate into their designated pitch minutes. Then, almost too quickly, she was front and center, ready to get things going.

The lights went off, then two flashed in their direction. Spotlights. As though they were about to perform Shakespeare or something. A small red dot between the heads of two of the panel suggested they were being recorded too. Hmm, whatever happened would be documented for posterity. Great. No big deal. Just don't fuck this up.

She took a calming breath and spoke, wearing a smile. "Huddle Hope," Roux said to the four table people, choosing to ignore the loaded hottie in the shadows behind them. "I bet you've had all kinds of flashy, fun ideas tossed at you over the last two days. What we have for you is something different."

Deciphering audience reactions wasn't easy while caught in the dazzle of the lights. Their presentation glowed from the wall between her flanking colleagues.

"What's the challenge?" she asked, broadening her smile. "Most people start with the positives, right? That's the thing about Huddle Hope; it's almost all positive. We only have twenty minutes to impress you, and the positives speak for themselves."

"Regulation. That's our challenge," Helena said,

coming to her side. "Huddle Hope will require regulation. Negotiating what's best for our clients will be extremely important. It lays a great responsibility at Huddle's feet, but it's one we can handle."

"Too often, corporations shy from social responsibility," Franco said as the women stepped out of the path of the screen. "Huddle Hope will embrace that responsibility."

"Our users have proved they accept the gravity of their words and actions. We're there for our people for debate and for the good times. But not so much for bad times."

"On numerous occasions, Huddle has experienced users reaching out to the service, to others when they are in need," she said. "We have no provision for handling this officially… until now." Their placeholder logo appeared on the screen. "We want to create a safe place to support those in need. Initially, we would pilot a befriending service. A buddying system. Something for those who need support. Moving up to group sessions. Therapy. A secure environment to talk about more difficult issues."

"Mental health."

"Trauma."

"Domestic abuse."

"Any number of issues that we can form a network of support around."

"It will not be a substitute for appropriate medical or other professional help. Though we would prefer our structure involve a foundation of appropriately trained professionals. And we shouldn't branch into uncertain areas. We must take advice at every stage…"

"Let us show you our vision," Helena said, stepping into the spotlight.

Her boss glittered. Roux could be charming… in

the right light. She could be unpredictable too. Volatile. She got that she wasn't everyone's favorite cookie, but her great rack excused many sins.

The panel consisted of two men and two women. Equal opportunities. Would that work? Franco did okay with the ladies. She wasn't sizing up the panel's sexual preferences. It was just a fact that people were nicer to people they liked. They weren't exactly getting a great opportunity to project their personalities. If the panel liked the pitch of twenty different groups, they'd use non-pitch reasoning to narrow down the candidates to a shortlist.

Helena was good at this. Excellent. Even she was enthralled by the speech. Franco did the technical stuff with the presentation. Helena's honeyed tones tempted; at least that was the hope.

The woman could dazzle with charisma. Thank God someone could. Maybe she was a hothead. No. Yeah. She was a hothead.

Helena was so good that she almost missed her cue.

Standing perpendicular to the presentation, only the peripheral view of the final slide prompted her to talk.

"We have a great passion for this project," she said, covering for her almost slip. "We welcome questions and are willing to work hard. Very hard. For this worthy cause."

"Your cost projections are conservative."

A chill went down her spine. That didn't come from anyone at the table.

"We took median figures," Franco said, clearing his throat. "But vastly overestimated our contingency, aware that the budget has to be realistic."

"It's lazy accounting." Okay, what was going on? That was Mr. Loaded Dude at the back. Had to be. "I want accurate figures."

Was that a…?

Franco was a whisper away from pulling at his collar. "We can…" another throat clear, "I can tidy that up. Get more accurate numbers."

"We're nowhere near financial scrutiny," one guy at the table said and twisted to look over the back of his chair.

So Table Guy wasn't interested. Loaded Dude was. Good. If they were going to get anyone on board, the higher up the ladder, the better.

"I can't assess the proposals without an accurate forecast."

"You are not assessing anything," Table Guy said to the boss man. "This is not your duty. Delegation. It's what you're good at. This is not my first rodeo. Just trust me, would you?"

The brow raise was subtle; she only just caught it as she turned to disconnect the laptop.

"Yippee-ki-yay."

She stopped. Everything went completely on pause.

"Okay," someone at the table said. "Thank you for your presentation. Someone will get back to you."

She knew it was someone at that table because it wasn't that voice. That voice…

Hotshot's voice.

Spinning on the spot, mouth open, she fixated on him and damn, he was looking right back, right into her. Fuck.

Did he know? Of course he had to know. A guy like him had access to everything. Like everything. Shit. What had she told him? So much more than she'd ever tell a guy in real life. That was what made him different, safe, they'd never have to look each other in the eye. Except they did because… they were doing it right then.

"Thank you very much for your time," Helena said. "All of you. It's appreciated and a great pleasure to be before such instrumental players in the Mosaic machine. It's an honor."

A few beats of nothing passed.

Someone grabbed her arm to pull her toward the door.

Don't be a hothead. Stay quiet. Stay calm. Say nothing. Walk out. Just turn and walk out the door. Don't wreck their chances.

Fuck their chances.

She snatched her arm away from the tugging hand. "You have some nerve," she said, narrowing her focus on Hotshot. "Some real fucking nerve."

"Language," he drawled. "Watch your keywords."

"Miss Radley..." Table Guy said but was ignored.

"You don't have any idea what decency is, do you?" she demanded, marching closer to the table, still fixated on Hotshot. "What choice is. What fairness is."

"I'm so sorry, I don't know what's gotten into her," Helena was saying in the background. "Roux!"

But she couldn't take her eyes off the smug smirk at the back of the room. "You couldn't keep away, you just couldn't even... do you know the damage you've caused?"

"Roux!" Helena chastised her as the men from her group hissed too, desperately trying to silence her. It was too late for that. Way too late. "What is the matter with you?"

"He is the matter with me. Him. There..." she said, pointing. "And look, he doesn't have a damn thing to say for himself. He knows what he's done. He knows he's wrecked everything. He knows it. But he stands there smirking, like he's not the biggest asshole the company's ever seen! The company? The country! The world!"

"I'm so sorry. So, so sorry."

"He's not sorry," she said, glaring. "No, Mr. Bigshot doesn't have to be sorry, he owns huge chunks of the world."

"If I own it, shouldn't I have the final word on how it's run?"

"No. No, you shouldn't. It's called free will, and it's not your right to take it away."

"My right to keep mine."

"I'm not so sure," she said, a hand landing on her hip. "It's clear you can't be trusted with it."

"Just as you cannot be trusted with discretion."

"Oh, I'm discreet, Hotshot. I'm discreet over the whole damn place."

"Miss Radley…"

Someone stepped into her line of sight, blocking her view. He wasn't the only one nearby. The panel and her own people surrounded her.

"Okay," she said, holding up her hands in surrender. "Okay, I'll take a breather." Turning around, she started out within the tight cordon formed by her vigilant colleagues. "This isn't over!"

"You see me walking away?" he called back.

She slowed, intending to about-face, ready to pick up that gauntlet. Her damned teammates literally tore her from the room and down the corridor to the lobby. They pushed her forward and spun her as Helena began her tirade.

"The man asked a question! And he was right," Helena said, whirling on Franco. "I told you to get those numbers cleaned up weeks ago. Take Myles, go upstairs and get it done. I don't want to see either of you until those numbers are blindingly shiny." The guys shuffled off, in a hurry to comply. "And you…" Helena was on her again and sighed. "Go up to your room. I don't want to see you again. Full stop. Stay in your room until it's time to fly home."

"What? But I—"

"I can't guarantee you still have a job after speaking to him that way. Don't interact with anyone else. No one. Now, go. Go on. Go!"

Marching away from her boss, seeking the elevator, one thing was for goddamn sure: she would never talk to Hotshot again. Maybe she would lose her job, but at that minute, she wasn't even sure she wanted it.

FOUR

CAGED IN THE COMPANY-supplied hotel room, her aggravation only grew. The standard room with its queen-sized bed, tiny closet, and claustrophobic walls stifled her.

Who the fuck did he think he was? Her relationship with Hotshot was on Huddle. Only on Huddle. What possessed him to change that? How long had he known who she was? He owned the company. Would have access to employee records, her personnel file. Everything.

Maybe if she could go for a walk… Eat. Drink. Breathe before she screamed. Frustration scalded her insides. She wanted to pound the walls and stamp her feet. How could he have ruined everything?

Obsessing wouldn't get her anywhere. She needed a distraction. Sitting on the bed, she yanked her purse toward her.

Usually, if she had time in the day or needed a distraction, she'd go trawling to see what Huddle trouble might be around. Some limited capacity booths were visible in advance. Users could reserve their spot to guarantee it. Contemplating how each debate may go gave her something to look forward to. Not anymore. Her safe space wasn't so safe anymore.

Retrieving her phone from her purse didn't help her mood. Notifications. Huddle notifications. From him.

Two missed calls and a Huddle message.

HOTSHOT: NOTHING?

Yep, that was it. Nothing. Except he'd done something. And she was supposed to just let that go?

The door beeped. It sounded like the door. Did Helena have a key?

Leaping from the bed, she got one step before it opened and who came storming in? Hotshot himself.

"Who the hell do you think you are?" she demanded as he stalked toward her.

"You know damn well who I am."

When he got closer, she backed up into the open space by the bed. "I know you're an asshole! What gives you the right to unilaterally—"

"Free will, Babycakes."

What an asshole!

She whirled around to find him five feet away. "What we had worked, and you decided to change it!"

"Yeah, I did!"

"How long have you known? Was it all some big joke to you? Bet you got a real laugh!"

Four feet. "I didn't have a damn clue until you opened your mouth downstairs!"

"Yeah, right!"

"Yeah, you told me you were Huddle. I knew you had a pitch for the conference—"

"I told you I had a work weekend, and you never thought to tell me you'd be here too?"

Three feet. "I wasn't supposed to be here! I was never meant to hear the pitches!"

"And you just happened to stroll into mine? What a miraculous coincidence."

"I knew you'd be in one of them, and if I could figure you out—"

"See!" Two feet. "You were here for me!"

"Did you hear me denying it?" A foot. "Yeah, I am here for you. So the fuck what?"

"No swearing."

Another step. "We're not in a Huddle booth now, Radley."

No booth meant no rules, no boundaries. How had they got closer? So close she could feel the huff of his shallow breaths fogging her hair. The heat of those dark eyes narrowed on her. Hotshot. Holy fuck, Hotshot was right in front of her.

"No."

"I can do whatever the fuck I want," he snapped.

"No rules?"

"None."

"Freedom, huh? What you going to do with it, Mr. Bigshot?"

Their mouths clashed. Frantic. Angry. Charged. Lunging forward and down, he scooped her off the floor to rush her against the wall. Her back hit hard, but she didn't care about tomorrow's bruises. Panting breaths. Heat. Aggravation. Passion. Her arms were already around his neck, coiling around his head, forcing his kiss deeper as she pushed his invading tongue back. Their mouths had fought for months, over a year, they were old friends, old enemies.

The bastard wasn't going to win. Wasn't going to dominate. Not her. Fighting back was her style. And not just in debate.

Slanting her mouth, she tasted more, taking what she wanted. Needling. Baiting. Goading. He wanted this. Wanted her. Did he think she'd just surrender?

Toeing off her shoes, the ferocious kiss fueled a burning need that wouldn't be satisfied by this feeble effort. The searing desire had to be quenched. To be fulfilled. Shoving his jacket from his shoulders, her message spurred him to spin away from the wall, knocking over the nightstand lamp as he dropped them onto the bed.

His palm skimmed her outer thigh, ascending to push her skirt up, caressing all the way to her hip. Damn, he was good. Zinging needles of aching need followed those fingertips until his lips diverted her focus by trailing down her throat. Her rebellious body arched against his domineering force. Fuck him. Fuck. Fuck. Shit.

Control, she needed it, and he wouldn't expect timid. Screw that. Somehow, she found his tie and wrapped it round and round her knuckles to pull him up again. Her mouth wanted his, wanted more of what he'd started. He didn't resist but fought for dominance.

No, she wouldn't. Give in to him? Play it meek? Did he remember who she was? She wasn't one of his weak starlets. Wasn't a woman who needed to be taken care of or given handouts. She'd take anything, any way she wanted it.

Just as quick as he gave his kiss, he snatched it away. Planting his hands on the bed on either side of her head, he stared down at her. Not mad. Not arrogant. Not teasing or... The genuine shock blazing from him kicked hers into gear.

What the hell were they doing? The chance of salvaging their friendship would drop to nil if they got physical... more physical.

Her jaw moved because it felt like she should say something, but… what? Ask him to leave? Demand he leave? Apologize?

Boosting himself from above her, he didn't linger and went for the door. She was still lying on the bed when it closed. Hotshot… What the hell was that?

FIVE

THE NEXT TIME the door opened, she was the one with the handle. Someone had knocked. Again, she expected Helena. Instead, it was Franco. Suited, looking dapper.

She smiled at his slow perusal of her body.

"Wow, and I thought I'd need to persuade you," he said.

"Why would I miss the welcome dinner?" she asked, stroking her hair from behind to bring it forward over her shoulder.

"Helena said she told you to stay put."

"Mm," Roux said, stepping back to showcase the long sparkling dress with spaghetti straps and a wide slit that showed off her leg, all the way to her hip. "I spent a fortune on this dress. Do you think it should stay in the closet?"

Smiling, he offered his crooked elbow. She slipped her keycard into her clutch and closed the clasp before taking his arm.

They started down the hallway.

"You look incredible," Franco said. "You're the

hottest woman in our department, maybe the building…" They stopped at the elevator; she pressed the call button. "You know, you'll laugh, but…"

When he didn't continue, she sought his gaze. "But what?"

"I promised myself if you broke up with Joyner…" He cleared his throat. "I'd ask you out." She smiled. "Stupid, right?"

"I broke up with Greg four months ago."

"I know," he said on a sheepish laugh. "Making a promise isn't as easy as keeping it."

The elevator doors opened. "Story of my life, Franco."

They went inside and selected the ballroom floor. "You're the most intimidating woman I've ever met," he said. "Most guys I know are terrified to talk to you."

"I'm not intimidating," she said, then thought about it. "Am I?"

"You're independent."

"A lot of women are independent."

"You're opinionated."

"Most women have opinions too," she said, touching the long diamond earring dangling from its hook in her ear. "Is there something wrong with women forming their own opinions?"

"No," he said hurriedly. "Nothing at all. You just… express them… vehemently."

"Hmm," she said, taking his elbow when the doors opened to let them out. "Do you know where our table is?"

The ballroom was directly opposite the elevators. Suited attendants stood by the wide, open doors. The scope of the place was impressive. A glittering chandelier hung over the dozens of tables beneath. A podium in front of the small symphonic band suggested someone was going to speak at some point.

Champagne was offered at the door. She took a flute and let Franco worry about them finding their table. If they wandered around long enough, Helena would catch sight of her and make herself known.

Sure enough, just as Franco found purpose, someone rose in her eyeline. Helena. Her escort let go of her not long before they got there. He wouldn't want to be blamed for tempting her out of her room. What Helena didn't know was that she'd never intended to stay put. Cowering wasn't her style.

"I thought I told you to stay in your room," Helena leaned in to hiss when she sat.

"I apologize," she said to the table. "To everyone… for my behavior at the pitch."

"Guess we shouldn't have expected you to keep a lid on it," Myles said. "You were super passionate about Huddle Hope."

"I *am* passionate about it," she said. "I don't think of it in the past tense."

"Do you think we still have a chance?"

"No," Helena said. "Not after the way she laid into Xavien Rourke."

"The guy on the panel said Rourke wasn't assessing anything," Myles said. "Maybe he wouldn't—"

"It might have helped if the figures were rock solid," Helena said, glaring at Franco. "Did you fix them?"

"Yeah, I… I'll sleep on it and go over them again tomorrow."

"I can't find any way to submit additional materials," Helena said. "I tried to ask about it, but everyone else handed out their packs at the pitch. We don't get a second shot."

She could get additional materials to the panel. Through Hotshot. Rourke, is that how she was supposed to think of him? Xavien. It was too weird. And that kiss.

What was that about? He'd just kissed her. Boom. Taken charge and… Helena was still talking; servers were somewhere in her periphery passing out plates. Her fingers ran through the loose curls of her hair on her shoulder.

Meeting him. Kissing him. It was still processing. Getting ready for dinner had given her a distraction, something to take her mind off him.

After that weekend, if he stuck around for the conference, they'd have no reason to talk to each other again. The safety of what they'd been was gone. Their security. Their carefully crafted personas, hidden in a digital world, had been blasted to shit. God knew what the guy was really like. Sure, she'd figured Hotshot was no slouch, he'd told her he had a business. Mosaic was more than just a simple business. It was a massive multinational with interests in many industries. Huddle was just a tiny piece of the man's overall empire.

Empire. Hotshot had an empire. Was successful. Rich. Powerful. A model dater… What the hell was he doing hanging out with her night after night on Huddle?

They got through dinner. She didn't say much. The guys talked about their figures and got excited about the possibility of reaching the next stage. Helena wasn't optimistic.

Huddle Hope meant something to her. Yet the idea of moving to California wasn't as appealing now knowing Hotshot lived there. Overbearing, infuriating, rude Hotshot.

Her clutch vibrated on her lap.

Helena was again talking about how they'd lost their chance. She switched off and opened her clutch to check the screen.

HOTSHOT: EXCUSE YOURSELF.

What a dick. Did he think giving orders would be endearing? At least now she understood why he was so goddamn arrogant.

Ignoring the message, she slipped her phone back into her clutch and picked up her wine. Downing the last of it, she didn't hesitate to pick up the bottle and refill it.

"We worked for months on this," Helena said. "All that work's just disappeared because Roux couldn't keep her mouth shut."

"You've said that," Roux said. "Repeatedly." Helena was a grade above her, technically her superior, but she wasn't a supervisor. "I said sorry. What else is there to say?"

"This was a massive opportunity. We could've been catapulted to… We could've been successful. Lived the LA life!"

"Mosaic isn't based in LA," she said.

That was true. Why were they in LA for the conference? Wasn't it just a big inconvenience for the executives to travel south for the party? Maybe they needed the separation to drag themselves away from the office.

Another vibration. She slid her phone from the clutch just enough to read her Huddle messages.

HOTSHOT: COME OUTSIDE.

Apparently, this guy didn't take no for an answer. Why was he so persistent? They couldn't hang out in public. Couldn't hang out at all.

HOTSHOT: THE TERRACE DOORS IN THE BAR ARE OPEN. WALK OUT AND DOWN THE STAIRS.

Was it his compulsion to treat people like idiots? Just because she didn't follow his instructions didn't mean she didn't understand them. They were clear. Unlike his reason for breaking what had been working for them.

More wine. That would help.

HOTSHOT: YOU GOING TO MAKE ME COME GET YOU?

Blackmail? Really. If she didn't leave, he'd come in and get her. What gave him the right? Someone needed to set this guy straight. Somewhere along the way, he'd confused her for a pushover.

Her glass was still in her hand when she stood up. She gulped half of its contents, then put the rest down. Her colleagues could wonder. With the adrenaline amping her, she couldn't make polite excuses.

The bar was by the entrance; she'd seen it as they came in. There were matching glass doors to the terrace from the ballroom, but they weren't open. The doors in the bar were, and it was busy enough that she doubted anyone cared who went outside.

Smokers used the beautiful deck. With dinner not long over, plenty of people were getting their nicotine hit. The glass perimeter barrier around the raised wooden terrace continued down the stairs to the path into the grounds.

A trickling fountain at the end drew her closer. Light beneath the water shone up, illuminating the pool in a sparkling glow.

"You're a cheap date, Radley."

Spinning toward the male voice, she found him seated on a carved stone bench, hidden between ten-foot hedges. The fountain didn't matter to him. The grounds didn't. The people. The party. He fixed his smirk on her and didn't flinch.

"Don't deal idle threats," she said, grabbing her dress at her thigh to hold it up as she crossed the grass.

"Never do. Never would."

She stopped in front of him. "So what was that don't make me come get you message?"

"In thirty more seconds, I would have."

"No, you wouldn't," she said. "You don't want the world to know about this. If you did, you could've posted a company memo."

"Saying what?"

"That you get your kicks arguing with subordinates. Did you talk to my boss? Ask him for all the gossip? Any rumors about me?"

"Why would I do that? You tell me shit every day."

The reminder heated her blood, though a chill crossed her shoulders. "I can't believe you're… You know, it's probably illegal… Isn't it catfishing?"

"Which in itself isn't illegal. And I didn't claim not to be me. You didn't ask."

"Why would I?" she asked, exasperated. "You've been in the perfect position to know everything about me from the beginning. I bet you stalked me, didn't you? You stalked my personnel records."

"No. You think I have time for that shit? I'm a busy man. I never looked you up."

"Yeah, right."

"Didn't need to," he said and snickered. "Why are you mad? I didn't extort or seduce you. Our friendship was mutual."

"Changing it, this, wasn't."

Resting back against the bench, he laid an arm along the cool concrete. "You going to sit down?"

"No," she said.

"Because you pace when you argue with me." He reminded her of their connection. "Walk it out, baby."

"Don't," she said, pointing at his face. "I am not arguing. We are not arguing."

"Because we'll end up making out again."

Ignoring that, she got back to her point. "You had no right to do this. No right to change everything without my consent."

"I'm your best friend, Babycakes."

Because who else did she speak to every day? Colleagues. She spoke to colleagues every day… and just hadn't known he was one of them.

"Were. You *were* my best friend."

Though it pained her to admit it.

"Still am."

"No," she said, unable to believe he could be so insensitive. No, wait, this was Hotshot. Of course he could be insensitive. Insensitive was his nature. "Friends respect each other's wishes."

"You never said we couldn't meet."

They'd never talked about it in anything other than jest. "You screwed me over. Me and my team."

"How the hell—"

"Huddle Hope's dead. We can't progress in See It Through. Our whole damn point for being here. Helena is ready to hand me my ass and when she finds out—"

"SIT isn't up to me," he said, saying each letter. "It's the panel's choice. Completely. Nothing to do with me."

"And when they figure out we know each other? You don't think your subordinates will want to impress you? Charm you by choosing your friend?"

"Not after what they saw downstairs," he said. "It's not like we get along."

"I don't even like you," she said, dropping onto the bench beside him. "You're a jerk."

"Yeah?" he said, leaning over to nudge her body with his. "You're a hothead."

"Not the first time I've been told that today… This seat is cold."

He straightened to take off his jacket. When she took her back from the rest, he swept it around her shoulders. As she threaded her arms into the sleeves, he sank into a relaxed pose with an exhale.

For a score of seconds, they sat in silence. He opened his hand, presenting it to her. Should she? This was Hotshot. Jackass extraordinaire, but her Hotshot. Slapping her palm to his, their fingers interlinked as his knuckles dropped to her thigh.

"You were never curious?"

"Never enough to hoodwink you," she said, not that it was within her power. "This was a really shitty thing to do."

"Guess I owe you… one trivial… or two."

Except their identities were no secret. Where they lived, what they looked like, it was all available now. They didn't have to restrict themselves to trivial.

Meeting. Knowing the truth of each other. It opened doors she'd never considered. They could call each other "friend." In life, in real life, they could look each other in the eye and judge veracity. Did he argue with her because he believed his position or just to be aggravating? Probably the latter. She'd been guilty of that too.

His trivial questions usually related to what she wore. Her habits. Sexual and otherwise. Typically, she'd answer without disguising being unimpressed. They played with each other. Played up qualities to provoke the counterpoint in their opponent.

"You own Huddle," she said. "You created it."

"Neither of those were questions."

"I want to know when you knew you were coming here," she said, setting her unapologetic glare on his profile. "When did you know for sure you were coming here to look for me?"

"This morning."

"Bullshit," she exclaimed, throwing his hand back to his lap, shooting to her feet. "You knew before today!"

"I talked myself into it and out of it a dozen times," he said, then frowned. "I don't apologize for who I am or the decisions I make. I came here to lay eyes on you. I came here because it wasn't enough to be in the dark anymore."

"And it didn't occur to you to talk to me about it?"

"To get your permission?" He scoffed. "No, Radley, it didn't occur to me. Shit, how can you talk to someone every day and not know them at all?"

"Me?" she yelped. "I know you. I know you all too well. I know you're arrogant. Selfish. Small-minded—"

"Intelligent. Witty. Ruthless," he said, surging to his feet in front of her. "You know who I am, Radley. You've known it since the beginning. You always knew I was capable of a move like this... I'm capable of anything when it comes to getting what I want. Now you know who I am, you can see exactly the lengths I'll go to. I succeed. When I want it, I don't stop until it's mine."

"This decision wasn't yours, Hotshot," she said, prodding his chest. "*We* decide about *our* friendship. We. Together."

"And if I'd talked to you about it, you'd have run and hid. You hid behind that screen, behind that headset, because I'm the first guy to encourage that goddamn attitude. I'm not afraid of it." He stepped closer, forcing her to crane her neck. Damn his height. "I came here to meet you. You, Roux Radley. I have never, and will never, ask you to apologize for being you. Don't ask me to do it."

She wanted to growl at him, to curse and argue, except there was a problem… he was right.

The ferocity in his gaze was just like he said, unapologetic… and something else… Fuck, he turned her on. The arrogant asshole. Overbearing. Domineering. Stimulating. Stirring. This friendship was going to be unique. He got her endorphins rushing, her temperature rising. There was need. A desire for triumph. For battle.

"So that's how this friendship works? We do whatever the hell we like whenever we like? Damn everyone else?"

"Yeah," he said. "That's it. If it feels good, we're allowed to do it."

"You're such a dick. People don't live their lives that way. People consider other people. They consider the consequences, they don't—" he grabbed her arm as she turned away. "Like that…" she pointed at his grip, secure on her arm. "People don't manhandle other people just because they want to."

"Are you afraid of me?" he asked. "Do you think I'd hurt you for kicks?"

"No," she squawked, insulted by the ridiculous suggestion. "You're an asshole. You're not an indiscriminate abuser… I don't think anyway. Though I didn't think you'd barge into my life and suit yourself, so I guess I have some things to learn."

"Oh, I harmed you?" he drawled, bowing back, letting her pace away. "You're damaged. Broken by my intrusion."

"Uh, no," she said, turning on him. "Do I seem damaged? You pissed me off—"

"How is that different from any other day?"

It wasn't. "And when you piss me off, don't I let you know it?"

"Too much."

She arched a triumphant brow. "I thought if it felt good, it's allowed."

"You know what else feels good?" he asked, marching over.

"Yes," she said, turning away with a flourish of her skirt to speak back over her shoulder. "Making a dramatic exit."

Leaving him wanting more gave her some time to get her head around their new setup. Hotshot in her life. Hotshot the hot property, hot as sin billionaire tycoon. Yeah, there was a lot to wrap her head around.

SIX

FIREFLY: I'M MEETING MY COLLEAGUES FOR BREAKFAST. STAY AWAY FROM ME.

HOTSHOT: THAT'S THE DIFFERENCE BETWEEN THE SUCCESSFUL AND THEIR MINIONS, BREAKFAST IS BROUGHT TO ME.

FIREFLY: PRIDE IS A DEADLY SIN, YOU KNOW.

HOTSHOT: DEADLY SIN IS WHAT I EAT FOR BREAKFAST, BABYCAKES. HOW DID YOU KNOW?

FIREFLY: IT'S THAT GLINT IN YOUR EYE.

HOTSHOT: GRATEFUL I BROKE THE SEAL NOW? TOLD YOU, I'M A GUY WHO GETS WHAT HE WANTS.

FIREFLY: TO A POINT.

HOTSHOT: HAVEN'T FOUND A LIMIT YET.

What a dick. Her best friend was a complete

jackass. She should cut him off cold, prove to him he had a limit, that she'd give him one. Except their game was too much fun. He enjoyed being cocky and arrogant, and she enjoyed shouting him down.

They were as bad as each other.

Entering the breakfast room, she scanned for her colleagues. It was difficult to miss Myles and Franco because they leaped up to gesture her over. Offering a brief wave, she went to pour coffee before joining them at the table.

"Where's Helena?" she asked, pulling in her chair.

Usually, Helena was prompt. A model employee. Always on time. Always impressive. Either the woman was concealing an inferiority complex, or she was eager to rush up the ladder. Back in the day, Helena would've been the teacher's pet, a role she'd never got along with herself.

Deference just wasn't in her nature. No wonder she struggled in personal relationships. They often suffered because she worked so hard to keep herself in check in professional environments. By the time she got home, she just couldn't keep it in anymore.

"We don't know," Myles said. "We went by her room; no one answered."

They went by Helena's room but not hers? Interesting.

"You don't know if she's in there or not."

"True," Franco said. "Maybe she's in trouble. Maybe she fell in the shower or something."

Was that the hope? If they had to go in and check on her, naked would probably be the guys' preference.

Sipping her coffee, she appreciated the heat of the java. "Did you try calling her?" Neither of them spoke; they just looked at each other. "I'll take that as a no." Her phone was already in her hand. She scrolled to

Helena's name and pressed call only to be greeted by a recorded message. "Hmm… voicemail." Putting her phone on the table, she looked from Myles to Franco. "Are you two on top of those numbers? Whenever she shows up, that will be her first question. You've got to give her hope."

"We were going to go over them again after breakfast," Franco said. "Do you really think there's still a chance for us on See It Through?"

"Unless we can't figure out how to give the panel more accurate numbers."

"I think until someone says otherwise, we work off the assumption there's a chance," she said, resolved not to ask Hotshot for help. "Get the numbers immaculate. Helena and I will work on getting them in front of the pertinent eyes."

She could do it without the help of Xavien Rourke. Her independence meant everything to her. She'd never relied on a guy for anything and never would.

Franco's phone rang. "Helena," he told them before answering. "Helena…? Uh huh. Yeah… They're here… Okay. Yeah." He hung up. Expectation hung between her and Myles. "She wants us to go to the room we waited in before the pitch yesterday."

Franco was quick to stand up. Myles wasn't far behind.

She took her time sampling some more coffee. "Why?"

If there were going to be revelations or disappointments, she'd need as much caffeine as possible. If something was going on, there was always the chance of Rourke being behind it. With the way he'd come into her life, he'd proved he was capable of anything.

"She didn't say," Franco said. "She wants the three of us there as fast as possible."

And from the men's actions and expressions, they were willing to follow orders.

Don't rock the boat. Be amiable. Okay, this would be tough. Maybe she should just stay silent. She almost scoffed aloud. Yeah, that was likely.

She took another couple of slugs from the mug, then got up to join them on the jaunt to the boardroom. The guys may be in a hurry, she was less dutiful.

Some part of her was skeptical. Almost expecting Rourke to appear from around any corner, she kept her wits high. What was happening? He hadn't told her to keep their friendship a secret. If she walked in there to him tossing his weight around, she'd be ready and wouldn't be shy.

The previous day, with him saying almost nothing to her, she'd been full of fire. If he actually opened his mouth, he'd get both barrels. She took no prisoners. The adrenaline high wasn't all her fault. Something about him provoked her. Not that she hadn't had cause.

Franco was the first to arrive. He hurried in with Myles close behind. The latter held the door for her, but both men fixated on Helena, seated beside a basic desk at the other side of the room.

"I was right," Helena said, dropping a pointed finger to a small stack of documents on the desk.

"Right about what?" Franco asked. "The numbers? We cleaned them up. Give us an hour, you'll see your face in them."

Another suck up. Maybe she should take lessons from those closest to her.

"We're out of See It Through," Helena said. "We won't progress any further."

"What the hell?" she said before she could think if it was smart to speak out… again. "They can't do that. They haven't heard all the pitches! If the rest of them are—"

"We've been offered a contract," Helena said, silencing her.

It was only then she noticed the glitter behind the woman's cool eyes. Whatever she was trying to conceal was right there, just behind the fragile shade.

For a moment, no one said anything. The guys were probably, like her, expecting their colleague to continue.

Myles broke first. "What kind of contract? A contract for what?"

"They want to buy the idea," Roux said, anticipating a ruthless response. "The higher-ups have decided they like it and want to cover their asses by offering us—"

"They want us to develop and institute Huddle Hope," Helena said. "Not as part of the SIT scheme, completely for real, everything all the way."

She couldn't believe it. The guys were cheering, and Helena was on her feet. They hugged and gushed, and she was just… astounded.

"What do we have to do?" Myles asked. "What's our operating budget?"

"Another team had a similar pitch," Helena said. "We've been asked to work with them on a feasibility study."

"Another team?"

"Yes, and they want us to get to work as soon as possible," Helena said. "We'll be based on the executive level of MHQ. The squeeze will be tight at first, but we'll need to keep the top brass in the loop every step of the way. We'll be working very closely with the highest level of management."

"Here?" Franco asked. "In California?"

"Yes," Helena said, dialing back a little. "We were prepared to move if we progressed in See It

Through. I told Mr. Cornish that wouldn't be a problem." Moving to the Golden State. Relocating her entire life. She'd been willing to do it before. Why did it seem like such a big step now? "We'll get a moving bonus. There are employee apartments on the Mosaic compound. It's like its own little village. We'll live there until we decide we want to get something of our own somewhere else."

"What if we don't want to move away from the Mosaic Village?"

"I don't know," Helena said, returning to lay a hand on the paperwork. "I haven't got through everything yet. They're flying in a lawyer for us… I can't believe this is… it's like a movie." She laughed then took a deep breath. "We're still employees of Huddle. So our employee contracts don't exactly change. These are just add-ons to cover what it means to work with Mosaic. We have a meeting set for tomorrow morning. If we're a go, they'll transport us to Mosaic HQ, and we'll have the weekend to settle in. Work starts Monday."

"Just like that?"

"I think so. We'll have to go home to get our things. They said someone would do that for us, but I'd rather get my own things."

Why? If it was as simple as giving someone a list, she had nothing to hide.

"This is incredible…" Myles said, falling into a nearby chair.

"He said Mr. Rourke is like this, he's a really decisive leader," Helena said. "I didn't meet him. Leon Cornish from the panel yesterday came to me. He said Mr. Rourke only takes such bold steps when he's certain. But it's a minefield of an area. That's why so many social media platforms shy away from anything like Huddle Hope. If we can crack it, with the help of this other team, we could make a big difference in millions of lives."

"He gave you the hard sell, huh?" Roux asked.

"This was your idea, Roux," Helena said, frowning. "Why aren't you jumping for joy? You didn't screw it up. Huddle Hope will happen… despite your outburst yesterday."

"Maybe because of it," Franco said. "I've heard Xavien Rourke likes passionate people."

"One thing we know for sure, Roux is passionate," Helena said on another laugh. "This is everything. For all of us. Executive level management stuff… overnight. We could never have got here with any other company or going out on our own."

She was right. The opportunity was undeniable. A new life in a new place with a new job… maybe even a raise, she'd be a fool to say no. Who would say no?

SEVEN

"NO."

"I haven't said anything yet," Hotshot's voice came through her cellphone's speaker.

"And to whatever you're going to say, I say no," she said, combing her just blow-dried hair. "I spent all afternoon yesterday with a lawyer thanks to you. Then on calls to long-haul movers. I'm moving my whole life."

"You're welcome," he said, oozing cocky condescension.

"I'm doing this because it will help a lot of people… and because I won't let my aversion to being your friend come between me and professional progress."

"You're a smart woman."

He believed he'd won. Maybe he had. What war were they fighting? At that precise moment, she didn't know exactly. But he certainly sounded sure of himself, good for him.

"Do you actually believe in the idea or are you flexing some macho misogynistic muscle?"

"Who cares?" he asked. "If you do your job right and this gets off the ground, do you think the people you help will care?"

"I won't help anyone," she said, amused by the prospect. "Of all the people in the world who someone might charge with caring for others' sensitive needs, I'd say I'm the last person on the list. No, sorry, second to last. You'd be right underneath me."

"When we got horizontal, it was the other way around," he said. "We'll see how you do taking control next time."

"There won't be a next time," she said, smoothing her flyaways with a straightening iron. "You only got so far because you took me by surprise. I was being polite."

"I have no problem scratching your itch anytime, Babycakes. This friendship needs an incentive. Keep those benefits coming. So long as you don't go getting ideas, we're good."

"Ideas?" she asked, trying to quell her outrage. "Of what exactly? Decency? Trust? Loyalty?"

"I'm all of the above, Radley, and then some. Free love and equal rights, whatever. Just know I won't be putting a ring on it."

"Mm hmm, and why exactly would I want a ring from you?"

"You're a woman," he said. "Your life's purpose is to find a guy to take care of you."

Scowling into the mirror, she kept straightening her hair. "It's a good thing you're rich. No woman would put up with you if you didn't provide her with a gold card. She'd need it to whisk herself away to some tropical paradise. Alone. Away from you at a second's notice."

"Do you know how many women have tried to tie me down? Pick a number. Doesn't matter what they start out saying, it always ends the same."

"That's the beauty of friendship, Xavien," she said, wearing a sarcastic smile. "It keeps going long after the love has faded. I'm not one of those women you pick up in a bar or pass little notes to after gym, I'm your friend. Your *best* friend. So there can be kissing and sex talk and flirtation, whatever, you're still going to pick up the phone the next day and talk to me. It's in the contract."

"We have a contract?"

She put the straightening iron on its heat mat and looked her reflection in the eye. "Yes, you changed this, Mr. Rourke, your choice. You made this real world. You found me; you're stuck with me. Isn't this what you wanted?"

"I just wanted to know if you were as hot in person as your voice suggested."

"Disappointed?"

"That I didn't cop a feel when I had a chance? Yeah, now that you mention it, I am."

Again, she frowned. "Your hand was up my skirt."

"Yeah, but the real potential's in the bra."

"You know, it doesn't surprise me you're a breast man," she said, returning to her hair. Today's style was poker straight. "Somehow you seem like the grab and grope type."

"So this contract between us…" he said, gliding right on by the accusation. "If it feels good, we do it—"

"Your clause, but what about it?"

"Yours seems to be, find reason to bitch at him as often as possible."

"No, mine is: friendship is real and permanent, whether you like it or not."

"Good call," he said. "You want to come upstairs?"

"I have a meeting with your Leon, whoever he is,

downstairs in a few minutes."

"I can tell him to be late."

The smooth transition from asshole to seductor came in the tone of his voice. It went from provocation to soft as bassy silk in a heartbeat.

"Tempting," she said without sincerity. "I think I'll leap into the fire."

"Rather than fan the flames with me?"

"It's a wonder you ever got a woman to go out with you, Hotshot."

His brief laugh tickled her. "Leon is a cool customer. He's levelheaded, no nonsense, a guy who gets things done."

"Which is why you like him."

"Which is why I like him," he agreed. "He'll be your team's point person on this. If you need anything, he has a direct line to me."

"More direct than this?" she asked, switching off the styler and running her fingers through her hair.

"Still haven't given me your phone number," he said. "You can only get me on Huddle if I'm logged in on Huddle."

They talked every night, or they had before his big reveal, through Huddle, at designated times. They didn't often talk earlier in the day. Now knowing who he was, she could understand why he couldn't hang around social media all day, every day... though he did own the site. Being logged in was his right, given he was in charge. But the guy had a business to run, several actually, he had things to get done.

"I'm sure I'll survive a day without you."

"I'm in LA through the weekend and out of state from Monday."

"Until?" Was she worried or just asking the obvious question? "Until you feel like coming back, I bet. What is it? Monaco? Yacht in the Mediterranean?"

"New York, then London. I could be back in New York for a while after, depends how negotiations go."

"Acquiring something shiny?"

"Potentially partnering with an old friend on a new deal." She didn't understand but didn't have to. "I have a dinner in Washington coming up in a couple of months, Labor Day, if you want to join me. Some people get excited about that kind of thing."

"Washington State?" she asked, wondering what took him up there.

"D.C." he said. "Your call. We'll talk about it later. There's a party in LA tomorrow night too, but you're not ready for that."

"Oh no?"

"You've got enough going on." Yeah, thanks to who? "Leon is suspicious of beautiful women, Radley. Don't be surprised if he takes a while to warm up to you."

Her smile curled slowly. "Oh, I can handle men, Hotshot, don't you worry about me."

"About you? No. Him…? I'll tell him to wear a helmet and pads."

EIGHT

"THIS IS INCREDIBLE!"

Driving past the raised barrier to enter the private complex immediately signaled they weren't in Kansas anymore. What a picture-perfect scene. Gleaming security boxes flanked three lanes of flawless tarmac that cut through greenery so lush it had to be artificial. The three lanes blended into one road that went no more than a hundred meters when it came to a fork. Two options: Mosaic to the right, Dyce Tech to the left.

They went right.

So many questions. She hadn't been on Huddle or talked to Rourke since their morning conversation the previous day. Life had been manic. And she was making a point. What point? That he wasn't as powerful or important in her life as he probably thought.

She'd survived without him before. He had to learn he was part of her life through choice, their individual choices, not necessity. It was not obligation or reliance.

The seamless asphalt sliced through the verdant

grass as they drove toward the spherical building up ahead. Yep, it was a reflective glass sphere, gorgeous, large, and completely wrong. How did it support its weight? How did they keep it from tumbling one way or the other? It shouldn't be possible, yet there it was.

Rolling by another guarded entrance, they stopped right in front of the magnificent building.

Damnit, did it have to be so impressive?

Thank God Rourke was still in LA. She shouldn't have to think about him that weekend. It would be easier to settle in if she didn't have to worry about him popping up here, there, and everywhere.

A guy opened the car door. A broad, hunky guy. Mmm, hello. As her mouth was about to introduce herself, another female voice roused the air.

"Hi, yeah, okay," the woman said, clutching a tablet, a stack of files, and a cellphone. "I'm sorry, I'm not totally organized. This happened fast." The laugh was little more than awkward, and their confusion didn't ease the little brunette's contrition. She swallowed. "So I'm Mieux, Penrose. Pronounced Mew, but not spelled that way. Mieux Penrose and… I'm here for whatever you need."

"Whatever we need," Franco said and nudged Myles, his grin bursting. "This place is amazing."

"It is, it really is amazing," Mieux said, passing the files from her tablet hand to the forearm of her cellphone hand, cradling them against her chest. "I'm not exactly qualified to give you a full history of Mosaic, but I can say you will not find Mosaic HQ lacking."

"If you're not qualified, why are you here?" Helena asked. "Don't you work here?"

"I'm on contract from the Brooker Agency," Mieux said. "I go wherever they need me. I've worked with Mosaic a few times. It's one of my favorite places to be."

"You're a temp," Helena said.

She didn't have to be so snide, did she? Why was Helena sneering at the woman there to support them?

"Something like that," Mieux said with half a shrug. Walking backward, she tried to gesture for them to follow. "As you were all, are all, Mosaic employees, your security credentials are on the system. You've been upgraded…" Even as she walked backward, the smooth glass doors inset from the exterior wall slid open. "So you're already authorized to go where you can and can't go."

"Where can we go?" Myles asked.

"Where can't we go?" was Franco's question.

"As you can see…" Mieux did her best to open her arms, "there are food and drink establishments, convenience and clothes stores. Anything you could need is available here at Mosaic. Everything on this floor is accessible to everyone. You need office supplies? Coffee at two a.m.? You can get both here." She kept on going backwards. "Gym and pool facilities are available to all. Spa and other recreational facilities too." She read the top file. "Who's Franco?"

Oops, yeah, maybe they should've introduced themselves.

Franco held up a hand to receive a file. As Mieux said each of their names, they got their own documents. Security logins, policies and procedures, employee handbook, maps of the building, the campus, the village… and a lease, hmm, interesting.

"I'll show you around down here, the different facilities we have, and then upstairs, where you'll be working. It seems overwhelming now, I know, but you have the weekend to settle in."

"Are the other team here?" Helena asked. "I'd like to meet them."

"Not yet, they are on their way though," Mieux

said. "You should be able to meet them before your flight."

Helena had elected to go home and arrange her things for the move to California. She wasn't as particular. The movers could pack her essentials. She'd brought her laptop and could get a new vibrator. What else was there to worry about?

"Have you met him?" Franco asked, stalling Mieux after one step.

"Him? Mr. Rourke?"

"Yeah," Franco said. "We haven't been introduced. We've been in the same room as him but Roux—"

"Okay, she doesn't need to hear about that," Helena said. "We have a fresh start here."

Somehow, she didn't think that was Helena's way of protecting her. No, she probably wanted everyone to forget about her fit at the pitch.

"I have met him," Mieux said. "But he meets fifty new people a day, don't be surprised if he forgets a name or sends others in his stead. Mosaic prides itself on collaborative working. It's part of their schtick, I guess you could say."

"Dyce Technologies shares the campus."

"It does," Mieux said, smile growing. "Mr. Rourke and Mr. Dyce have known each other since they were children. They share many of the same resources and often meet to brainstorm or help each other through dilemmas."

That felt a little like the brochure spiel.

"Have you met Mr. Dyce?"

"What is your obsession with who's met who?" she asked Franco. "What does it matter?"

"I want to meet them," Franco said. "Everyone wants to meet their heroes."

"Oh, God," she groaned, turning her head away.

Suck their cocks why don't you?

"They live here, right? Mr. Rourke and Mr. Dyce. Somewhere on campus?"

"Mr. Rourke's house is a half mile away from here. It's private. Accessible by invitation only."

Internally, she scoffed, how often did that happen? Models weren't exactly lining the halls.

"Right there," Franco said, excited. "Bet we have the same zip code."

The guy was crazy. Had he always been crazy? Why was she only noticing now?

"Does everyone agree with the plan?" Mieux asked, sticking to the itinerary. Good. At least someone was doing their job. "There will be time for food and refreshments when the other team arrives."

"Let's get to it," Helena said. "We want to know this place backwards, so we can hit the ground running on Monday."

"Excellent attitude," Mieux said, turning her back to march on. "Please follow me."

Follow her. Follow the new team. Suck up Rourke's ass. Hmm. Why did it feel like she was failing already?

NINE

THEIR TEAM. In addition to her, Helena, Franco, and Myles, Doctor Johann Ellis and Guillermo Hurst completed their squad. For two weeks, they'd been searching for a rhythm and hadn't quite hit it yet.

Mieux was in and out, helping with admin and anything else they needed. She was a great liaison and took a lot of the daily grind from their plates. The assistant kept minutes, collated documents, sent memos and reports to Leon, their supervisor.

Not that he supervised. As far as she could tell, he wasn't even on the premises most of the time. Whether he traveled independently or just kept his head down, his appearances were sporadic. They were based in a glass conference room on the symmetrical executive floor. The only time they saw Leon was when he passed by to go to his office or worked in the conference room opposite theirs.

Lunch was less than an hour old and already the debate was hot.

"That's good. I'm glad you're confident," Roux

said to Johann, their doctor. "But we can't let Huddle Hope work that way."

"It's an established process."

"That's great, if it works for others."

"We're not reinventing the wheel."

"That's exactly what we're doing," she said without disguising her amusement. "Venturing into this arena on a digital platform gives us a latitude other forums don't. We can erase geographical lines, social constraints, even break down economic and political boundaries."

"Ah, that's risky."

"Good! That's what we want to hear. We want to take risks for maximum rewards."

"We can't play with people's lives."

"How do we break down economic barriers?" Guillermo asked. "If people don't have access to technology…"

"We'll give them access," she said. "Mosaic has charitable affiliations."

"People don't want to feel like charity."

"If you're struggling with mental health issues, a little kindness can go a long way."

"You think a free tablet will cure mental health issues?"

"I think being noticed is a start," she said. "Acknowledging the struggle is real. Showing someone they are worth the effort. There are so many reasons it would be valuable. We have to look at this from many angles, but we cannot lose sight of the people who will benefit from this. They are the driving force, the motivation here."

"And I don't think you understand the seriousness of this. There's no way that—"

"Yes, there is—"

"In your opinion, Roux! You think because you

shout louder you'll win?"

Her smile was smug. "No," she said, dropping into the chair at the head of the conference table. "I'll win because I'm right."

No one responded because they were all fixated on the glass wall behind her. What was so fascinating? She turned her chair and—

Hotshot.

Of course. He and a stream of his entourage departed the elevator to cross the executive floor. Most everyone in the vast glass space was gawping or whispering. She rolled her eyes. At least now his gargantuan ego was making more sense.

"Am I the only one working here?" she asked.

"My God, he is ridiculously hot," Helena murmured, maybe to herself, but it startled everyone else. Her colleague blushed. "Sorry."

"Okay, let's get back to it," she said, yanking the chair beneath her toward the table.

"Oh my God, is he coming this way?" Franco exclaimed. "Shit."

Not very professional, Franco, but he was right. Rourke's people funneled up the stairs into the bottleneck between their conference room and another. He rounded the curve of the transparent wall and Myles was there to open the door.

Rourke strode in like he owned the place. But, uh… okay.

"Sir, it's an honor to have you here," Johann said.

Rourke came straight to her. "Get up."

She didn't even *look* up. "Kiss my ass."

"Not with an audience," Rourke said and turned his back on her. "What's the disagreement?"

"How do you know there's a disagreement?"

"Radley's in the room," Rourke said, blocking her view of the others. Rude much? She'd told him to kiss her ass, so, yeah, maybe the slight was allowed. "What's the argument?"

Johann inhaled. "Sir, I believe it's important that each individual who wants to use Huddle Hope services undergo examination by a medical professional."

Rourke rocked back on his heels. "I don't even have to look at Radley to know she didn't go for that. Let me guess, here's her argument, it's cost prohibitive, no, that wouldn't be her first argument. Her first argument is it's impossible to get two doctors to agree on anything. That no one doctor in a single meeting can successfully diagnose a person's feelings and slot them into a clean, neat box. It's also a barrier that may prevent users from joining. And, if that's not enough, it could get litigious. We are not and never will be a substitute for medical advice or treatment. What if we don't let in someone who needs Huddle Hope and something happens to them? Are we letting in more of one demographic or another? Are we favoring or prejudicing ourselves with particular brackets of patients—wait, she wouldn't call them patients."

"Clients," she muttered behind him.

"Clients," he said like she hadn't just fed him the word though everyone else would've heard. "That's before you get to the agoraphobics and imposter syndrome. Who believes they deserve the time of another person or not? Do we set up facilities for these appointments? And if we do, are we like any other healthcare provider? We're not running a hospital, we're a safe space, a safety net and all are welcome." His head moved a little her way. "How am I doing so far?"

"Dial down the arrogance and you'd be pretty close."

"You can be damn haughty yourself, Radley." He didn't turn, just marched toward the door. "As you were."

"Mr. Rourke…" Johann said.

Myles opened the door again.

Rourke spun to address everyone. "Until future notice, Radley's in charge."

The phone in his inner pocket buzzed.

Johann sputtered. "You agree with her?"

"Hardly ever," Rourke said, fishing his phone from his pocket. "But her rack is better than yours." He raised the phone to his ear. "Speak."

And out he marched.

Before the door was fully closed, she was on her feet. "Excuse me."

Myles opened the door wide again, and she went striding out, crossing past other executive offices and up the half dozen shallow stairs that led to his office.

She didn't even look at those congregating inside the door, just stormed through them.

"Hotshot."

He turned to her. "I'll call you back," he said, putting his phone away. "The rest of you out." When she heard the door close, she folded her arms and waited. "Miss me?"

"Want to tell me what that performance was about? I have to work with these people. Why would you put me in charge?"

"I want in your pants," he said, sauntering toward his desk. "Is it working?"

She wasn't amused. "Hotshot!"

"Don't get shrill," he said, dropping into his chair. "Tell me who else I know better in that room?" She faltered. "These people will work under your purview and you'll work under me."

"Under your purview."

"That too."

"Hotshot," she warned. "These people don't know about us. That we know each other."

"Why not?" he asked, rocking his chair in a slight arc back and forth.

"They're my colleagues, our colleagues," she said, trying not to show her surprise. "You want them to know?"

He shrugged. "We know each other."

"Yes, but—"

"But nothing," he said, smirking. "I don't tiptoe around in cover-ups. We're friends."

"I wouldn't go that far," she said, brightening his smile for a flash. "I want a raise."

"Nope."

"Bigger apartment."

"Nope."

"Perks? Benefits?"

He inhaled like he was considering it, then sighed out his words, "Okay, you can suck my cock. I won't make you beg."

"Oh ha-ha," she said. "You're a comedian."

"If I'd chosen another path in life…"

"I'll text you if I ever get desperate."

"Or wasted. Pussy pics always welcome. Upskirt it for me anytime."

"What do you need me to do?" She was quick to hold up her hand to delay his response. "With Huddle Hope."

While opening a hand to the chair opposite, he slid in at the desk. "I need Leon on SIT full time until the choices are final and the ball is rolling. But I can't lose the reins on Huddle Hope; it's too important. I need eyes and ears in that room. Yours. This is a minefield."

"I know."

"Why shouldn't we have people cleared by medical professionals?"

She went to sit at the desk. "Take the cost out of it—"

"I have the money."

"Exactly, and I already have you donating tablets and tech to users who need them. Don't worry, I plan to spend your money. Plenty of it. But we can't take the place of real, honest to God healthcare providers. We're a support, not a replacement. Being cleared by a medical professional takes time, it takes practical steps. If someone needs support at two in the morning, they need it then, not when it's been okayed by some grump in a white coat two weeks, or two months, later. That's not to say we can't hire a team of medical professionals to monitor interactions and look for red flags."

"And if they don't see them?"

"I considered maybe…"

"Don't temper yourself," he said, pushing back in his chair. "I feel you holding back. Remember who you're talking to. If you restrain yourself, I'll send you back to the switchboard. Give it to me, Radley."

"I do that, and I'm likely to get up and start pacing."

"You want to scream," he said, opening his arms, "do it. No need for headsets here." No, there wasn't. "You haven't been online."

Had he checked? "Been settling into my new place."

"Kept waiting for my alarms at the house to go off."

Coy didn't work on her. "I thought about sneaking up there and checking out your pad."

"Why didn't you?"

"Wasn't sure if the orgies and virgin-sacrifice continued in your absence."

"Oh, yeah, I have people who take care of that for me when I'm not home. They water my plants too."

"Yeah, right. You're ridiculous. There's no way I believe you have houseplants."

A beat passed. Shit, was that tension weighing in her gut? It was something. Looking him in the eye changed what had always been between them. The thrill? Yes, that was expected. Even in voice chat they had that. But there was greater exhilaration in person than she'd have predicted.

"What did you think about the red flags?" he asked.

"What if we have user flagging? We have our professionals, but we also foster an environment of support. So others online can flag or highlight concerns about another user."

"We'd need safeguards."

"Obviously. We monitor the monitors too. This needs to start as a pilot program."

"It'll have to run at least six months."

Her head tilted. "A year would be better."

"Yeah, a year would be better, but we don't want to miss the train on this."

"You think there are others in the field?"

"Others who won't mind poaching or cutting corners."

"Then I guess you have to decide," she said, waiting until his wandering eyes came back to her. "You want your lady to fake it or make it? Sometimes getting to the top takes time. That doesn't mean she isn't worth the climb."

One side of his mouth rose. "I love it when you make things about sex."

"Got to keep it in your frame of reference to help your understanding," she said, playing it straight though some part of her enjoyed him enjoying her. "Anyone else who wants to play on this field will have to play by our rules. They rush, they make mistakes, and someone gets hurt. That woman isn't calling you again. That woman makes headlines with words like 'horror' and 'suicide' and 'avoidable.' When you stand in front of your business journalists and tell them we're in this, you're going to tell them we're doing it right, not fast."

"On the money, not for the money."

"Exactly, which leads me to—"

"Don't worry about that," he said, opening his laptop.

"Worry about what?"

"How we monetize it. I have enough money," he said, typing in his credentials. "That's not what this is about."

She couldn't deny her curiosity. "What is it about?"

"You need something to distract you."

"Distract me from what?"

"Baiting me."

And if that didn't just prod her hard. "Excuse me? You think—"

"Go back to work, Radley," he said, amusement twisting his lips.

He wanted a rise and she'd given him it. "Clever," she said, turning to go. "Be online tonight, we'll see who's baited then."

"No," he said, stopping her just before the exit.

"No?"

"We're having dinner tonight."

"I eat dinner every day," she said, being deliberately obtuse. "I'm sure you do too. Or does the blood you suck from your victims sustain you longer than that?"

"A virgin's blood can last me a whole week. If I keep it chilled."

"I'm sure," she said with a smile that was more of a sneer.

He spoke again before she could leave. "But I meant all of us. There's a group."

Oh, yeah, he was just back from his trip. He hadn't spent much time with her colleagues and would want to get to know them.

"What time?"

"Car will pick you up at eight."

"A car? Don't you live on the—"

"You don't want to walk around the lake in heels or hooker boots, and they're the only thing women are allowed to wear in my house."

"Clothes optional?"

That corner of his mouth ascended again. "Forbidden… for females."

"You know you're a pig," she said, swinging the door open.

"Noted!" he called after her as she sashayed out. "Back to work, Slacker!"

TEN

DINNER HER ASS.

The car showed up just like he said. With a chauffeur to open the back door like she couldn't do it herself. Someone had already poured the champagne. Sick. But she had to smile as she sipped from the flute. What a dick. Yes, there was flash and glamour, but he wasn't fooling her.

Except he had.

The mansion appeared as they rounded the ascending road. Glittering, it was fully alight; the driveway lined with twinkling lights that glowed in the trees on either side.

"What the hell…?" she murmured, sliding closer to the window as she buzzed it down to stick her head out and…

People stood on either side of the entrance. The line of cars in front of her were dealt with by the valets scurrying around efficiently, parking the vehicles… somewhere.

Like a conveyor belt, one stopped them, another

uniformed someone opened the door, a third took the keys, and a final handed out tickets. Each shifted role in rotation as the car was driven away and the guests escorted inside.

"Fuck. Me."

This wasn't dinner. She didn't know what the hell it was, but it wasn't some casual dinner party, colleagues getting to know each other. This was… an event. More than a function, it was a damn ball. Like the Oscars or some shit. Whoa, boy.

She swallowed. Yep, the women wore gowns. The men were in tuxes. This was a full tilt, no expense spared, no holds barred, balls to the wall damn jubilee or something.

When the car got to the front of the pack, she had to back off for the valet to open the door. And she wanted to leave. Wanted to pack up her corporate smart casual and go right back to where she came from.

For about three seconds.

He could show off as much as he liked. Could launch curveball after curveball. Bring it on.

Licking her lips, she smiled and slid her hand into that of the suited man outside.

Rourke wanted to have dinner? Wanted to boast to his cronies, congratulate himself on an excellent piece of misdirection? He wanted to win… but not as much as her.

The marble stairs were shallow and flanked by burning torches. The lobby was full of people mingling. The stairs curved up and around to a broad landing above that overlooked the cavernous space. No sign of the master himself. No. Why should he show up to greet his guests?

Flashing a smile here and there, she went to the sentry at the bottom of the stairs.

"Restroom?" she asked. He pointed to the wide

corridor to his left. "Thank you."

A woman was coming out of a room to the side. She was quick to swerve in and hurried over to drop her purse on the vanity. What kind of person had a restroom in their home with actual stalls? Partying had to be his thing.

"Thank God for heels," she whispered, kicking them off and yanking the pins from her hair to toss it over, boosting her volume.

Without caring who else may walk in, she took off her top and bit the plastic from the end of a bobby pin to pick out the seam of the sleeve. One went, then the other. She put her top back on, pulling the wide straps left onto the balls of her shoulders, tucking in any loose threads.

"What have I got?" She opened her purse to pull out eyeliner. Thickening it up, she added a flick and slathered on the mascara. "Damn him," she muttered, smudging on her matte lipstick and pinching her cheeks to give them a little color. "Think you can get over on me…"

A gaggle of women entered, giggling. They stopped to gawk; their surprise joined her in the mirror. Whatever. She kept on working and just winked, sending them back to their business.

They were probably his type, the kind of women who got him going. All preened and perfect. She could do preened and perfect. Though, tossing her hair again, she stepped back, preferring her rough around the edges look. Yanking down her top, she plumped her breasts in her bra. Something was missing…

The chain strap of her clutch would be perfect. Prying the links from the purse, she looped it around her hips twice and tied it in an uneven knot.

And there it was.

Slipping on her heels again, she fluffed her hair.

The women not in stalls were watching, but she didn't care. This wasn't about them.

Sailing out to the party again, she sashayed her way to the server with champagne and tucked her purse under her arm to grab two flutes. One she downed and put back, the other stayed with her.

A few long stairs past the front door took her down into a huge space clearly designed for entertaining. Open doors led to a deck on two sides. A group. For dinner.

Okay, now she was getting the game. Screwing around was one thing, but this was war. If he wanted to shake her, he'd have to try harder. There were no rules. No sportsmanship. Only a winner and a loser. She wouldn't be the latter.

Strangers swarmed the house, no familiar faces, but she didn't mind wandering around, smiling, nodding, absorbing the interest of the partygoers. They no doubt thought she was in the wrong place by her lack of diamonds and grace.

Some people outside were eating. A buffet was laid out to one side and movement took her in another set of glass doors to a kitchen bustling with staff.

The shrimp was so good; she ate a few more pieces. Oh, and there was sushi, right over there.

"Miss Radley."

A server slid into her path, halting her dead. "Come to throw me out?"

Someone probably flagged her presence. She didn't exactly fit in with the champagne and caviar crowd.

"Mr. Rourke requests your company."

She scooped her hair over one shoulder. "Well, he can suck it," she said. Shock hit the guy right between the eyes. "But I… I can tell him that." She put the flute on the counter. "Where is he?"

"Follow me, I'll show you."

They crossed past the island of food and the giant refrigerator and went through into a darker hallway. No people there. No fancy guests. Maybe the hall led back to the front of the house.

Rather than go out anywhere, he took a sharp turn into another hall and then they were ascending stairs. To… where? She'd been kidding about the orgy thing… Was he playing chicken with her?

Light rose from the head of the enclosed stairway. At the top, she turned to look back. The whole wall beyond was glass. The light came from outside. From the party beneath.

"This way," the guy said, going to a set of double doors to knock.

"Yeah," came a call from inside.

The guy took both door handles and leaned into them, rolling them apart. Just a couple of feet later, he let go and nodded into the darkness.

She was to…

Passing him, she went inside, unable to deny her curiosity. The vast room had to be thirty feet wide. More maybe. Split level, the right was down a few stairs. He had a thing for split levels. At that same end, an array of screens covering the wall provided the only light. So many images. Too much to take in. Video footage? Various news channels. Business and stocks. No voices. No volume. Security footage. Code. Server data. What the hell was all that? Numbers. Letters. Symbols scrolling constantly.

"Take it to twenty-four, but no more. That's it."

His voice startled her. A door next to the screens closed at the same time the pair shut behind her.

"Radley."

Ignoring the vast desk opposite the double doors, she went toward the screens and stayed at the top of the stairs looking down at him tossing something between his hands.

It was impossible. She wanted to absorb and deflect. But as her eyes traveled up his body and back down again, she couldn't suppress her amused disbelief.

Bare feet, gray sweats, a tee-shirt that had seen better days. The guy hadn't shaved. Hadn't even combed his hair.

"This is your dinner party?"

"You hungry?" he asked, heading away from the screens. Recessed lights flickered on in the corner, revealing a bar for him to slink behind. "Figured you'd get wasted faster if I didn't feed you."

"You know there are people in your house."

"A lot of 'em," he said, opening a fridge. "I made you something."

She couldn't see what he was doing but was intrigued and incredulous. "You made me something?"

"Yeah, come over here."

"I'm on tenterhooks," she said insincerely, descending the stairs.

"Got you something too."

"A present?"

"Yeah, there in that box," he said, nodding backwards as he turned around to put a tall glass on the bar next to a box with a bow on it.

"What is that?" she asked, approaching with caution. This was Hotshot after all. He opened a hand to the glass filled with red slush. "Daiquiri. You made me a daiquiri?

"Impressed, aren't you?"

"No," she said, picking it up to sniff it. "You lace it with something?"

"Touch of spunk, Babycakes. A little manseed."

Ha ha, she sneered, provoking his smile.

As he went back to the fridge, she sipped. "You

made this?"

Wow, it was amazing.

"I made it," he said, popping the cap off a beer bottle. "Told someone to make it. Same thing."

"That is not the same thing. One requires effort."

"Took effort to tell the guy," he said, smirking as he drank. As he lowered the bottle, he gestured at the box. "Open your box."

"What's in it?" She turned it around. "Should I have witnesses?"

"No, I deliberately cut you off from everyone. No one will hear you scream up here." He shrugged. "Open it. Don't open it. Whatever." Rounding the bar, he passed to head toward the massive couch facing the dynamic screens. "Come over here. I've got something to show you."

She left her purse and took the drink. "You take your cock out of your pants, I'm claiming workman's comp for the trauma. I need danger money being alone with you."

He dropped onto the couch. "Afraid of me?"

"Don't flatter yourself."

"Did you win?"

"Win?" she asked, sliding one knee onto the seat and then the other to rest her side against the back of the couch, facing him. "Your cock's still in your pants, so, yeah, I guess I did."

"It's there whenever you're ready for it, Babycakes, but I meant with the doctor."

That soured her mood. Thank goodness for the fortifying daiquiri. "Hmm," she huffed. "Johann. He's so far up his own ass. I thought you won the award for worshipping yourself, but he's stiff competition."

"You don't like him?"

"Obviously you did, or you wouldn't have hired him. That should be enough for me to dislike him. You have terrible judgment."

"Not to burst your bubble, but I never met the man before today. The panel heard their pitch."

"And it was better than ours?"

"No one's was better than yours, Radley. Yours was the most memorable. What a finish."

"So why do we need them?" she asked, ignoring his mocking. "I'm better. You don't need them."

"Gets into a legal gray area to favor one idea or group over another when they're so similar." He drew in a breath. "That said, make up cause and fire him. I don't care."

"Fire him?" she asked, jolting in surprise.

ELEVEN

HE REACHED AWAY for something on the end table. "Sure."

Putting his feet up on the low coffee table, he tipped his head back to drop whatever he'd scooped up into his mouth.

"I can fire people?"

"People under you," he said, jabbing at the tablet on the arm of the couch. "People I don't care about."

Like Johann. Authority worked for her. "Nice!"

"Doesn't include me. I'm above you. In everything."

"Until I stage a coup."

He opened his arms, beer in hand, attention on the screens. "Want to be on top?"

She drank some of her daiquiri. "If I fire Johann, does Guillermo go too?"

"Got a thing for the protégé?"

"Maybe."

"Ever screwed around with an underling?"

"Says the guy who obviously has."

"Baby, I'm the pinnacle. The apex. The top banana. There is no one over me. Every woman I screw is a subordinate. I'm your alpha, Babycakes."

She ran her fingers into his hair at his crown and sighed. "Such a big brain and such little sense." Her fingers stayed in his hair. "Is this where you talk to me? When we're on Huddle? In this dark, secret lair of yours?"

"Here or upstairs," he said. "Want to find a booth?"

"Don't have my headset."

"We have plenty."

"Yeah, right! You expect me to login here? Like I'd trust putting those details in your system."

A slow, sly smile crept onto his face.

Uh oh. Her eyes narrowed, but he smacked his lips and held his bottle toward her. "Hold my beer."

She did, and he slid the tablet from the couch arm.

"What are we doing now?"

"Is your laptop on? Doesn't matter, I'll turn it on."

"Are you kidding me?" she asked, just as one screen in her peripheral vision changed to her desktop wallpaper. Not just the wallpaper, her icons too. That was… "Oh my God." He laughed, a low snicker, and opened her browser to navigate to her saved passwords. "Hotshot!"

His laughter came louder this time. "And that's me going in the easy way. Want me to show you the fifty other ways I could've done it?" He opened her history. "Let's see what we've got here…"

See, she'd been totally right all along. "Stalking. I knew it! I said it, didn't I? You're a creepy stalker. Thank you for proving my point, jerk."

"First time I've been in here, but it won't be my

last. I'll check your incognito history when I'm alone."

"I don't use incognito browsing, honey. Why would I? What do I have to be ashamed of?" She leaned a little closer. "Sex isn't a dirty word, Boy Scout."

"Yet I see no porn listings."

"That's what work computers are for," she said, shrugging and swigging his beer. "I've got to pass the time doing something all day while raking in the billions for you." The corner of his mouth rose again. "Why do *you* need porn, top banana? Can't you afford to make your own? Hire a few pornstars, make some home movies. Cast yourself in the starring role."

"You don't have to hire pornstars. Get a woman liquored up and turn on the camera. When there are diamonds involved, no woman says no."

She laughed, somehow knowing he was kidding. Maybe it was that smirk or the last year of hearing his tone without other cues. His voice betrayed teasing. It told her when he was serious. Angry. Hurt. Annoyed. Playful.

Sitting there, looking at him, the flesh and blood three-dimensional human being, it was difficult to comprehend that he owned the same disembodied voice that had filled her senses night after night.

"More power to any woman who uses you for your money. I believe in a woman's right to choose."

"I know you do," he said, hitting another couple of buttons, all confidence and swagger. "And I believe in a man's right to choose."

The debate was one they'd had before. From many different angles.

"It's the woman's body," she said, releasing his beer when he took it. "It's her choice whether she puts it through the trauma of pregnancy and childbirth. Never mind—"

"A man can raise a child just as easily as a

woman."

"And how often does that happen?"

"This isn't the kind of thing where generalizations hold up."

"Yes, it is," she said. "Because by your reasoning, a man can have an ideological objection, a general objection, with no intention of raising or supporting a child, and still force a woman to go through with a traumatic and life-changing process."

"Isn't it life changing to take another life?"

"You ever knock a woman up?"

"Not that I know," he said, drinking his beer and setting it on the end table.

"See! How does that not prove my point? You could go around impregnating twenty women a day and your life wouldn't change at all. You think the twenty women's lives would change?"

"I can afford to start my own sex cult," he said and tilted his head. "Maybe a project for next year."

She smiled, but quickly erased it. Not that it mattered. His focus was back on the screens and his tablet.

"You have enough land here for it."

He shook his head. "Dyce would never go for it… Kinloch, maybe. He has land."

"Your billionaire bachelor friends? Think you could share power?"

"Kinloch, K2, wouldn't get in my way. He prefers to be left the hell alone."

"Says the guy sitting alone in the dark with a hundred people in his house." He didn't react, though his brow dropped. Something up ahead caught his intrigued focus. "Why invite them if you didn't want them here?"

"I throw parties all the time." Whatever was on the end table, he scooped up some more and tossed it into his mouth. "They're boring as hell."

She laughed. "Why throw them?"

"Why not? I can afford it. This isn't your scene?"

Couldn't be further from it. "Not exactly."

"People like parties. Food, music, fancy lights, people are easy to impress and they like schmoozing."

On an exhale, she looked closer. "You don't. You're bored as hell."

"Yeah, do something interesting. Work a little. Pep me up."

"Call those pornstars if you want that kind of show."

"Sex is boring too."

"Then you're doing it wrong. You should try harder."

When he glanced her way again, it wasn't her eyes that got his attention. Her breasts had somehow become more interesting.

"Bet those aren't boring."

Snatching his jaw, she jerked his head up as she leaned in. "I am a whole package, Boy Scout."

"Shame about your warped view of the world."

"My warped view?" she asked, releasing his jaw to push away the hand he slithered up her thigh to her waist. "You want to have sex with me, but have you thought about contraception?"

"You have an IUD."

"So? That mean it's all on me? You shouldn't trust so easily. Maybe now I know who you are, I want to trap you and your billions."

"I've spent a year vetting you."

"Thought you didn't stalk me."

"Didn't have to, you're a font of information."

"Which I gave to a guy I thought I'd never have to look in the eye."

"You're welcome, Radley," he said, showing an

unapologetic smile. "Come on! You can't deny it. Your life's better with me in it."

"Is it?"

"You live in an exclusive zip code. Have a management position. And an office of your own on the top floor."

That lightened her. "I have an office?"

He shrugged. "I'm working on it." As she shoved him, he laughed. "What does it matter? You wouldn't fuck a guy for a promotion."

Climbing off the couch, she swiped up her glass. "I already got the promotion."

"I can take it away. Dangle it in front of you until you submit."

Her? Submit? Hell would freeze over first. Unless…

Going over to the bar, she opened up the fridge and found the expected pitcher of daiquiri in a separate section of the freezer. "If I was horny enough, I might let you."

"I could get you there. You think I don't know what turns you on?"

"I think you do," she said because, begrudgingly, she admitted to herself he'd done it more than once since they started talking over a year ago. "Some things anyway."

"Oh yeah, what don't I know?"

On a snicker, she filled her glass. "Trust me, that's not a door you want to open."

Sucking a few ice crystals from her fingers, she put the pitcher back. Etiquette dictated offering him another beer. Yet the words didn't materialize. She slipped off her shoes while returning to him, enjoying her refreshed drink.

"Think about getting me a beer?" he asked.

She just smiled, pleased with herself. "I thought

about it. For a second."

"And?"

"You haven't done anything to deserve it," she said, kneeling on the couch again.

"What about you?" he asked. "What have you done to deserve my hospitality?"

"I'm here. My presence is enough. I could walk right out that door any second."

"Then what happens to your promotion?"

"You can't fire me without cause."

"I can do whatever I like. I own the building. The company. The land."

"Thought Dyce owned the land."

"We both do, and he's more likely to side with me."

Her head angled. "You think? Is your rack better than mine?"

His gaze dropped again. "Those babies could get you a free pass."

"Could they?"

"If you tell me what you meant about a door I shouldn't want to open."

"Men don't like a sexually liberated woman. They say they do, but they don't."

"Didn't we already say if it felt good, it was allowed? Be as sexually liberated with me as you want, Radley."

Slowly shaking her head, her shoulders flexed. "You're not capable of rising to my challenges. You'd break way before I did."

"You think?" he asked, ignoring her feline smile to bob his brows. "What makes you think you could rise to mine?"

"The very fact that I challenge you arouses you."

"Does it?"

"Mm hmm," she said with a slow nod, arching

closer. "All I have to do is show up."

"The boundaries between men and women are arbitrary."

"The sexual lines?"

"The physical lines," he said. "Why should we conform to societal norms? Don't women always harp on about defining their own rules? About embracing their right to choose?"

"We do have a right to choose."

"So if you have that right, why not use it?"

Sounded more than a little self-serving. "To have sex with you?"

"Not me specifically, not any man specifically. Physical boundaries that are placed on you by a patriarchal society—"

"A woman who follows her instinct, sexual, physical, or otherwise, also faces the possibility of being judged by those around her. How many times have we heard a woman was 'asking for it' by wearing revealing clothing? People impose their own judgments on others."

"You judge people."

"I do," she said, slurping more of her daiquiri then handing the glass off to him. "I own that though. That's something about me. And I'd hazard we all do it." Leaving the couch, she went back to the fridge to get him a beer. "I'm just more honest about it than most."

"You're right that we all—"

"Oh, I'm sorry, what was that?" she asked, cupping her ear as she strutted back to him. "I'm what?"

"If you'd let me finish…" He gave her back the daiquiri and took the beer, twisting off the cap to toss it aside. "I was going to say you're right that we all judge people, we judge situations, setups, trust our instincts—"

"Which is really just an innate judgment."

"Maybe. But the rest of us don't assume the worst, you do."

"I do not," she said, strolling around the coffee table.

"You do," he drawled. "Radley, your defenses are so damn high, even you can't see over them. You're in your own world."

"We all exist in our own world. It's not possible to put yourself in anyone else's shoes. People might say they do, but it's bullshit. You can't live my life any more than I can live yours." Glass in hand, she wandered to the end of the screens and back. "We know each other about as well as any two people can. Conversation, words, are the only way to learn what's in a person's head, them telling you directly."

"That relies on honesty," he said. "Don't we hide our perceived flaws and present the best versions of ourselves?"

She snorted and spun to pace back the other way. "Is that what you've been trying to do? Might want to brush up that game for next time."

"Next time? Your clause in the contract stated, *'friendship is real and permanent, whether you like it or not.'* You're stuck with me." Which was what she'd told him. "You're the last friend I'll ever make."

"Providing you're honest. Honesty is a requirement of friendship."

"I'm more honest than most because I have less to lose."

"Less?" She frowned. "You own a massive multibillion—"

"The business is my bedrock. The money gives me the leeway to be as daring, as bold, as out there as I want. I have a direct line to the White House, I can—" She stopped to blink at him and he just snickered. "Yes, Radley, I know those at the top. I do some work for the

DOD… on the side.”

"On the side," she mocked his words. "You can be a real asshole."

Beaming with pride, swagger bled from him. "I know. You're welcome."

TWELVE

"YOU CAN LITERALLY do whatever the fuck you want with friends that high up. Why wouldn't you?"

"Right," he said. "Knowing those at the top has its benefits. Also has its drawbacks."

"Because you're automatically tainted," she said, returning to her pacing. "You celebrate the victories and are dragged down by their failures."

"Which is part of the reason I don't holler about it."

"You keep it a secret."

"It's not a secret; I don't advertise any of my friendships."

"You know Zane Dyce."

"Yeah," he said, crossing one ankle over the other on the coffee table.

"Can I meet him?"

"He's in the Pacific."

"Ocean?"

"On an island. Not just floating around out there."

Hmm. "For? Business or pleasure?"

"Business," he said. "Pleasure if it presents itself. Guess he's open to it."

"Is he seeing anyone?"

He laughed. "Want me to hook you up? He's not always the most outgoing guy."

"I can't even picture him," she said. "He's not like you."

"Meaning?"

"You might not advertise your friendships, but you're not shy about flaunting your women."

"You know that because you work for me."

"Which I only just found out."

"No, you just found out you knew me. You always knew you worked for Xavien Rourke." Valid point. "How did we get back to that anyway? Do you enjoy reminding me how pissed you were?"

"I was pissed because you murdered our friendship. You were there in this place I didn't expect you to be. The presentation was stressful enough and then there you were. It was inconsiderate. You can't make choices for me and shouldn't make decisions for us."

"If it feels good, it's allowed." And if life was that simple… "You weren't stressed about the presentation; you lap that shit up."

"I can tell it's been a long time since you stood up in front of strangers."

"I stand up in front of strangers all the time."

"Strangers desperate to impress you. How often do you stand in front of people you don't intimidate?"

"Oh, am I intimidating, baby?"

Was he? No, not to her. "Maybe if you hadn't given me open access to your cock." He flashed another quick smile. "You're a long way from intimidating."

"Good. I don't want you to hold back with me."

"I don't."

"You didn't before you knew who I was," he said, swiping across on his tablet. "Now it'll be your urge to temper yourself. You did it today."

"Being your friend does not mean giving you access to everything. I am allowed my own thoughts. Are you aware of that? Are you aware others can have private thoughts that you're not entitled to?"

"Not us," he said and side-nodded. "Come here."

"No."

His smile grew fast. "Come sit beside me, Babycakes. You're not intimidated, right?"

"No. That doesn't mean I want to sit by you."

"What are you afraid of? We'll watch movies. We watch movies together all the time."

"And you always end up talking about sex."

"*We* always end up talking about sex." His eyes glittered with that same mischief twisting his lips. "If it feels good…"

And it felt good. Just being near to him. Having his voice in her ears without the headset relaying the words. Maybe too good.

Going around the coffee table, she sank onto her knees, facing him again. "If I'm your best friend, I should get a raise."

"Okay," he said. The tablet went back to the arm of the couch. "And what do I get in return?"

"What do you want?" she asked, aiming for sultry despite knowing it was a loaded question.

"Know where I'll start."

He cupped her breasts, squeezing, pushing them together. He leaned in, opening his mouth in an inhale on the swell.

"Those are D-cups," she said, tipping more of her daiquiri into her mouth. His teeth dug in deep, the gentle suction grew more powerful. "I get your obsession with my breasts now. All those supermodels from your past would barely fill an A-cup collectively."

He slurped his mouth free, though his tongue wasn't so quick to depart. It trailed to the edge of her top. "I date underwear models too."

"Playmates?"

"Back in the day," he said with a semi-shrug. "I can make a call if you're interested in a career change."

"Are you kidding? I just got a promotion. Where are we on that raise?"

"Want the house?"

"I don't know, I haven't seen all of it yet." As he drew the straps of her top down, she stretched her shoulders back, pushing her breast deeper into his mouth. "Why have none of you wealthy bigwigs put money into developing contraceptives for men?"

"It's a woman's responsibility." Pig. "You don't want to have a kid? Either protect yourself or keep your legs closed."

"And if a man doesn't want children?"

"We're biologically driven to spread our seed. It diminishes our manhood to limit our fertility."

"You're a dick."

She gulped down some more of her daiquiri.

"With a dick," he said, taking her glass to put it on the coffee table.

And this guy thought that meant, what? That he was in charge?

"One that doesn't rule the world. You can't just go around doing whatever you want, ruining women's lives for the sake of a few seconds of pleasure."

"A man has a right to make decisions about his progeny. If a man's generous enough to put a child in you—"

"Generous enough?" she said, grabbing his

shoulder to shove him back.

He groaned in deep ecstasy. "Temper, temper, baby."

Riling her was his favorite hobby. "If a man wants to make the decisions," she said, grabbing a handful of his hair, "he first has to take the decision to control his seed. If we had male contraceptives—"

"The long-term effects could have a bearing on our later fertility." He dared her with a brow arch. "Would you deny a man his right to ever have a child?"

"Any new drug requires study to prevent negative side effects. Instead of delving into the more responsible course, you prioritized Viagra research."

"Personally? I didn't. It's not something I need and I'm not in pharmaceuticals. No one consulted me on that decision," he said. "You know who is in the medical field? Your friend at work. Maybe lay this on him tomorrow."

She sighed, mocking in her disappointment. "You sow the seeds of discontent…"

"Why would I do that?" he asked, fondling and kneading her breasts. "Your ire's mine. Your indignation. Your incredulity. I prefer it focused on me. I'm the only man who can keep you under control."

Is that what he was doing? Because she was the one with her fingernails in his scalp. "You're a masochist."

"Only if it turns you on," he said, ducking to kiss one breast then the other.

"I must be one too. I keep showing up." And her fingers loosened, combing up into his hair again. "Our friendship. Our rules."

"Mm hmm," he said, kissing the corner of her mouth.

"We've never agreed on anything."

"Then we've got to keep sparring, don't you want

to know who comes out on top?"

Her hands drifted down to his body. "I want a raise."

"You get one after I get one."

Her fingers curled into the fabric of his tee-shirt. As he straightened her leg over his lap, slanting her back, she yanked his shirt over his head.

He swooped as though to kiss her, but she dropped onto her elbows. "Ah ah," she scolded, wagging a finger at him before picking up his hand to guide it to the zipper on her pants.

Smiling, it was clear he relished drawing it down and taking her panties off right along with the pants that disappeared over the back of the couch.

"You prepped for me," he said, smoothing his fingers down the crease of her leg to her smooth folds beneath.

"I prepped for me, Boy Scout," she said. "You have to pass the audition before your cock gets its part." The searing heat in his gaze sped her heart as the huff of his shallowing breaths fogged her body. "Your cock want the part, baby?"

"Oh, he does. I'm not worried." And as the length of his finger slid against her clit, he curled the tip just to circle her entrance, and drew it back. Up and down, just like that in long, slow, strokes that tightened some muscles and loosened others. "Damn wet already, baby. She's so happy to come out and play."

"You know what will make her wetter? Happier? So much more grateful?" On a sigh, she sank onto her back and raised her hips, undulating with his caress. "Your tongue, Boy Scout."

"If it feels good..." he grumbled, the warmth of his mouth a whisper from her pubis.

"It's allowed," she exhaled because what other choice did she have?

He kissed her there and ran the stubble on his jaw down the curve of her body. Shit. Had she told him she liked that? The rasp of that rough hair on her most sensitive corner. He shifted. She heard it but, with her eyes closed, didn't see the new position. She let him raise her leg over his shoulder and breathed out in bliss when he kissed her inner thigh, taking his time in crossing the other and skipping her clit.

That didn't matter.

If he hadn't learned it already, she wasn't shy. He was an added extra, not a necessity.

Raising her knee, the sole of her foot skimmed up his shoulder blade. Her fingers sank into his hair, enjoying the sensation of his soft locks in contrast to the shadow on his jaw. But that wasn't her only pleasure. Her other fingertips descended her abdomen and touched her clit. Rubbing herself in gentle circles, the flood of her juices sped her widening caress. But he kissed her nails and forced his tongue between them, riding the motion of her hand with his own tease.

"Mmmm…" she groaned.

The motion of her body worked against the delight of his mouth. His tongue retreated, slid lower, and thrust into her. On a gasp, she arched, forcing his mouth so close his teeth rasped her flesh.

"Easy, babygirl."

"No," she whined, her fingers working faster. "I'm close. Oh, fuck I'm—"

"You'll go when I say," he commanded, snatching her hand away, pinning it on the couch as he drew her clit between his lips. "I'm in charge here. You want me in charge."

"I want you working for me. You get me off or I'll go downstairs and—oh!"

When he plunged two fingers into her and pulled them back, she hummed in the pleasure he gave.

Mimicking her hum, he sank his mouth against her clit, warming it with the vibration. "Like that, baby?"

"Mmm," she moaned, clenching her fingers in his hair. "Shit, Xavie—"

"I know, you like it. You love it, baby." His tongue lengthened its strokes, almost mocking in how it played with her. She growled. "Temper, baby."

The laugh in that tone was enough to snap her.

Shoving her foot into his shoulder, she forced him away. "I'll go and find myself a real man. A man—"

He snagged her wrist and whipped her onto her back before she could fully rise from the couch.

"Forgive me, babygirl," he murmured from on top of her, sweeping her hair from her face.

Except he wasn't contrite. Amusement still dripped from his bedroom voice.

"I'm going home."

"No, you're not," he said, still smiling.

"I'm going home. You're pissing me off."

"How's that different from any other day?"

"This what we do now?" she asked.

"Fuck?"

"We're not fucking," she said, wriggling beneath him. He was bigger than her, heavy, in that horribly comforting way that didn't do her arousal any favors. "You're being a dick."

"Stay the night and you'll find out just how much of that I can give you."

"I'm not staying. Why would I stay with you anyway?"

"We're having a slumber party. Don't friends do shit like that?"

"I don't want to slumber with you."

"No," he said, drawing a fingertip along her hairline down her temple. "You like getting your own way."

Her brow arched. "Pot?"

He grinned. "Okay, Kettle, your point. Tell me what you want."

He knew what she wanted; it was written all over his face. Her whole body was ready for it. For him. He wanted her to say it. As she drew in a breath, her breasts pushed against him, and he pushed back. Wasn't that just exactly their way?

Ah. What an idiot. Her snit evaporated as satisfaction crept in. "Nothing you don't want to give, Hotshot," she said, parting her legs to coil one around his hip. "You want to give it to me, baby? Are you hard, Xavie?" Her sultry voice came from the back of her throat as her leg slid up and down his. "Does your long, thick—oh." Switching to a pout of innocence, she widened her eyes before cringing. "Is he just a little, itty-bitty—"

"Ain't nothing itty-bitty over here, Babycakes."

She subdued her smile and dared him with a gaze. "So says you, and we both know you're not the most accurate barometer of truth."

"Mm, so says me."

And when his hips rose and his hand disappeared between them, it wasn't so easy to contain her glee or her triumph. Goading him was about to have a reward she'd never expected to receive from him. Yet, in that moment, every raw nerve-ending anticipated the completion that would come if he sank himself into her.

The blunt head of his cock pushed against her. She held her breath. He kept it there, sliding it up and down, coating her with the moisture seeping from her body. Rocking against him, she tempted the stimulation higher, lower, wherever she could get it. Their eyes met as her teeth caught her lip and that was it. His mouth opened just a little at the same moment he pushed into her.

And then it was her turn to express her bliss. No itty-bitty nothing was right. She'd never felt so full.

"Xavie, baby," she said, arching as she draped her arms around his neck. "I knew you could do it."

He thrust so hard that she yelped at the unexpected depth of his intrusion.

Smug pride plumped his cheeks. She socked his shoulder, but as he moved within her, warming her, rousing her, the flat of her palm caressed his shoulder, his defined arm, up to his neck and into his hair.

"Mmm, yes." She couldn't help herself. Just like she couldn't stop her knees from rising and her hips from moving with his. "Xavie."

"Not yet," he growled, getting faster, thinning the air between them, lessening the oxygen they got per breath. "Wait for me, baby."

He hadn't got the warmup she had. Her whole being was ready to explode in response to the pound of need tightening her muscles.

Squeezing tight, her pelvis pulled back. "Xavie—"

"Shit, baby, go!"

With that permission, she bucked and braced, holding onto the waves of ecstasy that milked him deep within her.

"Oh, Xavie," she breathed out when he dropped on top of her, his weight sort of braced on the elbow he had on the couch above her shoulder.

"Know how many times I've thought about doing that?" he panted. "We'll last longer next time."

"Next time?" she asked, ready to tease him again. But he scooped her off the couch and carried her across the room. "Where are we going?"

"Upstairs. Slumber party needs a bed."

And he opened the door by the bookcases behind the desk she'd ignored earlier.

"Oh, your bedroom?" They went up a sweeping spiral staircase that occupied the cylindrical hallway. "Aren't I honored?"

"You should be," he said when they got into the huge room at the top of the stairs. "Now it's your turn to impress me."

THIRTEEN

MMM, MORNING. In the heat of the smothering pillow, she almost couldn't breathe. But it didn't matter. She didn't need to breathe when the bed felt so good. The pillow might be a melted marshmallow, but the mattress was firm. The sheets sandwiching her were feather soft, so light they were barely a tickle on her skin.

Morning.

Bed.

Her eyes opened in the same instant she pounced onto her elbows.

Fuck!

Scrambling out of the empty bed, she ran away from the bright floor-to-ceiling drapes to the spiral staircase downward.

"Fuck," she said, darting across the dormant room to grab up her clothes from the previous night. "Fuck!"

Again and again, she wanted to scream at him. Unfortunately, he wasn't around. The jerk left her sleeping. Who the hell did that? Who the hell just—what a jackass!

After slamming the front door, she came to a crashing halt. A car, right there, door open. Could he have…? Did he…? She was wearing heels and…

It wasn't technically stealing if she wasn't leaving his land, was it? That was on the assumption he even owned the car. Maybe it belonged to a staff member. The keys were on the dash. And there was a note on the steering wheel. "*If it feels good…*"

"It's allowed," she said, getting in to gun the engine and speed down to her apartment.

This didn't excuse him abandoning her. Why was she behind the eight-ball with him all the time? Not all the time. Since they'd met in real life, that was since when. She never used to be, but now he was kicking her ass, keeping her off-kilter. In her defense, she wasn't prepared like him. He'd known they were going real world and technically his life hadn't changed.

Her world was upside down, in a spiral after a few backflips. She lived in a new place. Worked in a new place with new people. Her home, her work, her social life, even her economic bracket had changed. Everything was different.

That was no excuse.

If he wanted to play, she had to raise her game.

In her whole life, she'd never showered and changed so fast. Not that it mattered. She was already late. Seriously late.

It was a couple of minutes past noon when the elevator doors opened on Mosaic's executive floor. Striding out, she held her head high. No one would see shame. She didn't have anything to be ashamed of.

The bunch of people in the jerk's office may not have noticed her, but he did. Their eyes met, and he raised his chin from the fingers that had propped it up.

Without an ounce of hesitation, she extended an

arm to flip him the bird. Yep, and she'd leave it there, hanging in the air as long as possible. His lips puckered in a quick kiss and he winked.

What a dick.

Rounding the conference room, she tossed her hair and went inside. "What did I miss?"

"Are you okay?" Myles asked. "We were worried. You're never late."

"Were you sick?" Helena asked. "If you're sick, you shouldn't be at work."

"My body's not even cold and you're trying on my shoes," she said, going to drop into the chair at the head of the table. "I ask again, what did I miss?"

"You look good in charge," Franco said, tripping over his own tongue.

"Are you going to make me say it a third time?"

It wasn't fair. None of her team had left her lying in bed. None of them had abandoned her sleeping form after ravishing it over and over again.

What kind of guy did that?

Every time she wanted to turn over and go to sleep, he wanted to do it again. She'd reminded him they had work in the morning. Had he cared? No. Now she knew why. This was the jerk's plan all along.

"We were having a debate," Guillermo said.

The word titillated her excitement and calmed her in equal measure. "About what?"

"We need an investor," Johann said.

She frowned. "We have an investor. We're sitting in his building."

"We need someone with greater exposure," Helena said. "Someone to be the face of the program. Someone to draw in others' support. Maybe someone with a not so perfect past…"

"Because we don't want to look like we're preaching?" she asked, taking a shot.

"This could be expensive. It could get expensive fast. We also need…" Franco trailed off as he and Helena made eye contact. The latter nodded, and he exhaled. "We need to spread the risk."

"So if there's a disaster, we have pre-emptive support."

Not a bad idea.

"Huddle Hope can't make money," Helena said. "We don't want it to appear we're—"

"Cashing in on other's misery," she said, nodding.

Had Rourke reached that conclusion on his own? Was that what he'd meant about monetizing it? They couldn't. Well, they could. Plenty of healthcare providers made money from others' misfortune. But that wasn't the point for them. They wanted to be universal. Available to all. No matter their background or location.

"The larger the pool of connected parties, the wider our network. The more influential people we can reach, get invested in this, the greater the publicity. And we don't want to be seen as a place for losers and lost causes."

"We are a place for losers and lost causes, rather people who think they fall into those categories," she said. Her phone buzzed. "But I understand what you mean. If we can be a place for the cool kids too, then it's something people will talk about. The more they talk about it, the more likely they are to approach. Acceptance helps Huddle Hope be inclusive. You're so right."

"Think that's the first time you've ever agreed with anything without a fight," Johann said.

She showed him a fake smile and opened her purse to retrieve her phone.

HOTSHOT: SLEEP WELL?

What the hell? She wasn't even logged into Huddle, how had he—except she was logged in. After witnessing his work with her laptop, his abilities shouldn't surprise her.

FIREFLY: No. An asshole got me drunk and kept me up all night.

"Political support would be an advantage," Johann said.

"Rourke has that," she said, considering what else they might need. "Celebrity endorsement would help with the exposure and recognition."

"We'll need medical people too," Helena said. "Lawyers. Businesses that may link into Huddle Hope."

"We need someone influential, with contacts. A wide network."

Her phone buzzed again.

HOTSHOT: I forget, how many times did you come? Six? Eight?

More than that, but she wasn't going to stoke his elephantine ego. Though she wouldn't be cruel either.

FIREFLY: We're on Huddle.

HOTSHOT: I noticed. Impressed?

FIREFLY: That you violated my personal boundaries again?

"We could make some calls," Helena said. "See if we can get local business interested?"

"We need to do our research first."

"Do we want local?"

"No," she said. "Johann's right, we have to think bigger. Think about someone high profile. Someone not only known in this echo chamber."

HOTSHOT: VIOLATED PRETTY MUCH EVERY ONE OF THOSE LAST NIGHT. COMING OVER TONIGHT?

FIREFLY: NO. BECAUSE YOU CAN'T BE TRUSTED.

HOTSHOT: TRUSTED TO WHAT? I DIDN'T SHOW EVERYONE THE NAKED PICTURES I TOOK WHILE YOU WERE SLEEPING.

FIREFLY: NOT EVERYONE?

HOTSHOT: YEAH. SHARED THEM WITH THREE OR FOUR SITES MAX.

She laughed, stunning her colleagues.

"Oh, uh… What were we talking about?"

"Collecting backers."

"You know that's important too," she said, pointing at the frowning Myles. "Fundraising will be so much easier the more people we can get logistically involved. One network leads to another and another and so on."

"What about Zane Dyce?" Franco asked, pepping up the others. "He's like right on the doorstep."

She shrugged. "Wouldn't hurt to ask, I guess."

"Think he could see us today?"

"Think he'd see us at all?"

"He's in the Pacific," she said. "But that's not prohibitive, video calls are in right now."

"A guy like Zane Dyce won't have space in his

schedule, probably for months," Helena said. "Do we know anything about his network?"

"He basically stocks every home and office with every piece of tech they own. People know Dyce Technologies."

"But not Dyce," Helena said and frowned. "I can't even picture what he looks like."

"Tall, dark, and handsome," Franco said, rolling his eyes at the other guys. "And super rich. How do the rest of us have a chance?"

"He's usually only seen at product launches," Myles said. "Only people who pay attention to that stuff would know him."

"We need someone more gregarious."

"Someone who'll fight for Huddle Hope."

"That said, we can't kick Dyce out of bed," she said. "If we ask, he might lead us to someone else."

"Good point."

"But how do we get to him?"

Leaning back in her chair, she turned ninety degrees, craning to look back to the opposite side of Rourke's office. To the boardroom table he and his cronies sat around.

"There's one obvious way," Franco said.

Exactly her thought.

Turning back to her colleagues, she didn't expect them to be intent on her. "What?"

"No one else will get in," Myles said. "You went walking in there yesterday like it was no big deal."

Maybe it had been a big deal. But she'd been following the man, her friend, not their boss. Not exactly.

"We should run it through Leon," Johann said. "He's our contact."

"Supposed to be, but we never see him."

"He's dealing with the SIT candidates," she

muttered.

Her phone buzzed again.

HOTSHOT: WHAT YOU TALKING ABOUT?

FIREFLY: NOTHING THAT'S YOUR BUSINESS. GIVE ME ZANE DYCE'S PHONE NUMBER.

HOTSHOT: WHAT'S IT WORTH?

FIREFLY: I DON'T NEED YOUR PERMISSION; YOU'LL LEAVE YOUR PHONE LYING AROUND EVENTUALLY.

HOTSHOT: YOU'D INVADE MY PRIVACY, RADLEY? YOU SHOULD KNOW IT'S AGAINST HUDDLE RULES TO PRESSURE A USER FOR PERSONAL INFORMATION.

Man had a point. Just what were the rules now? And, shit, who was monitoring them? The guy at the top might be exempt from monitoring, but she wasn't. And was his profile linked to him? The real him? If it wasn't and he was "undercover," monitors would treat him like any regular user.

"Roux?"

Again, she snapped back to the moment. "Hmm?"

"What do you want to eat?" Myles asked, rising from his seat. "We're going to get some food and do some research. Narrow down the list of people we want to approach."

"Smart," she said. "Get me a—"

"Club hold the bacon, light on the mayo, and a strong black coffee," Franco said, proud of himself.

"Yeah," she muttered. Was that guy okay? "Whatever. Let's get to work."

Okay, so it was kind of rich of her to say that when she'd been the one to walk in hours late. But she was there, and that was what counted. Now they had to lock down the money and influence. Piece of cake.

FOURTEEN

"ZANE DYCE IS the closest to home," Myles said.

At the end of the day, their list was impressive. Maybe too impressive. Getting that number of people, high profile people, on board would be a mammoth task.

"You think if we can't get him others might wonder why," Helena said. "Mr. Rourke must know him. They chose to share a campus, to have their buildings side by side."

Except there was so much space between them that she'd seen no hint of Dyce or his technologies. Just how much land did the men own?

"That's a good point," Guillermo said. "If Mr. Rourke's good friend and close associate won't get involved, why should anyone else?"

"Mr. Rourke's endorsement may be enough," Johann said. "If we can use his name."

Were they there? Could they use his name? Maybe they didn't want to use his name. Could be some people and businesses they were considering had beef with the man at the top of Mosaic.

"Give me the list," she said, reaching over to snag Franco's tablet.

"What are you going to do?" he asked.

Leaving her seat, she headed for the door. "Find out."

What other way was there? Besides, much as she might like to downplay his abilities, Xavien Rourke had risen to the top in a competitive field. The man had to know something about what he was doing.

There were three people in his office when she went in. Rourke, Leon, and another guy she didn't know.

Standing by the door, she just smiled when the three men quieted to look at her.

"You should knock and wait outside—"

"She doesn't know how to knock and wait outside," Rourke said and stood. "Doesn't matter, we're done anyway."

"But, sir, we were—"

"We're done," he said and looked at Leon.

"Actually, we might need him too," she said of Leon.

Rourke shook his head. "We don't need a third."

Leon and the growly guy with him passed by to exit. Her smile grew, not that either of them appreciated it. On an inhale, she raised the tablet toward Rourke, but said nothing until the men were gone.

"Did you break something?" he asked the moment the door was closed.

"I didn't break anything, thank you," she said as he came over. "Though I considered setting your house on fire."

Mr. Oblivious carried on despite the threat. "I'm hungry. Are you hungry?"

"No. Thanks to someone, I'm only halfway through my day."

"Good," he said, taking the tablet. "You can do

all the work tonight."

His focus narrowed on the device.

"What are we doing tonight?"

"What is this list?" he asked. "People you want to have sex with before you die?"

"Before *they* die," she said. "Some of those people are old. Especially the women. And some of them are married. We'll need to extort them."

"Do you have the cash for that?"

"No, but we can hack their Huddle data. Link into their other accounts online. There has to be one or two incriminating pictures in there, right?"

"We can hack them?" he asked, seizing her wrist to pull her closer. "*We?*"

"I'm sure I have something you want."

He snickered. "Do you? What's the list?"

"Potential backers for Huddle Hope."

"Others? My money isn't good enough?"

"We have multiple reasons. One of which is—"

"Risk dissemination."

She smiled and ruffled his hair. "See, you're not just a pretty face."

"Fundraising too. Took you time to catch up to it," he said. "We can't profit from this."

"No."

"So your list is…"

"People we'd like to talk to, maybe put a presentation together and see if we can tempt them to join our endeavor."

"You're good at tempting."

"Anyone on that list you're feuding with? Anyone's wife you're screwing? Or husband? Teenage daughter? Housekeeper? Or is the pool boy more your thing?"

"Maybe."

"Can you put us in touch with any of the names

on the list?"

"Maybe."

Maybe. Maybe. Maybe.

Walking up against her, he kept going until her back hit the door.

"Can we use your name?" she asked, coiling her fingers around his tie.

"You've gotta launch yourself out there on your own one day, kid."

"Yeah, but this isn't that day, is it?" she asked, increasing the pull to draw him lower. "You want to help me."

"I'll think about it." One corner of his mouth curled in such sinister seduction, a wave of anticipation swept her prickling skin. "If you make it worth my while."

"How would you like me to do that?"

"Use your imagination, pretty girl. What you got that I want?"

Slowly, her tongue swept across her upper lip. "Maybe... one thing."

"Oh, you have more than one thing I want," he said, his fingers curling in her hair right at the base of her skull. "I can think of three right off the bat."

And it wasn't easy to restrain her smile. The innocent thing went better, especially when it was such an obvious ruse.

"Maybe... maybe if I dropped to my knees for you, sir..."

"Maybe," he said, pushing himself against her.

"Such a shame your office is glass," she said, running the tie through her hands over and over. "We wouldn't want the world to see the power I have over their alpha."

Without breaking eye contact, he pressed a button on his watch. "Now we're all alone."

Glancing left to right, the wall she was leaning on was no longer transparent. It was black. Completely opaque.

"Impressive," she said.

"Dyce glass."

"Mmm, resourceful man that Zane Dyce," she said, pulling on his tie until his mouth was just a whisper from hers. "Are you calling my bluff, Mr. Rourke?"

"Was it a bluff?"

Withholding her smile, her fingers drifted from his tie to loosen his belt. "You'll help me whether or not I do this," she whispered, wrapping her fingers around his cock. "You're playing the big, bad, exploitative boss."

Laying his hands flat on the glass, his lips came even closer. "Are you calling my bluff, Ms. Radley?"

She brushed her lips over his. Not kissing him, but not not kissing him either. "I love role play, Mr. Rourke," she whispered and sank down to take him into her mouth.

His sharp inhale fired her satisfaction. Yes, he got to pretend he had power over her, but it was only pretend. Right then anyway. With him deep in her throat, her hand tight around his shaft, chasing her lips, no one had more power over him than her.

Moaning her own pleasure shook him in her mouth. Closing her eyes in a long blink, the moment they opened, she found his gaze. With gritted teeth, his splayed fingers drove through her hair, pulling tight, his grip steering her with increasing urgency. Oh, he wanted her, needed her right then. She didn't mind him losing control. The mask of teasing indifference was difficult to maintain when he wanted what she offered so bad.

"Shit, Roux," he hissed.

Sucking hard, she dipped in and retreated, pulling back until her lips were only on his tip. "Something wrong, Mr. Rourke?"

"Yeah, you're talking," he growled. "Open."

And with a broad, satisfied smile, she did exactly that, and he fed himself into her throat. God, it turned her on. Had blowing a guy ever felt so good? The mechanical suck and retreat, the licking and kissing and humming, it was all practiced, acts she'd done before. But it had never given her such raw gratification. This man. Her friend. Was at his weakest right there. He couldn't stop his fist from tightening in her hair or his eyes rolling back as he clenched his jaw.

Fuck, she was horny. Yet, she didn't want him in her pussy. She wanted him to come right there, in her mouth, in her throat, any way he wanted to. Her pleasure came from his. Their boundaries were gone, their friendship consummated in every way it could be.

"Roux," he barked and surged in deep, coating her throat with the seed she swallowed down.

Perfect, just perfect. Her smile rose as she did. "I'm picking the movie tonight." Tucking him back into his pants, she was careful about putting him all back together. "I want sushi for dinner." Because he'd deprived her of raiding the sushi bar at his party. "And you'll help us recruit every person on the list."

The tablet was on the floor next to them. He must've dropped it, maybe it was busted, she hadn't even heard it hit the ground.

"Fine. No problem and... no, I won't."

He sauntered away to the desk as she scooped up the tablet. "You better be joking," she exclaimed, storming to the desk. "I just—"

"Trust me, Radley," he said, descending into his chair with a satisfied exhale. "Work smart, not hard. You want the people on that list?" He smiled. "There's only one person you need. One person who can deliver them and many, many more."

"One? Who?"

"Trust me, Babycakes. Prepare to wow, and I'll deliver the candidate."

Did she believe him? He had to know what he was doing, wasn't that what she'd told herself not long ago? Okay. They would prep. But Xavien Rourke better be right.

FIFTEEN

LEON CORNISH SHOVED into their conference room. "Are you ready?"

"Oh, God," Helena said, pressing her hands to her stomach. "Is he here?"

"We're prepped for the presentation," Johann said. "Can you tell us who it's with?"

Frustrating Rourke had been tightlipped about the identity of the person due to meet them any minute. They'd prepped, just like he told her to do less than forty-eight hours ago. But even she felt ridiculous waiting there for some unknown entity.

"Where is he?" she asked. "Rourke, where is he?"

"On his way," Leon said, checking something on his tablet.

"Who could it be?" Guillermo asked. "Who could deliver all the people on our list?"

Helena shrugged. "It must be someone important."

"Someone rich."

"Someone influential. You think he's in politics

or—"

"Politics are divisive. Not everyone on our list was from the same side. If this person can deliver everyone, they have to be neutral."

"Or incredibly charming."

Her gaze tracked to the elevator as the doors parted. When Rourke came out with another guy, her mouth opened. Shit. Was that…?

"Zairn Lomond," Helena whispered the name that stuck in her throat.

She swallowed.

"Oh, shit," Franco said. "Oh, no, this is bad."

"How could he do this to us?"

"What's the problem?" Myles asked. "Zairn Lomond knows everyone in the whole world. Everyone. Literally."

Helena spun around just as she put her back to the sight of the smirking billionaires crossing the floor together.

"Yes, he knows everyone," Helena said. "Which means if we fuck this up, we're finished. All of us. In every arena. Industry. Everywhere!"

"Were you this nervous presenting to me and the SIT panel?" Leon asked.

No one had a chance to answer that, thank God. Myles opened the doors and the duo came in.

"Zairn Lomond," Rourke said, slapping a hand onto his buddy's back. "These are the people I was telling you about. You don't need to know their names." He pointed at her. "Except that one. That's Roux Radley, watch out for her." He leaned closer to stage whisper. "She makes the Kyst-meister look like child's play." He patted his friend again. "Go to it."

"You're leaving?" she asked, taking an involuntary step toward him.

His brows rose a fraction. "You nervous?"

"No!"

"Good. Didn't think so," he said and winked. "I'll swing by at the end for the big finish. Radley does it like no one else. Hope you're up on your movie quotes, buddy."

He departed. Leaving them alone. Her team. Leon. And Zairn fucking Lomond.

"You're in charge," he said to her.

She blinked.

"Roxanne is the most beautiful woman in the world," Myles said from absolutely nowhere, giving her whiplash.

Zairn took the random comment in stride and turned just enough to look at the speaker. "Her name's Roxanna," he said, "and she knows." His head twitched in a tilt as he approached the chair at the head of the table. "Though Knox Collier would disagree with you."

Way to start them off on the wrong foot by insulting the man's girlfriend.

And Collier.

The man really did know everyone.

"I watch her streams all the time," Myles said, rushing over. "She's just…"

"Beautiful?" Zairn asked, sitting down. "You said that already. You know I have met her."

"Stop slobbering on the man's girlfriend," she said, marching down the room.

"Fiancée," Myles said. "You're engaged, right?"

"Some say," Zairn said. "She has single friends we're trying to offload."

The moment she reached the screen and spun on the spot, Leon hit a button on his tablet and the glass walls went white. More Dyce glass. "Mr. Lomond, let us tell you about Huddle Hope."

They talked for more than an hour. Each of them took their turn to say their piece and dazzle the billionaire with their presentation.

At least, that was the idea.

She was feeling good about it until Leon put the lights back on and she got a better look at Lomond's impassive expression.

"We're happy to answer any questions," Johann said with an optimism she sure didn't share.

"No," Lomond said and stood up.

"No?" Franco asked. "What does that mean?"

"It means this isn't in my wheelhouse," Lomond said, retrieving his phone to type and swipe.

"You don't want to give it a chance?" Johann asked. "What exactly are your objections?"

"I'm sure it's a brilliant idea. It's just not for me."

"Wha…? Wha…? What?"

She understood the others' surprise. Why had the guy let them go on and on for an hour if he was just going to slap them down?

"I do know someone who will be interested," Lomond said. "A startup perfect for this."

Hope! Yes, okay, that was something, wasn't it?

"Who?" Johann asked.

"I can set up a meet, if you're interested."

"We're interested," Helena said.

"We are," their doctor said, "but we don't want to waste our time."

Was he really so arrogant? What was with the attitude? There had always been a chance the pitch wouldn't reap results. It was disheartening, annoying even, but that was the way the game went. Not every roll of the dice got you to the finish line.

When Rourke came in, there was an air of knowing around him.

"You knew this wasn't for me," Lomond said like he sensed it too.

The straight smile on Rourke's face tilted just a

little. "I sure did."

"Mr. Lomond—"

"You want me to set up the meet or not?" he asked, cutting Franco off.

"Yes," most of them said at the same time.

"Yes, please," Myles said after.

"My people will be in touch within twenty-four hours," he said and went out, taking Rourke right along with him.

"Well, that was…"

"A bust," Johann said, his expression tight. "Why did they put us through that? Is this some game?"

"He's right," she said. "Kind of. Zairn Lomond knows a lot of people, but he's not known for being the caring and gentle type."

"You ever see the video of him with Roxie when she was sick?" Myles asked and she shook her head. "Watch it. That'll change your opinion."

"Don't we need someone warmer? Someone more approachable?" she asked. "Look, it wasn't a bust. Rourke said he would connect us with someone who would deliver the list." Now that she thought about it… "He never said Lomond would invest."

The others considered this.

"We have to trust him," Helena said. "He knows what he's doing and wouldn't have gotten to where he is without some expertise. He's on our side."

"Is he?" Johann asked. "And a startup? How will they have the foundation we need? The stability? Does Rourke want this to succeed?"

The doctor's glare drilled into her. The others weren't quite so harsh, but there was a sense of expectation from them too.

"What?" she asked. "Why are you all looking at me?"

"There's something going on between you," the

doctor said. "The way he talks to you, and you go running in there—"

"We're friends," she said. "Is that a crime?"

"How did that happen?" Myles asked. "How do you get to be friends with—"

"You treated him horribly in the SIT pitch," Helena said.

"Worked for us, didn't it?"

"Is that how we got here?" Franco asked. "Because you yelled at him."

She wasn't exactly sure how they'd ended up there. Did Rourke love the Huddle Hope idea or was their relationship a factor?

"I never asked him."

But she would. If she remembered the next time they were together. Though that didn't guarantee an answer or honesty. They could just end up arguing again.

"What do we do now?" Myles asked.

"Wait," she said. "What else can we do?"

"Who do you think he's going to hook us up with?"

"God knows," Helena said, slumping into a chair.

"I won't be getting my hopes up," Johann snapped.

Wow, the guy needed to chill. Yes, she was disappointed. They were all disappointed. But they had cause for optimism. Her phone buzzed, so she fished it out of her pocket.

HOTSHOT: COME TO THE OFFICE.

His office? She started across the room.

"Where are you going?" Helena asked.

"Everyone stay here and tweak the pitch. An

hour's too long. We need to make it more interesting. Less of the facts and figures."

"Serious people like facts and figures."

"Serious people can take one look at our graphs and draw their own conclusions," she said, opening the door. "Just do what you can."

Thankfully, their conference room was still obscured by Dyce glass. Not only could it protect from the inside, but it concealed her path from the others. Already they were curious about her and Rourke and didn't need more to whisper about.

She scanned the room before going inside. Rourke was alone. So the friends hadn't spent much time together.

"…four at the end," he said into the phone as she went inside. "Yeah, later." He hung up. "Congrats!"

"Congrats?" she asked, going over to the desk. "For what? We didn't get a deal."

"You were never going to get a deal with Z."

"And you couldn't have told me that before giving us false hope?"

"These things have a way of working themselves out," he said. "It's a step closer. Z was your only guaranteed way in."

"Okay," she said, eyeing the boxes on his desk.

"Okay? You trust me?"

"In business, I do," she said, gesturing at the boxes with her phone hand. "What is this? You moving out? Am I getting your office?"

His tight grin was false but warmed her amusement.

"Thank you."

"For what?"

"Reminding me how catty you are. Now I don't feel so bad." He nodded at the boxes. "These are for you."

"What are they? Diamonds?" she asked, removing one of the lids. "Still won't grant you permission to put it in my ass." But there were no sparkling jewels. "Files? You're giving me files?"

"You didn't open the first gift I got you, so I'm trying again."

Putting her phone on the desk, she retrieved the first folder. "With files?"

"It's the semi-finalists."

"Semi-finalists of what?"

"SIT," he said, startling her. "Leon and his people narrowed it down to these forty-eight groups."

"Forty-eight?" she asked, trying not to gasp. "That's hardly narrowed down."

"Yeah, I want it down to fifteen before the end of the week."

"It's already Thursday. That's a lot of work."

"It is, which is why I'm not doing it. My time is way too valuable. Yours? Not so much. The pitch materials and panel's observations are in each folder, along with a video of the pitch and presentation on the USBs."

"Good. At least they're organized, I don't..." Trailing off, she put all the pieces together. "Wait. You want... You want me to..."

"Cull the list," he said, pushing back in his seat. "Yep."

"I have Hope stuff to do," she said, jabbing a thumb over her shoulder. "We have so much to— Lomond said we'd hear in twenty-four hours. Whoever he's referred us to—"

"That's what your team's for," he said. "Come over to the house tonight. You can spread out there."

"You just handed me a fuckload of work and you expect me to—"

"Come over and put out? Yeah, I expect that

too," he said. "And watch that language around the boss."

"The boss can go fuck himself," she said. "How will I get through this and—"

"I'm out for the rest of the day. Z and I are hitting the strip clubs," he said, getting up to grab his jacket from a hat stand behind him. "Work in here."

"You want me to work in here?"

"Sure," he said, rounding the desk to duck and kiss her head. "Have fun. I'll dedicate a lap dance to you."

Have fun? Screw him. Forty-eight presentations. She had to read and review… Inhaling, she held the breath for a second and blew it out as she went around to sit in his chair. She'd never finish if she didn't start.

Put out? Yeah, he could suck it himself.

SIXTEEN

IF ONLY IT WASN'T so damn interesting.

The Hope team didn't appreciate her bailing on them. What choice did she have? Rourke might be a jerk of a friend, but he was still their boss.

Getting through the SIT files was a mammoth task. Especially given she wasn't familiar with them or the pitches. She had less than forty-eight hours to get through something the original panel had six days to absorb and process.

She worked in Rourke's office for a couple of hours before packing up. Spreading out at his house would be a better option. At least there, people wouldn't push into the office to ask if she had permission to be there.

And he could supply sushi. She didn't know where it came from, but whatever delicacies she requested always somehow showed up at his house right on time.

Dragging the boxes out of the car… *the* car, that was how she thought of it because technically, it didn't belong to her. But it was the easiest way to get between work and Rourke's. She'd never given him the keys back. In her defense, he'd never asked for them. Until he did, they'd live with her. Like they had joint custody. Didn't seem like much to ask with her being orally available to him night after night. More than orally, but the other ways were more mutually enjoyable, so she was fair not to count them as credit to be repaid.

Her laptop was inside the top box. It would be a long night. She went inside, past the stairs and restrooms to go to the hallway that led straight through to the kitchen at the back of the house. The stairs to Rourke's man cave were halfway along it. His desk should be big enough for—

"…give it another week." His voice carried from the kitchen. She dumped the boxes on the stairs and went to see him. "I will, guy. I will…" He was on the phone and raised his brows when he saw her. Mmm, in sweats and a tee-shirt, he made an interesting view. How horny did she have to be to notice that or to be tempted by such little effort? "Yep. Thanks." He hung up and slid his phone onto the counter. "Have a good day?"

"Overall?" she asked, taking off her jacket. "I think Johann's pissed at you."

"What did I do?"

"No, actually, I don't think he's pissed at you." She went to the perpendicular edge of the counter his flat hands rested on. "I know he is."

"Good. I must be doing something right. Want a drink?"

She shook her head, buying time to yawn. "I don't want to lose my momentum."

"Your momentum, huh?"

Bending over, her elbows met the counter before her forearms. "I would've stayed at the office if it wasn't for people gawping at me in your prized space. I was like a damn exhibit at the aquarium. How often do you let people, other than you, use your office?"

"Mmm…" he pondered, his eyes rising for a second. "Don't think I ever have." She just smiled and let her upper body sink down to the counter too. The cool marble chilled her, but that was okay, she needed the stimulation. "Tired?"

"No," she said and stretched out her arms. "I am eager to get out of these clothes though."

"Funny, I was just thinking the same thing," he said with swagger and reached around to snag her hips. "Let me help you."

She laughed as he dragged her around the corner of the counter, pushing her down again when she tried to straighten up.

"Xavie—"

"You only call me Xavie when we're having sex," he said, his fingers gathering her pencil skirt up to ease it over her ass. No matter he hadn't given her a chance to say more. "I must be behind schedule."

"To take the skirt off, typically, it goes down," she said over her shoulder.

"Huh," he said, hooking his fingers into the band of her underwear to slide it down. "Like this?"

She laughed again. "Always get your way, don't you, Mr. Rourke?"

"I do," he said, massaging her clit. "Right now, that's working out for you."

It was. So much for not losing her momentum. Her hips moved as he aroused her; more than a few blissful whimpers left her lips. When he dipped his fingers into her, she pushed back. He was only checking if she was ready, but wasn't she always whenever he worked on her? It never took long for him to heat her up.

"Xavie," she whispered, opening her mouth against her arm.

"I love it when you make things about sex."

A laugh almost threatened, but she lost it when his cock pushed into her. Wasn't so funny when it felt so good.

"Shit," she whispered, her eyes closing tight as he advanced at a delectable pace. "That feels so good."

"Mm," he agreed, pushing his fingers up her spine, arching her hips further. "Your pussy takes it good, baby."

Trying to push back, she was stalled by him grabbing her hips. "Fuck me, Boy Scout. Make some effort."

His groan of approval was a prelude to giving her exactly what she wanted. Pulling back only to slam in, he forced her hips to advance and retreat as he drove into her. Yes! Shocked delight burst out of her in a yelp the second he hit her g-spot. Oh, shit, she hadn't expected that, but, fuck…

Taking control, complete control, he yanked her so high that her toes almost left the floor.

Fighting him didn't occur to her.

Not right then.

"Fuck, Xavie," she squealed. One palm landed on the counter as her other hand snaked between them to massage her clit. "Like that, right there. Oh, fuck. Fuck!"

Maybe he wasn't in charge. Everything she asked for, she got. He knew just how to hit her right, how to tease and satisfy her at exactly the same time. But she was a thing to him right then. A tool to deliver him to his pleasure. He hammered into her over and over, using her like he might a sex toy in the privacy of his personal space.

Her pussy swallowed his cock over and over, every minute craving more while climbing closer to the pinnacle of pleasure.

"Xa—Xavie!" she screeched as it consumed her, pulling her under, smothering her.

She couldn't breathe but didn't try. He fulfilled every part of her being when he spilled himself within her. That was it. What both of them needed.

As he growled and stilled, he smacked her ass and released her hips. She didn't move. Even when he slid out, leaving her draped across the counter, she just sighed in bliss.

"Okay, that didn't help my momentum," she murmured.

He drew her panties back up her legs and pushed her skirt down too. Wasn't like him to be dressing her or worried about things like decency or dignity. Whatever. She had work to do.

"All clear?"

She rose a fraction. That was a male voice. Not Rourke's.

"Yeah, you're good," Rourke said.

Planting her hands on the counter, she straightened her arms only to lose all muscle tone when Zairn Lomond came wandering into the room.

"Are you shitting me?" she asked, standing up just as Rourke raised a glass of wine into her line of sight.

"Evening, Roux," Zairn said like he hadn't just overheard his buddy screwing her. "Nice to see you again."

Snatching the glass, her glare landed on Rourke. "You're fucking me with our would-be donor in the next room?"

"He'll donate," Rourke said, beer in hand. "And he doesn't care about sex. That's Zairn Lomond, playboy extraordinaire." The men shared a smile. "You should throw a party for Hope, Radley. Stuff those coffers. Expand those contacts."

"I can't throw a party until I have my

consortium."

"I'll pay for it," Rourke said.

"You don't need a consortium," Zairn said, sitting at the separate long island that had held the buffet the night of the party. "You just need the right foundation beneath you."

"Our track record isn't great so far," she said. "Not easy to impress people when you're set up to have sex within twenty paces of them."

Zairn frowned. "Roux, I apologize if—"

"She doesn't care about the sex," Rourke said. "She doesn't mind an audience."

"I don't care about my opinion of me," she said because he was right that she didn't care about the sex. "How do I tell my group we're fucked on this because I got fucked—"

"You're not fucked, not that way," he said, resting a hand on the counter to lean in. "Zairn likes people who like sex."

"Do I?"

"Sure," Rourke said. "Kyst likes it, doesn't she? You're always fucking at it." The seated billionaire bobbed his head on a blink, a concession maybe. "With you, Kintyre, and Collier living in close quarters, I'm surprised it hasn't been going on twenty-four seven."

"Lilya thinks we're back in college."

Rourke laughed. "That's funny."

"Why is that funny?" she asked but was ignored.

"The food on its way?"

"Yeah," Zairn said and looked at his watch. "I don't know what—"

Noise from the front of the house stalled him.

"Casanova!" a woman hollered.

Zairn smiled and called back. "We're in the kitchen."

Something hit the floor, many somethings

maybe, and there was a shuffle before the clack of heels came closer.

"What the hell's she been doing all day?"

On a head shake, Zairn raised an innocent hand. "I gave up asking months ago."

Rourke laughed but stopped abruptly. "Wow," he exhaled, his mouth opening as he nodded from his friend to the gorgeous blonde who just walked in.

"You like it?" the woman asked.

"He like what?" Zairn asked and twisted to look over his shoulder, only to then turn his whole body that way. "Wow."

Mirroring Rourke's sentiment, Zairn seemed as surprised.

"What do you think?" the blonde asked, shaking her hair.

"I…" Zairn started. "Um… Why did we do this?"

"Why not?" the woman asked, going over to lay a hand on him and lean in. "Thought men preferred blondes."

"If you love it, I love it," Zairn said, kissing the beauty. "Do the cuffs match or…"

The blonde swept her lips back and forth on his. "You'll have to wait until later to find out, Casanova."

"Later, huh?"

"If you play your cards right."

"I have a few minutes now if—"

"Don't we have company?"

Not that an audience mattered, as Rourke demonstrated not long ago.

"Company, right," Zairn said, slipping an arm around the woman as he turned back to them. "Roux Radley, this is Roxanna Kyst. She prefers Roxie."

"Your fiancée," she said and received a nod. "It's nice to meet you, ma'am."

"Oh," Roxie said and shuddered. "Roxie is fine. I am not a fan of the ma'am thing."

"Sorry," she said and drew in a deep breath. "If you'll excuse me, I have work to do."

But when she tried to walk away, Rourke caught her shoulder to pull her back. "Do we want to eat outside or inside?"

"Outside," Roxie said, resting her lips on Zairn. "I don't have a drink, dear."

"Right," Zairn said, rising to take his fiancée's hand to lead her outside just as a bunch of suited servers came streaming into the kitchen from somewhere.

"Outside," Rourke said to the guy in the lead. "Follow the blonde."

The people came through with boxes and went onto the patio. One opened the pocket doors.

Rourke pulled her back, resting his mouth on her crown. "Schmooze."

"What does that mean?"

"Hang out with me and my friends."

"I have work to do."

"This is more important," he said, threading his fingers between hers. "Trust me."

"Trust you?" she asked, letting him pull her across the room. "That hasn't worked out so well for me so far."

He flashed her a smile. "There's always a first time."

Hmm, maybe. Trust him? To what? She shouldn't be drinking wine and hanging out while two boxes of files sat on the stairs waiting for her. SIT was important, and she wanted to do the job well. If someone fell through the cracks or she was too distracted to notice a worthy cause, it could make a difference.

Trust him? He'd been the one to give her the work, and now he was telling her to disregard it. If she didn't know any better, she'd say he was up to something.

SEVENTEEN

"IT'S RISKY," she said. "There's no denying it."

On the couch with Roxie in front of the faux-flame fireplace Rourke had switched on whenever they sat down, her enthusiasm burned bright.

"Mental health is such a hot button topic," Roxie said. "People have their own preconceived ideas."

"But isn't it the stigma we're trying to shake off? It's ridiculous. People tiptoe around so many other topics and classes of people, yet those with genuine health conditions are sidelined and judged. I don't think it's right."

"It isn't and services can't keep up with demand."

"Someone has to take it seriously. We've given the governments of the world their chance to take care of these people and they've failed. If business has to step in, then fuck it, we have to step in."

"You can't profit from it. No business could spin that to their advantage. At least if it's a non-profit, if something goes wrong, you can argue that the individual's care was at the heart of what Huddle Hope was trying to do. If you've made a mint from that person—"

"I know," she said on a sigh and sank deeper into the back of the couch. "But money is essential."

"Makes the world go round."

"Right. We need to get this out there, to spread knowledge, to make helping and respecting those with mental health issues mainstream. These people are mocked and feared when what they need is support. Whether that's medicinal or therapeutic. And we need to empower people. To show them they can make a difference and help others without putting themselves at risk."

"This is either an incredible watershed moment…"

"Or a complete disaster waiting to happen."

"You have to make it clear everywhere, over and over again, that the program is no substitute for—"

"Medical advice and support, absolutely," she said, shifting just an inch closer. "But I wondered… What if we were a gateway too? Rourke has the money, he won't care."

"You want him to branch into medicine?" Roxie asked. "That's another minefield."

"Maybe we don't need our own facilities. We could work in partnership."

Roxie nodded. "Z knows people who can help with that."

"People he trusts?" she asked. "Because it couldn't be that we're just handing the vulnerable off to people who want to gouge them."

"Absolutely not. But you're right, you'll need that cushion either way. There will be some people you can't help."

"We can try to—"

"It's like saying you can cure cancer through sheer will," Roxie said. "A lot of people will benefit from a support network and safe spaces to discuss their issues. But there will be some who need genuine medical support, medication, maybe hospitalization. You have to be prepared for that eventuality. And you can't expand too quickly. This has to be gradual, measured, considered. At every level."

"Yeah, I agree, Rourke wanted a six-month trial."

"Has to be at least a year," Roxie said, her brow coming down a fraction. "Two would be better. Baby steps, if you go too fast…"

"Mistakes will be made, and that could mean lives. I know. I understand why this is an issue business and government shy away from, but we have to try. Someone has to try. People are out there suffering. They're being told there's no way to help them or that they need help that just doesn't exist. Someone has to try. Maybe this prompts a bigger discussion. Maybe our step leads to someone else taking another."

Roxie smiled. "You're really passionate about this."

"Someone has to be."

Facing each other, the women had their legs curled in front of them, mirroring each other, even down to the wineglass each of them held.

"Where does it come from?" Roxie asked, surprising her with the question. She hesitated. "Come on, no one dives headfirst into something like this without a reason, a history. Have you struggled with mental health issues?"

"Yeah," she said. "All my life, but not my own. My mom's been in and out of facilities her whole life. My sister and I bounced around from my grandmother's to different foster or children's homes."

"What about your dad?"

She shook her head. "Wasn't interested. He lived with us for a couple of years, but my mom just got to be too much. It's not easy, I get that. And maybe talking wouldn't have solved all the problems, but I always thought…" Inhaling, she held the breath a second before releasing it. "If there had been someone, anyone, to even pretend like they cared for her, for us, it would've made a difference. There was no attempt to help her, to support her, even within the community, that might have allowed us to stay together."

"Oh, honey," Roxie said and took her hand, startling her. "Have you talked to Rourke about this?"

Sitting up, she put her glass on the coffee table. "He knows I have strong opinions on the subject. On a lot of subjects."

"You must really have hit it off at the SIT pitch if he's inviting you into his home."

Had Zairn not told her or was Rourke tightlipped?

"We met before the pitch, sort of. We knew each other online, through Huddle," she said. "If you can believe it." Roxie's neck relaxed. "What?"

"You're not the…" Slowly, the woman smiled. "Oh my God, I know who you are." She looked all around. "Where's my phone?"

"Who I am?" she asked, not following.

"I need my phone. Not *my* phone. Obviously. *A* phone."

"Why not yours?"

"It won't be charged," Roxie said quickly. "Where did our guys go?"

"Upstairs," she said. "Probably to Rourke's lair. I'll show you."

If Zairn had access, there was no reason Roxie shouldn't. They went up. She didn't expect to open the double doors and see the guys sharing the desk, stacks of files everywhere.

"What's going on?" she asked, frowning at the piles as she approached.

"Give me your phone," Roxie said, rushing over to grab Zairn's jacket from the back of his chair.

"I'm hiring someone to follow you around with a charger," he said as his fiancée fished his cellphone from his jacket pocket.

"We used to laugh at the couples who shared phones," Rourke said.

"Laugh. I'd laugh if it wasn't so infuriating. She thinks nothing of being cut off."

"You're used to people being around when you need them. Especially when you're being faithful to one pussy. Doesn't she understand the potential urgency?"

Files. Three piles.

She opened the first and then the second. "These are the SIT files."

"These are the no," Rourke said, pointing his pen at one stack then the next. "Yes."

"And the third?" she asked, switching to open the first.

"The maybe pile. You have to review them."

"You want me to review them? Review your work?" she asked, subduing a laugh. "Why are you doing this anyway? I thought your time was too valuable."

"Z can't look at work that needs done and ignore it. When the Kyst-meister isn't in the room anyway. When she's around, his priorities are straight: tits and ass. Same place every respectable man's focus should be."

"Mm, right," she said.

"There's still a box on the floor we haven't touched. You'll be up all night."

"Will I?" she asked. When her eyes slid up to his, the slant of seduction wasn't far from his lips. "We have work tomorrow."

"Maybe," he said. "Depends how well you do tonight."

"I haven't relinquished ownership of your office yet. If I have to walk right in there and take over, I will."

"You do that."

"Jane!" Roxie suddenly exclaimed, startling her. The woman turned her back to wander away, a phone at her ear. "Grab Lilya. You will not believe who I met tonight."

Her? Was Roxie excited because of her? Something didn't add up, but she did make some connections.

"Jane? Is that…? Is that the woman who married Knox Collier?"

Rourke's grin burst as a laugh came out under Zairn's breath. "Yep," Hotshot said. "One and the same."

EIGHTEEN

"I LIKE IT," she said, unsure it was really the best their collective could do.

Not that it mattered. Their meeting was scheduled in a matter of minutes. Time for tweaking had run out.

"You think he'll like it?"

"I don't know who we're presenting to anymore than you do," she said.

Her colleagues didn't believe her. Why should they? Rourke would tell her. If she asked… nicely. She could find some way to persuade him to reveal who their afternoon meeting was with.

The door opened and she leaped to her feet. Rourke? Not a happy Rourke. Without a word, he marched over, his glare solid as concrete, and grabbed her hand to turn and storm out, dragging her along with him.

"What is it?" she asked but could only trot after him. "What is going on?"

He threw his office door out of the way and

swung her around, propelling her into the room. When she stopped at the desk and turned, the walls behind him were black again.

"We have a problem," he snarled, stalking her way.

"Horny, baby?" The only time he changed those walls was to give them privacy. "I'd love to accommodate you, but I have a meeting."

Crowding her up against the desk, he didn't stop until she was down on her elbows, then he planted his hands on either side of her.

"We…" he said again, slower this time, his scowl still fierce, "have a problem."

"What is it?" Maybe it was something serious. She'd never seen him like this. "Is it SIT or Huddle Hope?"

"It's us."

Now she was frowning. "Us? What's wrong with us? Are you pregnant?" He didn't appreciate her grin. "What is it, Hotshot?" Sliding a hand under his lapel, she stroked it around to the back of his neck, holding onto him for balance. "I'm not pregnant, if that's what you're worried about. Kids? Me? Please. Not a chance."

Suddenly standing straight, he left her to drop onto an elbow again while he took something from his pocket. A wallet. And from inside, a black card. He held it up and tossed the wallet aside.

"You know what this is?"

"Uh… a penis extension?" she asked, rising to lay a hand on his chest. "You don't need fancy things to show off. You're above average, an amazing lover." Her teasing pout didn't amuse him. "Why don't you spell it out for me, Boy Scout?"

"It's a credit card." He stabbed it into her cleavage. "Without a limit."

"Hmm, okay, thank you." She put it on the desk

behind her. "But the sex was actually free, so—"

"Have I totally misjudged this?" he asked. "Misjudged you?" Now she was just confused. "I thought you got it. I thought we got it. That we were on the same page."

"I don't understand."

"Clearly."

"You want to tell me what brought this on?" she asked, wrapping her fingers around his tie. "What wound you up?"

"You."

She smiled and swayed a little closer. "That's nothing new."

"I like the games. I love the games and you turn me on…" Searching him, she couldn't figure him out. "But this goes deeper than that." He scooped a hand under her hair to cradle the side of her head. "Tell me you know that. That I didn't just make it all up in my head."

Now she was flat worried. "You're scaring me, Rourke."

His eyes narrowed as he looked deeper into her. "Why didn't you tell me?"

"Tell you what? Xavie, I don't know what—"

"Your mom."

Oh. Right. Damnit. Roxanna Kyst apparently couldn't keep her mouth shut. Not that it was particularly confidential information. It was the weakness, the vulnerability. She was not fragile and did not need protection or to be saved. Rourke was an invincible force, and she would not let him believe her strength couldn't match his.

An uncomfortable chill took some of her confidence. "It's not a big deal."

"Not a big deal that your mom needs constant care? She's in a state-run facility."

Her head snapped up. "How do you know that?"

"Because I checked," he said. "Whatever is mine is yours." His head shook slowly. "I shouldn't have to tell you that. I should never have to say those words out loud to you. Not to you, Radley, come on."

"She's looked after."

"Not as well as she could be. We'll get her the best."

"This isn't your problem."

"Then I misjudged this," he said and cleared his throat, putting a meter of space between them, his hand rising to the back of his head. "Shit."

"You didn't misjudge anything," she said, going closer to grab his tie. "Nothing's changed."

Except when she tried to pull him down for a kiss, he resisted and extricated his tie from her grip.

"Damn, it's so inappropriate," he muttered, though she wasn't sure the words were for her.

"No one does inappropriate better than us." But when she stepped closer, he backed away. "Hotshot—"

"No," he said, shaking his head again. "We will provide you and your team with everything you require."

"Rourke—"

"Don't you have a meeting?" he asked, giving her a wide berth as he went around to the other side of the desk.

She exhaled a laugh, pivoting on the spot. "What is it you want exactly? You want to save me? You want me to depend on you?"

"Yes, I did," he said. "To depend on me the way I depended on you. What we were was nothing to do with money and everything to do with… I'm sorry I took it too far. Like I said, I thought we were on the same page. I misinterpreted everything."

"I don't like this. I don't like you talking about us in the past tense. Why does anything have to change?"

"Because I thought we were friends. I thought that friendship was real. The kind of friendship… Again, I apologize—"

"It was real. It is. Nothing has changed."

"It's changed for me."

"Because my mother is sick? Because we're poor and you can't be friends with someone whose means don't match yours?"

"It's never been about money."

His calmness infuriated her. "I guess things have changed. I didn't know you were so elitist. I was fine for you when I was flat on my back." He picked up the card to slip it back into his wallet. "Look at me." He didn't. "Argue with me. Spout some superior crap so I can tell you how wrong you are." He opened his laptop, and she bounded a step closer. "Goddamnit, Xavien Rourke, fight with me!"

"Go to work," he said, glancing at her just long enough to bob his brows toward the door. "Go on."

He pressed the button on his watch. The walls behind her would be transparent again. Furious heat burned behind her eyes. How dare he call her in there to judge her and then refuse to argue back? Why would he do that? Why was he messing everything up?

"Can we have sushi for dinner?" she asked.

Maybe he'd be over whatever this was in a few hours.

"Mieux has the number of the place," he said. "I'll ask her to share it with you. If you call, they'll deliver to the complex."

The employee apartment complex. A place she'd hardly been.

"You'll want the car back too."

No reaction. "Leave the keys in it. A guy will pick it up."

No one would steal from the Mosaic campus. No

one would get away with it. Was he taking the car back because he didn't trust her with it or because she wouldn't need to be anywhere near his house ever again?

Her stomach roiled.

Still, anger provoked her adrenaline. "You're going to regret this later."

"I regret our relationship already," he said and sat down.

Noise rose behind her. People were coming into the office. He had his own schedule to keep. As he rose again, he smiled, but it wasn't for her. In his mind, he'd dismissed her already.

Turning, in something of a daze, she got a couple of steps and raised her head. Roxie. Coming out of the elevator with three other people. Three other women.

When Roxie saw her, she smiled and crooked a finger. Go there? Why? What was going on? They didn't aim for Rourke's office and instead waited just outside the Huddle Hope conference room. Roxie gestured her over again.

What was going on?

Leaving his office, she strode over to Roxie and her friends. "What's happening?"

"We're in," Roxie said, looping their arms together. "Introduce me to your team."

Her team? Was it still her team if Rourke no longer trusted her?

But Roxie was already taking them inside.

"Oh my God," Myles said, his mouth falling open.

"Don't cream in your pants, please," she said as the women fanned out behind Roxie. "As you probably already know, this is Roxanna Kyst."

"Mr. Lomond's fiancée," Helena whispered.

"I prefer to think of him as Ms. Kyst's fiancé, but…" Roxie stepped aside. "These are my friends.

Astrid Ballard. Lilya Kearns. And the beautiful Jane Simmons."

"You didn't take his name?" Guillermo asked. "You're married to Knox Collier, right?"

"Oh my God," Jane said, her shoulders dropping as she looked at Roxie, who laughed. "Rox!"

"I'm sorry, honey." Roxie gave her a quick hug, then addressed the room again. "We have a suite of offices available in the building. Some of us will continue to work up here. We'll need an executive liaison. And—"

"I'm sorry, Ms. Kyst," Johann cut her off. "But aren't you here to hear our pitch?"

"I've been briefed," Roxie said, taking her hand. "I'm up to speed."

Last night? That was a pitch meeting? And Rourke hadn't told her? Of course not, just like him. Not that he was who she'd believed him to be.

"And you're…"

"In?" Roxie asked. "Yes, we all are."

"You're Zairn Lomond's contact?" Franco asked, wearing a frown. "I don't get it."

"No one does," Roxie said. "But be assured, I do make contact with him… regularly." The flirtation of innuendo in that last word put smiles on the women's faces. The men still looked confused. "Are you worried we weak women are too poor and unconnected to help your cause?"

"No!" Johann was quick to say. "No, I didn't mean—"

"The men we have sex with allow us access to their bank accounts. Otherwise, we wouldn't have sex with them. And they like sex. All of them. Especially sex with us… though not collectively. Unless you believe everything you read." She sighed. "We also have access to their Rolodexes." Roxie frowned and turned to Lilya.

"That wasn't right. No one uses that word anymore."

"No," Lilya said, smiling at her friend. "But Zairn wouldn't deny you anything, and it wouldn't be the first time you've swiped his phone."

"It would not. Easiest to do when I'm playing with his cock." These were her kind of ladies. "So worry not, new friends. We can get a party started. Whatever Huddle Hope needs, one of us will find whoever we need. We have contacts in New York too. LA. Chicago. Seattle. All over really." Roxie's confidence never wavered. "People who can get things done fast. As fast as we need them done." The room just hung there, awed by the woman's authority. "Okay, great effort, team. Let's get started."

NINETEEN

ONE VOICE. Another. A laugh. Johann. Bringing Roxie and her crew up to speed was a quick pace adventure. For everyone else anyway.

What the fuck was wrong with him?

As her attention drifted again, it snagged on Roxie who was looking right back. The others were still talking, but Roxie laid a hand across her wrist and leaned in to whisper.

"Who put him in charge?"

It took a second but, seriously, what the fuck? How right was her friend? Her shoulders went back.

What was wrong with him? No! What was wrong with her?

Her spine straightened as her lips plumped. Fuck him.

Roxie just smiled when she stood up. Without bothering to excuse herself, she left the room, his office in her sights. Yep, there were five other people in there, but she didn't give a shit.

Tossing the door out of the way, she strode in,

unbuttoning her shirt.

"Miss—"

"If you boys don't want a show, you better get outta here," she said, clear as a whistle in her determination, her eyes locked onto his.

She kept going with the buttons, pulled her shirt from her skirt and tossed it aside as she rounded the desk.

"Out," a male voice came from behind her. "Go."

Grabbing Rourke's tie, she pulled him upward as she bowed. "You…" she enunciated, "are stuck with me."

Planting her mouth on his, resistance meant nothing. What gave him the right to dismiss her? Damn man got too big for his boots. Kicking off her shoes, she pulled him higher, his resistance evaporating with the rise of her skirt.

It bunched at her hips as she slid onto the desk, taking his cock from his pants.

Damn man.

The sheer bliss of completion filled her when he pushed himself into her. Planting his hands on the desk behind her, thrusting into her, all she could do was raise her hips to meet his. That look in his eyes. Shit. What was in his head?

Breathing out, she laid a hand on his cheek. "Xavie…"

His head turned to catch the heel of her hand in his teeth. Fuck, she wanted that. Wanted more. Freeing his tie, she threw it away to yank open the buttons of his shirt. Their gazes never wavered from their opposite. This was it. In the flesh. Them as they were supposed to be.

Running her hands across his torso, all of him was what she needed. On the desk, in the middle of the day, it would never be as intense as she wanted. But fuck that. She didn't even know if he'd obscured the glass to protect them from the rest of the floor… or to protect the rest of the floor from them. The world could watch. They were all that mattered.

Snatching a handful of her hair, he tugged it back, hard, to force his mouth against hers. Was there force? Depended on the meaning. There was strength, but always consent. He'd tried to say no, to dismiss her like she wasn't the most important person in his world. Right then, in that moment, no one else existed.

Gasping for air, no amount of oxygen could satisfy the clench of climax that seized every part of her in bliss.

"Xav—"

"Fuck," he growled, snagging her hips, propelling all of himself into her in one final advance.

Sitting there, panting into the humid air between them, his forehead dropped to hers.

She couldn't open her eyes, even as he stroked the back of her head to coil his fingers in her locks again.

"I'm your best goddamn friend," she murmured, leaning away from his head to find his gaze. "I don't give you this pussy for free."

On an exhale, his lips quirked. "You know we'll get sued for that stunt."

"You can afford it," she said, linking her fingers at the back of his neck. "You didn't misinterpret anything. Sometimes I forget…"

"Forget what?"

"That you're a man and thickheaded," she said and socked his shoulder. "Don't pout with me. Talk to me."

"You don't keep shit from me. Honesty is the rule now. No Huddle rules."

She patted his chest. "Where is it?"

"Ask your pussy."

"Hilarious," she said, presenting a flat hand to him. "Give it to me."

"Again? Already? Give a guy a second to—"

"The card you want me to break."

From a desk drawer, he produced a wallet. She snatched it away to find said card and dropped the wallet back into his desk.

"You never leave the campus," he said. "How are you going to use it?"

"Uh, there's this fabulous thing called the internet, digiboy. Try it sometime." She tucked the card into her cleavage and guided his hands to her ass. "Here's what we're going to do. I'm going to use the world wide web and make some calls to check out places closer to here for my mom. Expensive places. Really expensive." He smiled, which calmed her heart. "And I'm going to make appointments at really inconvenient times for your schedule, and we'll go together to check them out."

He slid her closer. "Inconvenient times I can make work. Another option is we buy her a place and hire a staff—"

"She needs people around. Social people. When she's by herself, it's worse."

"You want her to stay with us at the house?"

"Live with you? Geez, the woman has enough mental problems, give her a chance at sanity."

"Mm," he hummed, bowing to brush the tip of his nose across hers.

"Did I interrupt something important?" Her mouth edged nearer his. "I don't care if I did, it just makes me feel good to inconvenience you."

"Inconvenience me with sex? Yeah, that was disruptive. We should find a way to ease that transition."

"You found your rhythm quick enough," she murmured, their lips still touching. "Work on limiting your resistance."

"I'll do better next time, Coach."

His tongue touched her lip, and she opened for him. They could spend the whole day screwing on his desk, could get up and leave the building right then to disappear into bed.

Pulling away, she slapped a hand onto his arm. "Okay, time to go back to work."

"I'll talk to your boss," he said, pushing her back on the desk when she tried to slip off. "Guy's an asshole, but he owes me one."

"And I do not want every person on this floor to think you last longer than you do. My pussy is plenty tight for you to spill quick."

"Yep," he said, dropping into his seat when she slunk off the desk. "She got hers too."

His fingers met her clit. She slapped the hand away and crouched to retrieve her shoes. "If she didn't get hers every time, we wouldn't come back for seconds."

"And thirds and fourths."

This time he touched her inner thigh and again she swiped his hand away. "You're supposed to start with the fingers, Boy Scout. Not finish with them."

"Who said I was done?" Catching her hips, he pulled her between him and the desk. "Man, you didn't even lose the panties."

"You know this is sexual harassment."

He kissed her hip, her thigh, her abdomen. "I have witnesses you were the aggressor."

"Mm," she said, grabbing a handful of his hair to yank his head back. "Don't ever pout with me again."

"Don't hide shit from me."

Dipping to kiss his forehead, she smoothed his hair again. "This wasn't makeup sex."

"No, who wants to make up?" he said, finally

letting her go.

"It's better when we're fighting."

"It is."

Slipping on one shoe and then the other, she got her shirt and his tie from the floor. She tossed one to him and fed her arms into the other.

"And it doesn't mean I like you."

"Fuck no," he said, looping his tie over his head, despite his shirt still being open. "I can't stand you."

"You want me to send your worker bees back in here?"

"Oh, I think they're long gone, Babycakes."

"I want sushi for dinner."

Wearing a grin, he winked, and she departed. The walls went clear, and her own lips curled. If that wasn't making up, she didn't know what would be. Fuck. Hotshot was way more than she could ever have expected.

TWENTY

"YOU SAY YOU want sushi and then don't turn up for dinner," Rourke said, striding into her apartment like he had every right.

Like she did at his.

"You took my car away."

The open-plan kitchen and living space presented a balcony beyond. A little skinny one, but a balcony all the same. The bedroom, bathroom, and closet were grouped through the door just next to the couch.

She was on the floor, paper spread out on the coffee table above her outstretched legs.

"You can't walk ten feet or pick up a phone? And I didn't take it away. It's still in the parking lot wherever you left it."

"You're here now. What's the problem?" she asked, finishing the last of her wine. "Did you bring wine?"

"Did I bring wine?" he asked, fake offended, and went back to the bag he'd dumped on the breakfast bar while taking off his jacket. He produced two bottles, showed both, and then brought them to the table. "I want to get laid later."

"So you brought the panty loosening stuff?"

"Cheap and potent, just like you."

"You and I have different opinions on what's cheap."

"Us?" He feigned surprise. "Opposing opinions? That'll be a first."

And she wasn't going to laugh despite the joke. "Open one. Now. Please." Her sickly smile was totally false and didn't pretend not to be. His snit lifted to a snicker when she batted her eyes too. He went off into the kitchen. "We have an appointment for a tour with a residential facility tomorrow. For my mom."

"Okay."

"And Roxie thinks we should have our Hope party in LA."

Opening drawers, he sought something. A corkscrew, no doubt.

"You don't like LA?"

"I know very little about LA other than it's full of pretty, rich people, but will that be a problem for Mosaic?"

"Will pretty, rich people be a problem for Mosaic?" he asked and gave up, slamming a drawer. "Where the fuck is your corkscrew?" Sliding aside a file, she picked it up from the table beside her. "You couldn't have told me you had it?"

"You didn't ask."

"If you had it, why do I need to open it?"

Although he asked, he came to take it from her to twist it into the cork.

"Why have a dog and bark myself?" she asked, showing his glare another manufactured smile. "It amuses me to make you feel needed. Though, my ex-boyfriend had one of those utility knife things. Carried it everywhere."

The cork popped from the bottle.

He opened his arms wide, bottle in one hand, corkscrew in the other. "Look around, beautiful. I own absolutely every single thing you can see. You want that or a utility knife?"

Taking her focus back to the files, she raised her brow and inhaled. "Things I don't care about," she muttered under her breath. "Your dick is *way* bigger than his; that was the choice I made. Screw ownership, I know where to get mine."

He filled her glass. "Good girl."

Her eyes slunk up to his. Not another muscle moved, but their exchange told him plenty.

As he retreated into the kitchen, she shifted onto her knees. "Roxie said we can use the club. Crimson."

"Yeah, I've heard of it."

"You ever heard sarcasm is the lowest form of wit?"

"Must be why you're so good at it," he said.

She wasn't going to smile. Nope. "Is Crimson respectable? Can we invite rich people?"

"I'll be there. Zairn, Knox, if Jane is there, Kintyre for sure. We've got a few bucks between us. How many rich people do you need?"

"If we could get away with just the four of you, we'd fuck it out of you. Why go to the expense of hiring caterers and stockpiling champagne when we could just lay you down on your backs?"

"You could fuck the money out of us," he said, putting food on plates.

"Except you gave us limitless credit cards. Bad move. Now we don't need to break a sweat."

"True. Shame this is about exposure, not money."

"Money helps."

"Money always helps, and money attracts money. With the four of us there, you won't get a single no…" He paused. "Actually, with the Kyst-meister involved, you won't get a single no. She doesn't accept no as an answer. If people say no, she visits them. To get rid of her, they agree to whatever she wants." He returned to the plating. "Maybe she's a distant Collier."

Whatever that meant.

"Franco's excited. Myles, Helena, I think even Johann's looking forward to it."

"That we own the club helps," he said, bringing over food and flatware. "Makes scheduling easy. You can do it whenever you want. We had Roxie's birthday party there last month."

He sat with her on the floor, putting the plates on top of her papers. "I thought Zairn owned the club."

"We don't care about that shit in our group," he said, taking the wine from her.

"You know what I own?"

The glass only just left his lips. "A sweet, tight pussy."

"And…?"

"Surprise me."

So she pushed aside the glass and grabbed a handful of his shirt to pull him into a kiss. So not where she'd been going, but it was no hardship.

"Mmm," he murmured as she pulled back. "You read my mind."

"Damn, and you asked to be surprised. Better luck next time." Laying a hand on her paperwork, she scanned what lay before her. "I have SIT stuff to get through and pitches to approve."

"Pitches for what?" He pulled the collar of her shirt away from the back of her neck to kiss her there. "I thought we were past that for SIT."

Her palm found his thigh beneath the table. "Everyone got into it with ideas about themes and concepts for the fundraiser. I told them to write everything down. I'll see what I can make of it."

"Efficient," he said, tracing his lips toward her shoulder.

A laugh escaped. "If you keep kissing me like that, I won't get anything done."

The wineglass appeared on the table, freeing up his hand. "Then don't get anything done."

His fingers skimmed across her cheek to draw her head around. "Xavie…"

He kissed her. "Mm?"

"Did you approve Hope like you did because we're friends?"

"No," he said and kissed her again.

"Was that a lie?"

"Was it the right answer?"

"Yes," she said, feeling his lips curl against hers.

"Then who gives a fuck?" He guided her hand down to the bulge in his pants. "I'll help you if you take the edge off."

"You brought me sushi," she whispered.

He kind of nodded. Their mouths stayed open, bonded in a semi-kiss.

"Got an even better source of protein for you right here."

Her laugh burst out and she pushed him down onto his back. "Okay, don't overexert the innuendo."

"Is there such a thing?"

Out of her shirt and bra, he was loosening his belt before she got through with his shirt buttons. Work was waiting. Food plated. But, shit, there was only one thing either of them needed.

TWENTY-ONE

THE COFFEE HAD to go faster. It wasn't that she was desperate to drink it, just watching it drip through was driving her nutty.

Impatience was not a virtue, but she had plenty of it.

"Coffee, coffee, coffee," she muttered, bending at the waist to get closer to the pot. Maybe proximity would speed it up. "Mornings mean coffee. Even on a Saturday. Play nice, huh?"

A knock at the door straightened her up. A visitor? Who would look for her there? Roxie maybe. Was it too early in the day for Rox?

Franco came walking in the second the door was out of the frame. "I was thinking about the theme thing."

"Please, Franco, come inside."

As she turned, it seemed to dawn on her colleague that she was only wearing a shirt.

"Sorry, I thought you'd be up."

"I am up," she said, going back to the coffee machine. "My coffee is on a go slow."

"Did you read my proposal?"

"Yes," she said, propping her elbows on the counter, supporting her head on her fists. "I think so. Which one was yours?"

They had read them all. It wasn't like they'd completely slacked off all night. Though the details were always second to his fingers, his tongue, his cock.

"I said the eighties," he said, his voice moved further away to the other side of the breakfast bar. "Pop music, Madonna, you know?"

"She prefers Cyndi Lauper." That was Rourke. Obviously, the boss was joining them. A yawn followed the words, and he smacked her ass hard. "Took my toy out of bed."

"We're waiting for coffee," she said, her jaw staying on her fists. "Why don't I have one of those bean to cup machines we have at the house?"

"I don't know. Why did we sleep here last night?"

In only black boxers, he opened the fridge to grab juice that he drank straight from the bottle.

"He builds a multibillion dollar multinational but can't figure out how to use a glass."

She snatched the juice from his lips, leaving him with a dribble on his chin. Snagging the back of his neck, she yanked him down to clean it up with the tip of her tongue.

"I know how you like to school me, Mistress," he said, reaching for her ass, but she swerved out of the way and put the juice on the counter. "When we going back to bed?"

"We have a guest," she said, folding her arms to lean back on the counter in front of the coffee. "Franco wants to talk about the party." Though he was kind of slack-jawed. "Who likes Cyndi Lauper?"

"Thought you were talking about Rox," he said. "On the Madonna score, she does an amazing 'Material

Girl' number."

"She does not."

"Calling me a liar?" he asked, grabbing an apple from the bowl on top of the fridge.

"Unless you can prove it, yeah. When did you see her—"

"On stage at her birthday gig." He took a big bite of the apple and spoke around it. "Bet there's footage somewhere. Seduce Z, he'll show you."

"You can't hack it for me?"

"I could, but my way's funnier." He nodded at Franco. "Who's this guy again?"

"A loyal employee. Ignore him, Franco. He aims for funny and misses every time."

Leaning in, Rourke buried his face in her hair. "There's one spot I hit every time," he grumbled.

When his hand swung toward her panties, she swatted it away. "You wanted to change something?"

But her colleague's mind was elsewhere. "What about…" Franco said. "What I said about… Joyner?"

"Who's Joyner?" Rourke asked. "Darts Man?"

"No, that was a one-night thing, and that's not what he meant."

"What did he mean?" Rourke asked, slipping his hand into her shirt to caress her breast, scooping her body in front of his.

She stepped away from him, not away from him because it was him, but toward Franco, the breakfast bar still between them.

"Franco, you're a great guy, and we can totally grab a drink sometime," she said. "Screwing Rourke does not change my availability."

Although it didn't help that he came up behind her and crouched to hold her hips.

"Good luck to the guy who follows my example," her arrogant friend said. "But I'll let you take her for a spin around the block if you've got something I want."

Her head turned ninety degrees. "What does he have that you want? And who gave you the right to pimp me out?"

"My house, my car, my building, your employment—"

"Oh," she said, spinning on the spot to glare. "I should be grateful?"

"You're beholden to me."

"Far from it," she said, serious in the face of his amusement. "Just because I allow you the privilege of pleasuring my body, does not give you the right to own or control it."

"What about the credit card?"

"No."

"The sushi?"

"No sushi is worth my self-respect."

"My charming personality?"

"Maybe if you had one."

"Because I'm male and superior to you?" His eyes glittered as they flared, daring her even as he addressed Franco. "Get ready for fireworks, loyal employee. You might need goggles and a cup for what she's brewing."

"Superior to me?" she spat back at him. "You're inferior to the coffee in that machine; I need it more than I need you. Superior? Men like you delude themselves into believing they are superior to make themselves feel better about their weakness."

"I'm weak?"

"If you're one of those males, you are."

"Didn't I prove that last night?"

"That you're male and weak? Yes. Only weak men find it necessary to exert dominance over women. Only weak men are threatened by strong women. Only weak men—"

"Ah! Shit, I get it. You need me to show you!" He stepped right up close, sandwiching her between him and the breakfast bar. Bending his knees on either side of hers, he crouched lower, leveling their eyes. "To take you to your happy place."

"I don't need you for anything."

But when he skimmed both hands onto her upper chest beneath the shirt and scooped the fabric over to the back of her shoulders, exposing them, he proved he didn't need permission. And then he started working on the buttons. One, then the other, and the next…

"You want me for something though," he murmured, his low voice thick and smooth.

Fuck him. Her lumbar trembled with the tickle of anticipation that accentuated the arch of her spine. "You don't deserve to touch me."

"Be a good little woman and submit to your superior."

"Like hell!" she said and tried to shove him away.

He shoved back harder, pushing the small of her back into the harsh angle of the counter. When his fingers curled slowly around her jaw to tip her head back, he held her lips in place to trace his across them.

Damn him. She jerked up, grabbing his lower lip in her teeth.

A rumbling groan shook his throat. That strain on his control put a smug smile on her face. If she wanted it, he did too. Neither of them lost, they both won. Though she didn't mind reminding him of her altruism.

Snatching her hips, he spun her around. "We're gonna do it whether you stand there and watch or not, employee," Rourke said, bending her over the counter. "Get! Go on. Shoo!"

Franco bolted, dashing away before the door slammed.

"That was rude. Xavie—"

"Stop talking…" he prodded her ass with the head of his dick, "or I'll put this in your mouth, and I won't be any gentler."

No, never. Gentle wasn't what she wanted. Her desire came when—slamming himself into her, he didn't take the time to test or tease her. His groan let loose when he was up to the hilt and a shiver went through both of them.

"I felt that."

"Quiet. There's etiquette for being a billionaire's whore."

"Good thing I'm not one," she said, stretching her arms across the counter. "Do your work, Boy Scout, and maybe you'll get a cookie after."

She didn't have cookies or know where the apple had gone, but fuck, he filled her up in all the right ways.

TWENTY-TWO

"AS YOU CAN see, our facilities are second to none," their guide said, strolling down a carpeted hallway lined with generic art. "We take our work here seriously. Your family is our family."

Uh huh.

"Thank you," Rourke said as they stopped in a bedroom doorway. "Could you give us a minute?"

"Of course," the woman said and widened her smile before walking away.

His hand curled around her elbow to lead her into the room. "What's going on?"

"It's beautiful," she said, going to the full height windows that looked out over the view of the grounds.

"Yeah, the fingernail crescents in the back of my hand scream ecstatic." She glanced down when he stopped beside her. "The scratches on my back, I can handle. They come with a happy ending." She bit the inside corner of her mouth. "What did I tell you about holding back, Radley?"

"I'm not holding back." Her head shook. "I

don't know it's…"

"If you don't like it, we'll look at other facilities."

"We have appointments with other places."

"Okay, so is this one out? That big-eyebrow guy we met at the front desk kept popping up to check out your tits." His own eyes dropped to them, and he nodded to the side. "Which I guess is fair for a guy not at liberty to play with them."

"It feels wrong."

"What feels wrong?"

"Relocating her life to suit mine. She has friends where she is, people who give her routine and stability."

"Okay, so we relocate them too. We'll relocate their whole families. No one will object."

Because he'd pay them not to. She wasn't mad. In fact, when he was being so generous, it was difficult to remember they didn't like each other.

She smiled. "What if I want to relocate Mosaic?"

"Then we relocate Mosaic," he said with a semi-eye roll and zero hesitation. "We'll make money wherever we go, baby. The location doesn't matter."

"Providing it has a bed."

"Now you're getting it."

"I'll talk to my sister," she said. "Get her opinion."

"She live near your mom?"

"She tends to… travel."

His brows got slightly closer. "Oh-kay."

"We're covering the cost, it's not like she has to pay anything. But I do have to tell her where our mom is."

"Do we know where she'll be?"

"Not yet. I prefer to see everything that's on offer before I make my final decision."

He moseyed in closer to embrace her, switching her angle to show the bed. "While you ponder, let's talk about payment."

"You want to have sex in a hospital?"

"It's not like a hospital, hospital, people aren't dying."

"So long as no one's dying, it's not disrespectful?" she said, containing her laugh. "The door is open."

"Never stopped us before," he said and crouched to kiss her. "I think you like the exhibitionist thing."

"I think I do too," she said, though sex and proclivities with him didn't always match up to her previous experience. "Helps that you have the money to pay off offended witnesses."

"That's what those babies are for," he said, eyeing her chest again.

Enjoying each other always came with a time limit. Work. Friends. Commitments. They used to hang out for hours just arguing with each other.

"Let's go somewhere, just for the hell of it."

"Where?" he asked. "Bali? You'd like Bali."

"Okay, braggart. You think I'd let you traffic me out of the country? I meant like a hotel. Local."

"That's unexciting," he said and sniffed. "Probably wouldn't get much for you overseas anyway."

"It just so happens I have a credit card we can use," she murmured, stroking a pointed middle finger up his chest.

"Lucky you."

"Belongs to a guy who just can't keep it in his pants around me."

"Bet he's grateful you give it up so easy."

"I humor him." Their eyes met. "There are people at home, and I've never had caviar."

"Oh, it's going to be one of those weekends?"

"If you play your cards right, maybe. You want to pamper me?"

"I want to fuck you."

"Then pampering it is."

"What would you do without me to look after you?" he asked.

Stepping back, she threaded their fingers together to guide him toward the door. "Read more, probably. Maybe broker world peace," she said, glancing back to show him a smile. "I'll start looking up hotels, if you do the 'we'll let you know' speech."

They went out and down the hall to be buzzed through the secure door by reception. "Speech?" he asked, pulling their joined hands across his body. "Check this out."

Their guide was there, waiting. "Did you—"

"We'll let you know," Rourke said without slowing for a beat.

They got outside and back into the car. "That was abrupt."

"Do you care?"

"No," she said, retrieving her phone from her purse. "Now about my hotel—"

"I know where we're going," he said, revving the engine.

Her phone dropped back into its previous slot. "You do, huh?"

"Yeah, only one place around here worth it if you want five-star."

"I don't care if it's a rent by the hour slut dump," she said, wriggling deeper into her seat. "I have an itch."

"Then I guess I have one too. Is it a cream or do I have to take antibiotics?"

That smirk went without an answer, and they drove deeper into the city.

"You never talk about your family."

"My family?" he asked. "You met my family. Zairn and Rox anyway. You'll meet the rest of them at the Hope party. Most of them. K2 won't crawl out of his cave, even for charity. Doesn't matter though, he hates people. More people talk about being connected to him than actually are. He wouldn't widen your exposure. You can use his name; he won't care about that." Apparently, he'd missed she didn't know this *K2* person's full name. "Truth is, he spends so much time in the damn mountains, he would never know anyway."

His friends were one thing. Yes, he cared about them. That was obvious. But she wanted to know more.

"What about your parents?"

"Divorced when I was young."

"Siblings?"

"A brother. Stepbrother. If that counts. What I should say is I have a stepbrother I know about. Haven't kept up with my dad for years. And you know, he could have twenty kids and his life wouldn't change at all."

Another smirk.

"Your mother remarried?" Slightly obvious question. "Do you get along with him? Your stepbrother? Where is he?"

"In the Pacific." She switched her frown to him and he laughed. "Yeah, terrifying, isn't it?"

"Dyce," she said. "Zane Dyce is your brother?"

"Stepbrother. We don't advertise it."

"I can't believe I didn't know this," she said, swatting his arm. "And you tell me I hide things?"

"You didn't ask."

"I want to meet him."

"You said that already. If you want to go to the island, we'll go to the island."

"I don't want to go now. We have this Hope party to plan."

"I'm not planning your party. Flowers and glitter. That's woman's work. Ah, but you need me to direct you. You need a man in charge, don't you, Babycakes?"

"You want to pull over and I'll prove who's in charge of this friendship?"

He flashed her a wink. "Anytime you want to be on top, Babycakes…"

"I can't believe I didn't know you're related to Zane Dyce. Forget the hotel. We're going home so I can embargo sex."

"Good luck trying. Do you want me to pull over and prove who's in charge of this friendship?"

She let that one slide on by. Wouldn't be right to gouge out his eyes while he was driving and all.

"When's he coming home?" she asked.

"Dyce? I don't know."

"Will he come back for the Hope party?"

"If I ask him to come, he will. Do you want me to ask him? He'll ask why, and if I tell him it's for a girl, he might expect a reward."

"And maybe I'll give him one. Is he richer than you? Better hung?"

He laughed. "He's *way* too easygoing for you. I don't think the guy knows how to argue."

"He's one of the biggest tech geniuses of his generation. He's CEO of a worldwide—"

"What does he look like?"

"What?"

"Zane Dyce, tell me something about him other than his name."

"He's your brother. Not mine. If you want to learn about him, pick up a phone."

"When you combine money and genius like that, you don't have to be aggressive or high profile. He gets his way. Every time. You know why?"

"Why?" she asked, slipping off her shoes.

"Because he's always right." Glancing at her, he grinned. "Yeah, imagine what it takes for me to say that out loud. Maybe I rubbed off on him."

"You are not always right," she said. "In fact, you're never right."

"Picked you, didn't I?"

"They say our bodies crave what we lack. You know, like calcium or iron or whatever. It's biology. A primitive drive. You probably picked me because what you lack is good sense and smarts."

"Know where I'm not lacking?"

His swagger encouraged her smile. "We could always build my mom her own custom facility."

"We can." And suddenly he was serious. "Put Hope on hold until you have that under control. Family takes precedence over business."

"Huddle Hope isn't business." Relaxing her head on the headrest, she admired his profile. Without looking, he reached over to lay a hand on her knee. "Or I could hand Hope off to Roxie."

"Hope is your baby, baby. I want both hands on the wheel. Your hands."

His generosity didn't surprise her. Neither did his faith in her. Yes, they made their jibes and belittled each other, but that was nothing. When it was real, it was real. What they were was completely genuine and innate.

Their security ran so deep, it didn't occur to her to question it. Hence why he'd been hurt when he thought she'd hidden the truth about her mom. They didn't hide things from each other. Embarrassment or shame couldn't exist between them, not really. In their friendship, they belonged to and owned each other fully.

Picking up his hand, she kissed his palm and tucked it between her ear and the headrest. That lasted all of three seconds.

"Radley, baby, appreciate it, but this is a manual and we're in city traffic."

Allowing his hand its freedom, she just smiled. "I could totally screw it up, you know? Hope. I could take all your money and ruin your reputation along with countless lives."

"Think it would stop me?"

"No."

"I screw up, you screw up. You screw up, we screw up. It's the circle of friendship, Babycakes. We have a contract."

She slid her hand across his leg to his inner thigh. "If it feels good, it's allowed…?"

"That," he said, adjusting his position and her hand, putting it to work, warming him up, not that he ever cooled down. Sometimes it was like being with a horny teenager. No judgment, she was no better. "And friendship is real and permanent, whether you like it or not. That's the beauty of it. It keeps going long after the love has faded."

"You think our love has faded?" she teased.

"Fades every time I shoot my load in you, Babycakes. Then I've gotta build it back up for the next time."

"You're crude."

"You love it." And he was right. As always, they jived with each other's wavelength and knocked as many out of the park as they did teeing up the punchline for the other. "I'm your best friend, Radley. No matter what, you're still going to pick up the phone the next day and talk to me. It's in the contract."

"You're a chauvinistic bigot," she murmured.

"You're a dandelion snowflake." His chin bobbed toward her chest. "Take 'em out."

Arching, she eased the fabric from her shoulders to widen her scoop neck. "That's as much as you get until you pony up. I want caviar."

"I am caviar. Luxury, rich—"

"And best enjoyed in small doses?"

"You want me to pamper you? Caviar?

Champagne? Orgasms?"

"Yes, please," she said, laying on a little sarcasm of her own. "Do a good job, maybe I'll let you be my whore full time."

"Better treat me right. Show a little gratitude. Make me feel appreciated." She wriggled her top further down. "Just like that."

He stole her hand to lay it on the stick shift under his.

Nothing wrong with a little time off, was there? They deserved a weekend of debauchery. Who was there to tell them otherwise? The business wouldn't suffer, and they could multitask. They could depend on each other. Not that she'd ever admit he'd been right.

TWENTY-THREE

"DON'T WORRY, she'll be here," Roxie's voice carried from the kitchen. "We have time."

Rounding from the hall, she strode over to the women at the island by the patio pocket doors. "I'm sorry! I know, I was supposed to be here a half hour ago."

Actually, the original meeting was scheduled for Monday morning at Mosaic. Somehow, it took her and Rourke until Wednesday to find their way out of the hotel suite. She couldn't be sorry. Turning off their phones and doing nothing but each other was exactly the medicine both of them needed.

"Don't worry about it," Roxie said, swirling red wine in her glass. "We've all done it."

"Done what?" she asked, grabbing the bottle to pour wine into the empty glass next to it.

Lilya sat opposite Jane and Roxie with her own glass of something orange. Fruit juice. Oh, the delights of pregnancy. The restrictions were just another in a long list of reasons she didn't plan to have children. Ever.

"Locked ourselves in a bedroom with our honeys." Roxie tipped her glass toward the other side of the island. "Lilya kept Kintyre locked up until he impregnated her."

Lilya straightened. "It wasn't a specified criterion. I can't help it if his sperm are super-swimmers."

Jane's focus stuck to Roxie. "We hardly saw Merci and Reid on Crimson Isle."

"Rainie and Gauge get the award for longest lock-in, that was like two weeks straight," Roxie said. "He came back from Australia for her; I guess she owed him some kind of reward."

"Zairn did a Tokyo round trip in like two days when you were broken up."

"Trust you to remember that," Roxie said. "Gauge bought the company who fired Rainie. That was hot."

Lilya picked up Jane's mantle. "Zairn gave you Lola's Liberty with a billion dollars in its account for your birthday. What did he tell you?"

Their friend rolled her eyes. "To go play."

"So romantic," Jane swooned.

Roxie raised a pointed finger. "Technically, it's a charitable donation, so he can claim it in taxes… or something. I don't know. He says I'll get the hang of the embezzlement thing soon."

That got a laugh.

"Is there a man alive less likely to embezzle company funds?" Lilya asked.

To which Roxie and Jane replied in unison. "Kintyre."

Another laugh.

"I could persuade him to be bad," Lilya said, leaning back to show the hand on her hardly there baby bump. "If I could tell him it was in our child's best interest."

"I think he'd do anything for you," Jane said.

Both Roxie and Lilya flattened their affects.

"Knox Collier," Lilya said.

"Do we have to say it every time?" Roxie asked.

Jane sighed. "I know."

"Your stalker's in jail in England."

"Not for stalking me!"

"No," Lilya said. "But that's how dedicated he is. You don't think Knox was behind the convenient arrest?"

"Even impressed me, and I don't like him." Roxie laughed when Jane whined. "I'm kidding, honey. You know I'm kidding. Besides…" When Roxie's head turned toward her, all three women's attention zeroed in on her. "We're missing the point."

"What's the point?" she asked, drinking some wine.

"What's the script with you and Rourke?"

Maybe she should start on the spirits. "The script? There's no script."

"You're all over each other all the time."

"They're doing each other all over all the time," Lilya said. "Are you together?"

"When we're having sex, yeah," she said, slipping onto a stool at the head of the island. "Hard not to be with him when he's inside me. I'm not always paying attention, but that's on him. Sometimes you have to let them do their thing, you know? Let them think they're good at it. Like when kindergarteners bring art home to their parents. They have to pat them on the head and stick it to the fridge, even if it's hideous. It's an unwritten law."

"Do you love him?" Jane asked, revealing so much of herself in those glittering, innocent eyes.

"He's my friend… unfortunately."

"That means?"

"Unfortunately, he's an asshole. I have an asshole as a friend. Yep, difficult to admit, but it's an unavoidable truth. A superior asshole who—"

"Are you exclusive?"

"When we're fucking," she said. "I could handle another guy, but I wouldn't ask any other woman to put up with his sloppy technique."

"You're being evasive."

Not deliberately. She laughed because that was the norm when Rourke was around. Sometimes she forgot when he wasn't in the room. Probably because he was always in her head, one way or another. And she often forgot that not everyone was like them.

"I don't know what you want me to say. It's not like that, we're not…" How could she explain it to three women who embraced commitment with stark, obvious boundaries and clear, articulated ownership? "I love him, yes." Jane perked up. "He's my best friend…" That deflated the innocent beauty a little. "I would never do anything to hurt him, and I know he wouldn't hurt me. What we are isn't like…"

"It's an open relationship?" Lilya asked.

"We don't have a relationship to open and close. Talking about forever isn't us. Neither of us are interested in that."

"What if he came in here with another woman right now?"

"He won't. Guy's been up to his eyeballs at the office since lunch." When they'd returned from the hotel. "He's got enough on his plate."

Had she distracted him? What had he done with his days before she was around, leading him astray? That was a joke. She'd distracted him even back before they'd met in reality.

"But what if he did?" Jane asked.

"Then I hope he has a ball with her."

"You can't not care."

She shrugged. "It won't happen. His focus is elsewhere. And we're sort of… unspoken."

"Do you want to get married?"

Simple question. "No."

"How do you know that you're… How do you know when to not…"

"Hit on other people? It doesn't work like that." Now all of them were confused. "Look…" She laid a flat hand on the counter. "We do what feels good. We do whatever we want whenever we want. It just so happens that right now, what we want to do is screw like rabbits. If I'm not in the mood, he accepts that or changes it. Same the other way around. We don't have language or rules, we have…"

"Feelings," Jane said.

Respect. Though that seemed like an ironic description given how much time they spent disrespecting each other for sport.

"We're each other's default." Was that a better way to describe it? "We default to each other. Whether that's talking something out, teasing each other, or getting each other off. We're open for each other twenty-four, seven."

"And if someone else got between you?" Lilya asked.

"Wouldn't happen," she said, shaking her head. "If we got involved with other people, that wouldn't change our friendship. Yeah, maybe he'll have to keep it in his pants around me, but so what? Soon as the lady's out of his life, if he needs a rebound, I'll be open for business, for whatever he needs. Just like he'd be for me."

"I don't get it," Lilya said.

Jane was as perplexed though there was a

curiosity there.

It wasn't as potent as Roxie's. "Are you kidding yourself?" She gestured at the trio. "We've all got into the fling mindset. We think it doesn't mean anything until we lose our guy and then it becomes... clear. If someone took Rourke away from you—"

She laughed. "No one can do that."

"If I was Rourke's girlfriend, I would hate you," Lilya said, lifting her glass. "Just saying."

"Me too," Roxie agreed and nudged Jane. "She won't say it, but she would as well. I put up with Kesley, I like Kesley, and Trish, Zairn's list goes on and on, but you're... You two are too..."

"Symbiotic," Lilya said.

"Thank you," she said, frowning, unsure if that was a compliment.

"That's it. That's exactly what it is. You're not co-dependent because you're completely fine, healthy, rounded individuals, but it's like... you exist together."

Okay. Now confusion closed around her. Apparently, everyone had to take a shot on the "what the hell?" train.

"Do you think he feels the same way?" Jane asked. "If you were with a guy, would he get mad?"

"Providing he gets something out of the deal, he's happy to pimp me out." As his interaction with Franco revealed. "He'd never get jealous and wouldn't need to be jealous. No third party changes our friendship."

"Maybe he loves her," Jane said, almost appealing to Roxie to make sense of it. "Maybe Roux thinks it's not a big deal, she thinks it's just sex and then..."

Roxie took Jane's hand. "I love you."

"That's not the same," Jane said, sagging into a slouch.

"Do you think he loves you?" Lilya asked.

"I know he does."

"Does he say it?"

"Would he say it?"

Restraining a laugh wasn't easy. If she wasn't in it, she might not understand it either.

Male voices carried down the hall. Not clear enough to be heard word for word, but loud enough to herald their arrival.

"Let's find out," she whispered, knowing exactly how it would play out.

Rourke and Zairn came into the kitchen. As Zairn peeled away to head for Roxie, Rourke's focus was the fridge.

"Did the beer come?" he asked.

"I love you, Boy Scout," she called out, leaning away from the island.

"Yeah, I love you too. Did the beer come?"

She shared a smile with the surprised and confused women. Zairn was frowning too. Yep, they were a conundrum.

"Will the world crash to a halt if our super special imported beer didn't show up?"

"It didn't?" His concern turned her around, just to laugh at him, but that was allowed. "You're screwing with me."

She gasped. "Me? I would never do that, baby." His hand was already on the fridge handle. "Open it and see. I haven't checked." And hadn't even thought to. The fridge wasn't high on her priority list. "These lovely ladies were already drinking when I got here."

"What a surprise," Zairn said, kissing the top of Roxie's head.

"Lilya has a friend for you in Boston, Boy Scout," she said, raising the rim of her glass to her lip. "She thinks you'd be perfect together."

"Nah, no, no, I don't think so," Rourke said, popping the cap off a beer bottle. Good, his foreign treat was there, maybe now he'd relax. "No more long distance anything. It's much easier to discipline a woman when you can spank her into submission."

Jane gasped and Roxie put an arm around her in a half hug. "Don't worry, honey. I'm sure Roux spanks him back."

"No, he enjoys it too much. I go straight for the CBT."

Roxie's mouth opened like she got it, Jane's confusion deepened. "Isn't that like a mental health therapy thing?"

"Yes," Roxie said, pronouncing her nod. "That's exactly what it is, honey. Talk therapy."

"Guess we know what Knox isn't into," Lilya murmured.

These ladies were funny. Despite being different in so many ways, their friendship worked. Opposites could attract in all walks of life.

Rourke's hand landed on her shoulder and kept going, sliding under her neckline to fondle her chest. "Are we going out tonight?"

Good grope. Yep, there were no words for what they were.

"I don't want to go out tonight," she said. "I want to have sex in the pool."

"Before dinner or after?"

"Don't they always say you shouldn't swim on a full stomach?"

"Swim? What the hell kinda sex do you want to have? We're not fucking dolphins."

"You won't be fucking anything with that smart mouth."

He kissed the top of her head. "Better I fuck yours."

"And who's hungry?" Roxie asked, slapping both hands on the counter to hop off her stool.

TWENTY-FOUR

"ARE YOU SCARED?"

"No," Roxie said to Jane after dinner. Outside at the patio table, the women sat opposite the men. "I've seen it."

"Are you scared?" Jane asked Zairn.

"I wake up scared every day, Jane," he said. "That's what being married to Lola means."

"You're not married yet," Jane said, her wide smile brimming. "I can't wait for the wedding. It will be magnificent. I'm pulling out all the stops. Roxie said carte blanche."

"Anything you want," Zairn said. "We want it to be perfect and this isn't our field."

"I promise you won't be disappointed. It's so exciting." Jane grabbed Roxie's arm but leaned toward Zairn. "She looks amazing in her dress."

"She'll look amazing out of it too," Zairn said.

Roxie laughed but was quick to stroke Jane's hair. "Don't upset her dream. Weddings are her catnip. She will breathe in every second."

"I'm sorry, Jane." So smooth. The ease of Zairn's honeyed words, the smolder with their confidence. She couldn't look away. "I'd love to hear the details."

That was the ticket to getting Jane going. The woman started talking so fast that it was difficult to pick one word from another.

Her phone buzzed, and she turned it over as she picked up her wine.

HOTSHOT: FEEL LIKE GETTING WET?

Oh, they were playing this game? She didn't even look at him and typed a response.

FIREFLY: UH, WE'RE ENTERTAINING. DON'T BE RUDE.

HOTSHOT: THE POOL'S RIGHT THERE. I KNOW YOU'RE THINKING ABOUT IT.

FIREFLY: AND HOW WOULD YOUR FRIENDS LIKE THAT?

HOTSHOT: MAYBE THEY WON'T NOTICE.

FIREFLY: US STRIPPING OFF AND GOING AT IT? WE'RE TALKING ABOUT WEDDINGS AND ROMANCE. NICE THINGS. NOT S3X THINGS.

HOTSHOT: AWW, LOOK AT YOU CENSORING YOURSELF.

FIREFLY: WE'RE ON HUDDLE.

HOTSHOT: WE'RE ON A BLIND SERVER. PRIVATE TO ME. RUN BY ME. YOU DON'T THINK I YANKED YOUR RESTRICTIONS THE MINUTE I PUT A FACE TO THE NAME?

FIREFLY: SO I CAN CALL YOU AN ASSHOLE?

HOTSHOT: IF YOU WANT. AND YOU CAN SEND ME PICS SANS CLOTHES. I'LL ADD THEM TO MY GALLERY OF YOUR NAKED AND ASLEEP PICS. WILL BE NOVEL TO HAVE SOME WITH YOUR EYES OPEN. I GET A LOT OF REQUESTS FOR THOSE. NOW I CAN CHARGE MORE.

FIREFLY: PRIVATE MEANS I CAN TELL YOU THAT YOU'RE AN ARROGANT PIG WHO DOESN'T DESERVE TO KISS A WOMAN'S FEET, LET ALONE SLIDE HIMSELF INTO HER BODY.

HOTSHOT: I KNEW YOU WERE THINKING ABOUT IT. AFTER TONIGHT, YOU'LL NEVER BE ABLE TO LOOK AT A SWIMMING POOL AGAIN WITHOUT THINKING ABOUT ME FUCKING YOU.

FIREFLY: YOU HAVEN'T FUCKED ANYTHING YET.

HOTSHOT: I'M READY TO GO RIGHT HERE. RIGHT NOW.

FIREFLY: OH, YEAH? YOU RISEN TO THE CHALLENGE ALREADY? WHAT DO YOU NEED ME FOR? GO SCREW YOURSELF.

Peeking up from her phone, she arched a probing brow when his eyes met hers.

"Anyone else feel like they're in a porno?" Roxie asked.

Everyone was looking at them. When had the others stopped talking?

"What?" Rourke asked, putting down his phone. "Nothing to see here."

"Not if you have your way," she said.

Rourke blew her a kiss with just his lips.

"You're circling each other." The corner of Roxie's mouth curled. "You don't even realize how you heat up a room when you're sparring with each other." Her friend sighed and looked at Zairn. "Have we lost our spark?"

Zairn laughed. "I'm ready to spark any time you are, Lola."

"Which leaves Jane and I to entertain each other," Lilya said.

And Rourke wasn't going to let that one go. "Maybe Kintyre should check whose kid that really is."

If there was something to throw at him, she'd have taken aim, but the wine was too good to waste.

"We should go back to Dyce's, Jane." Lilya relaxed. "I think there's still packing to do."

"She'll never fall for that." Roxie drank some wine. "We're leaving in a matter of hours. She's packed and repacked for everyone several times. Astrid doesn't know what to do with herself."

"You think I upset her?" Jane asked, obviously worried. "I didn't mean to offend her."

"You couldn't offend anyone, honey."

"Except Radley," Rourke said. "She offends easy."

"Because I don't subscribe to your religion that all men are gods?"

"Feel free to worship," he said, sliding down in his seat, linking his hands on his head. "Thou shalt not worship any god other than me."

"Thou shalt not worship. End of sentence."

"Everyone has the freedom to choose their own god."

"And it doesn't surprise me that you'd pick yourself." She sat up straight. "Were you dropped on your head as a baby?"

"Could be," he said with a shrug, though his hands stayed interlinked. "Maybe that's where the genius comes from."

"Learn a little humility. You'd be far more impressive if you practiced modesty."

"This is modest, Babycakes. I've got the goods to back it up and more than enough cash to sweeten the deal."

"Paying for it won't keep you warm at night."

"That's why I've got you. Why else would I keep you around? I've got to look after you and I have to be paid for the pleasure."

"Half the time I'm lucky if you're paying attention," she said. "I like it when you get like this. It reminds me how important contraception is. We have too many men like you."

"You need men like me. Men like me keep the world turning, Babycakes. And it's up to women like you to fulfill your role."

"Which is?" Lilya asked.

She held up a hand, eyes still locked on his. "Don't engage him when he's like this, Lilya, please. Be glad you found yourself a real man who knows how to treat a woman like a human being."

"Lilya's fulfilling her role, her biological imperative," Rourke said. "Carrying a man's child. His son. Making a man for a man."

"Oh, is that what she's doing? Not maybe that she has hope for the future? Hope that she'll be able to raise a man aware of his limits and equality to all other living things?"

"You think I'm equal to all living things?" His laugh was a blast of incredulity. "Sweetheart, I am the center of the fucking universe."

"Damn," Lilya said. "Now I want to punch him."

She sighed. "Unfortunately, I want to jump him."

Her fist met her chin to catch the weight of her head. "He comes to heel so quick for pussy."

The heat in his playful, arrogant eyes rose with the slant of his lips.

"And that's our cue."

"No!" she said, grabbing Roxie's hand before she could stand. "You're leaving tomorrow. Damn champagne and caviar."

Glaring at Rourke didn't lessen his swagger. "And cock. You prioritize the Cs. Champagne, caviar, cock, and coffee."

"Not necessarily in that order, but for maybe the first time ever, you might just be right, Boy Scout."

A phone rang in the kitchen.

Jane jumped up. "Oh, I—"

"Go on, honey." Roxie's calm permission prompted Jane to rush inside. "And she believed there was a chance she wasn't crazy in love with him."

"I'm desperate to meet this Knox and Kintyre too. He seems saintly," she said, crossing her legs beneath the table. "Unlike some people at this table. I have no idea what you two talk about, if he's so perfect and you're so not." She drew her eyes off Rourke to focus on the others. "Though Hotshot isn't the only one at this table with explaining to do."

Roxie, Zairn, and Lilya got the evil eye next.

"What did we do?"

"No one told me that my Boy Scout was related to wealth and beauty."

"You're obsessed with my brother," he muttered.

"Dyce," Zairn said. "You didn't tell her?"

"Uh, you didn't tell me, Casanova. I didn't know they were related. Who's older—wait, how do they have different last names? Oh, was there a sexy, salacious affair?"

"Rourke's mom married Dyce's father."

"Stepbrothers," Roxie said and looked at Lilya. "Did you know?"

"No, but being honest, it's not the kind of thing I would ask either. Zach and I don't spend a lot of time talking about Rourke's family… or Rourke in general."

Their host clucked his tongue. "That's 'cause you're busy making babies, Sweet Thang."

"Insult the woman one more time and I'll use my teeth tonight," she threatened his smirk.

"Your fangs? Better than your talons."

"I like leaving scars. Deep, deep scars."

"On my heart, Babycakes. You can have that; I'm keeping my cock."

"That's unfair," she grumped. "It's the only part of you that works… and the only part of you I like… sometimes."

"All the time, baby, don't kid yourself. You want it."

"Your cock? Yeah, and I'd want it more if it wasn't attached to you. I guess God had to give you something to work with, or you'd never have a chance of touching a woman in my league."

Roxie laughed. "Neither of you can help yourselves!" Her eyes met her fiancé's. "Is that what we sound like?"

She and Rourke weren't the only ones heating things up. When Roxie and Zairn made eye contact, their conversation was entirely silent, but no less potent.

"Do you really have to go back to LA?" she asked, interrupting their foreplay. "You're the sane voice around here. You can't leave me here with Rourke. That's cruel and unusual punishment."

"I'm sorry, honey," Roxie said, lacing their fingers together. "The first part of the documentary airs tomorrow. We have a watch party and reactions.

Streaming. Comments. The whole deal. It's press, press, press for a while. But we're in LA for almost three weeks, you can come hang out whenever you want. Jane has a big LA mansion. Superstar stuff. Lots and lots of space."

Her head tilted. "I didn't know she had money."

"Oh, yeah. Jane is loaded," Roxie said after finishing her drink. "She has a bunch of money. Bags and bags of cold, hard cash. It just happens to be in Knox's bank account."

Looking at Roxie and Zairn, there was no doubting their love. Knox and Kintyre were mysteries. Like Lilya said, they weren't a regular topic of conversation. She'd have to find the time to quiz Rourke about his friends. She already cared about Roxie and Lilya. Jane was such a sweetheart that it was impossible not to be protective of her. The Collier family, the media monolith, were strong, ruthless, bold. How did Jane fit in with that?

"I'll need to come down sometime for the party planning," she said because there was still so much to do, and her curiosity had to be satisfied. "Are you sure we can get it off the ground in two weeks?"

The countdown to the party had started. Only two weeks and three days to wait.

"Well, the invitations have gone out, so if we can't then those people will still have a great time at Crimson. One way or another."

Whether it was at a hip nightclub or a highbrow fundraiser.

"Will people have space in their schedules at such short notice?"

As usual, Roxie wasn't worried. "One thing you'll learn with the uber-rich is that they do whatever the hell they want. If they don't want to come, they're busy. If they do—"

"We lock ourselves in hotel suites with the

women we love," Zairn said. "You love the uber-rich, Lola."

"I love you. Uber-rich or not… You better start getting used to the idea that the time may come when I'll be worth more than you."

"I'm ready for that." Zairn was unfazed. "That's when I'll off you and rent myself an exchange student's uterus."

Hmm, maybe they weren't a normal couple after all. That was a strange kind of kinky.

"Dunlap's bringing the contract next week and I will read the small print. You don't have to be as thorough, not on my account," Roxie said, opening her mouth in an audible inhale before rolling her focus back to her. "Trust me…" Roxie took her hand. "The Hope party is not the kind of thing we do often. With the documentary and surrounding whatever, Z and I will be a hot ticket. Hotter than usual. We're always hot." She loved her friend's mock hair toss. "Whatever people think they have on, they'll cancel for us. They will. I guarantee the club will be past capacity."

"Especially when we have Knox out there ruining anyone who thinks about snubbing the invite," Rourke said. "Reid bringing Merci?"

"We said they didn't have to make the trip," Roxie answered even though Rourke had been talking to Zairn. "They'll contribute, obviously, and make the rounds in Manhattan. We don't want our group seen together too much, do we? And there are a lot of weddings coming up."

"I'm sorry I missed Jane and Knox's." Laughter rose from all angles. "Okay, why is that funny?"

"They're not actually married," Roxie said. "The media reported there was a wedding on Crimson Isle, but there wasn't."

"Oh. Oops."

Jane came hurrying out of the kitchen. "Knox says he has a surprise."

"Oh, I love a surprise," Roxie said. Growing suspicious, the blonde's eyes flicked back and forth between the men. "What do you two know?"

"If we know anything and say anything, it won't be a surprise," Zairn said.

Was that genuine or evasive?

"Z has surprises, Knox has surprises, Zach got Lil pregnant, surprise," Rourke said. "You pussies need to take your women in hand. I'll need to stage an intervention."

"With whom?" Zairn asked. "K2's off the grid."

"As always, these days."

"We lost Dyce to his deserted tropical island, and Cam has a lifestyle. Caspian's probably forgot there's anything more to a woman than her pussy."

"That's not a bad way to be," Rourke said. "I'll call the Wyldes. They must know men need to keep their women in line."

"All of them are single."

Rourke sneered. "You've changed. Where's our playboy gone?"

Zairn laughed. "Ask Lola."

Taking women in hand? No, the power was strong in the feminine camp. These men were their playthings, not the other way around.

She got up and slipped off her shoes while loosening her hair to shake it free. The tease in Rourke's countenance softened to a smolder.

"Is *this* our cue?" Roxie asked. When she took off her top and rolled down the zip on her skirt, Roxie jumped to her feet to kiss her cheek. "Come on, my minions, let's give the woman a chance to work."

The others retreated into the house as she strutted around the table.

"We're entertaining," Rourke said, his hands sliding onto her hips to push off her skirt, letting it fall to the slate beneath her feet. Rather than go down to his level, she put her hands on his and stepped back, tempting him out of his chair. "That was rude."

"You asked if I was in the mood to get wet," she said, unzipping his pants. "You a pussy tease?"

"Oh, baby," he said, surprising her by stooping to scoop her up. "The teasing hasn't even started yet."

Striding to the pool, he kept going, boosting them both off the edge and into the water, clothes and all. Fuck it. What an idiot. She twisted beneath the chlorine, righting her body intending to kick up, but there he was, already pulling her out and pinning her to the edge.

"You're an overachiever," she said, holding her own elbows after her arms twined around his neck.

"I think that's the first nice thing you've ever said about me." He grinned and focused on kicking off his pants. "You wet yet?"

"Which part?"

He winked and their mouths came together like opposite poles of a magnet drawn to each other. Yeah, he threw himself, them both, into the deep end, but she had nothing to worry about. He'd been there to catch her and always would be.

TWENTY-FIVE

"I GET THAT," she said to Johann in their conference room.

They'd like each other one day. As it was, just the fact they were no longer snarking was progress.

"We need to put together the bones of the system."

"That's not my area of expertise or yours."

Without Roxie, Lilya, and Jane around, their boardroom hub echoed. Even after a week without the trio, their conspicuous absence shook up the dynamic. Reduced to their original gang, decisions were more difficult with fewer votes. Especially fewer of those who sided with her.

Franco had been staring in the direction of Rourke's office all day. "What's going on in there?"

The walls were opaque. Yes, she was curious too, but that was exactly his game. Hence why she wasn't rising to it.

"I don't care," she said.

"Johann's right," Helena said. "We should at

least be interviewing."

"You think Rourke will let us pick anyone to code on his system?" It was funny. Actually laughing wouldn't go over well though. "He's on it. I know he will be. And I'd bet he'll pick someone in-house or someone unavailable."

"How can he pick someone unavailable?"

"You want to bet when Xavien Rourke picks up the phone that whoever he chooses will be immediately available," Myles said, shifting in his seat. "Is Roxie coming back?"

"You'll see her next weekend at the party," she said, getting impatient. "Can we please finalize these plans?"

"The people coming to the fundraiser will want information. They'll want to see that this is more than just an idea."

The doctor sure enjoyed being persistent. She couldn't judge him for that. When she got a bee in her bonnet about something, she didn't let it go either.

"We'll talk to him," she said. "Would you know where to start with recruiting an elite team? Short of putting a vacancy ad online. And, let's face it, no one worth having is trawling those ads."

"You mean you'll talk to him," Johann said, judgmental frown in place. Damn, and she'd just been praising their progress. "The rest of us don't have your access." And suddenly Franco was more interested in his feet than in the hidden office at the edge of the floor. "You're sleeping with him."

"I don't think I ever denied that. Not that it matters. My private life is my private life. And none of your business."

"He's our boss."

"Meaning his personal life is also none of your business."

"I don't like it either," Helena said. "But our project wouldn't have come so far if Roux didn't have his attention."

"Nice."

Although Helena was sort of sticking up for her, it was shade too.

"I don't mean… It's not like you're prostituting yourself or anything."

"Yeah, mm hmm."

"Is he good?"

Myles and his inappropriate outbursts saved the day. Kind of. The shock of the question wore off quickly, and she laughed.

"In bed? I wouldn't be fucking him if he didn't have potential. All it takes is a little guidance, a nudge or two in the right direction."

"How does that happen?"

"The nudging? I grab his cock and—"

"Roux," Helena hissed.

She didn't appreciate the scolding. "Aren't you in enough trouble already?"

Leon strode in. "We have to prep for a meet."

Okay, so maybe Helena had intended to give her a heads up on the approaching visitor.

"Where?" Johann asked. "What meet?"

"In here."

Something made her turn. In the distance, Hotshot stood in his open office doorway, arms folded, shoulder propped on the glass.

Closing her eyes, she turned her head away. "No," she said to herself. "You don't care why he's looking at you like that."

"He wants to see you," Leon said.

She shook her head. "Stupid grins like that mean nothing. He does that to wind me up."

"No, he told me he wants to see you."

"He can want all he wants. If he wants to tell me something, he can come here and tell me himself."

"You know he's the boss, right?"

But that smile, the dance of amusement in his eyes. Intriguing. How did he get her every time?

"So he likes to think," she muttered and exhaled a growl. "Damn him." Leaping from the chair, she kept her glare up as she marched across the floor to stop in front of him. "You didn't win. I'm only here for your cock."

"You'll have to get used to restraining yourself in here."

Catching her shoulder, he guided her inside. What was it…? Someone had moved his desk to an angle in the corner to the right. In the opposite corner was another desk, just the same as his, angled. The new arrangement of the long space put the seating area in the middle, slightly more on one side. A single pane glass partition perpendicular to the still black wall was another addition.

"I don't get it. Are we practicing our feng-shui?"

Still with a hold of her, he guided her to the other desk, the new desk. "You wanted an office. I got you an office."

Turning out of his grip, she put herself in front of him, stopping him dead. "You want us to share your office? Because I'm sleeping with you?"

"Getting laid will be easier if you're always in the room. Check this out."

Pressing a button on his watch, the single perpendicular pane revealed itself to be so much more. Another slid from it, pane after pane, until a new glass wall had formed between their separate spaces.

"An office."

"Yeah, we need to free up the boardroom you've occupied for weeks. With Rox and her crew on the road, we can put your team in the suite downstairs."

"My team."

"This is good. I like the short answers."

"Rourke," she said, curling her hands around his tie. "Do you know there's a difference between business and pleasure?"

"No," he said, backing off. With her still holding his tie, she went with him. "Business is pleasure. We had this conversation. I know you. I don't know them. And with Roxie in the mix, we need someone at the helm who's not afraid to stand up to her."

"Roxie and I agree on most things."

"Yeah, I'm trying not to focus on that," he said, directing her into the chair. "What do you think?"

Stroking the leather arms, she swung one way then the other. "I think it pays to have sex with the man at the top." Leaning forward, she snagged his belt loop to pull him closer. "I guess you want a reward for this surprise."

So much for taking their women in hand.

"Not a surprise, just logical, and damn right," he said, unhooking her finger. "But right now, we have a meeting." Touching his watch again, he opened the sliding glass wall. "Your door's being installed later."

"My door?" she asked, standing up. The only way in or out was on his side. "So you can just trap me in here until then? What happens if your watch breaks?"

"Then I guess you're stuck in there. It's fine. The restroom is on your side."

Hmm, that gave her an idea. "Where is our meeting? What are we meeting for?"

"It's Hope."

"We're meeting for Hope and I don't know about it?"

"Figured you'd want a framework for the system before next week."

Damn. Much as she wanted to restrain her smile, it crept up. "You're on it?"

"I'm on it. Did you think I wouldn't be? It's the only damn part of this that's my domain. I'm not giving you any reason to crack the whip on me." Bending, he murmured into her hair above her ear. "Not at work anyway. At home, crack out the black leather any time you want."

"You're on it."

She'd known that. She'd told the others that. Yet, as he eased back, their eyes snagged.

From teasing, he got curious. "What?"

Curling her fingers around his tie again, she pulled him down until their lips met. Fuck him. Even when he didn't surprise her, he surprised her. He anticipated her. Yeah, he didn't want her to get one up on him, but it was still an honor to know her needs and dreams were important to him too.

Reversing, her butt hit the table and she slid up onto it, hooking her legs over his hips, pulling his tie to bring him down as she slanted back.

He broke the kiss. "Ah, see, you got me there."

She smiled, yanking. "Get your cock out."

"No, because, see, I'm your boss and I didn't set you up in here to get laid."

"You get laid anyway," she said, sensing his teasing. "Is this inappropriate, sir? You don't want to ride the sweet, innocent, impressed underling."

"You're no more innocent than you are impressed," he said, straightening, sliding his tie from her fingers. "Meeting then pussy."

She sighed and hopped off the desk. "I'll catch up." Backing away, she went around the other end of the desk. "I'm going to use my private restroom."

He winked. "You going to charge me entry?"

"Don't I always? Did you hear from Zairn

today?"

"No, why would I?"

"They flew back this morning."

"They? From where?"

Did the guy pay zero attention? "Zairn took Roxie to Hawaii. They had dinner with Dyce. Roxie called to say they got in safe. I thought he would let you know."

A single laugh shook his shoulders. "Baby, Zairn can't piss without the media reporting it. If he didn't get home safe, that's when I'd hear, on CNN along with the rest of the planet. Go pee. Move."

Oh, he had no idea. Pee? No, that wasn't why she was sending him off to the meeting alone. He wouldn't believe himself on top of the pile after she was through with him.

TWENTY-SIX

LEON DID THE presentation. Of course. Rourke relished lording over everybody from the head of the table. Let him. She'd keep her binder hugged to her chest as Leon performed for the group. And when the time came, she'd launch her offensive. In the seat closest to the presentation with no one opposite her, the position was perfect to find out what their leader was: her boss or her bitch?

Eventually, her friend would get up to say something to the captive audience. The spotlight would entice him onto center stage; he'd never be able to resist.

"Does anyone have questions?" Leon asked after talking them through it.

Not only did Rourke have Hope's infrastructure on his agenda and under control, but he'd already built a skeleton system. And, damn, she hadn't wanted to be impressed.

"They have no questions," Rourke said, putting the lights on with his watch as he left his chair. "What they need to know is it's in hand."

"I have questions," she said, deliberately turning her chair away from her buddy to look at the presentation again. "Your timeline is broad. Shouldn't we narrow that down?"

Leon froze, everything except his eyes. Those went left, right, and back again. What was he looking for?

"Sit," Rourke said to the scared rabbit and replaced him by the presentation. "You want to do this here? In front of all these people?" She just grinned. "Okay, the timeline is whatever I say it is. If it hooks me, it'll be done by the end of the week. If it doesn't, I'll leave it as long as I like. Or until someone persuades me to use my skills for their benefit."

"Mm hmm," she said, sliding her binder onto the table. "You have a team?"

"Allocated exclusively to this?" he asked. "No—" His focus dropped as she pushed her shoulders deeper into the chair. That's right, boss man, feel the power ebb. Who was in charge now? His mouth closed slowly to a smile, but he cleared his throat. "My people do what they're told, when they're told."

"Some of your people."

"All of my people," he said, switching focus to others at the table. "Cornish, you tell these guys about their assignments?"

"Not yet," Leon said. "You and you will have to see me after this."

"We have assignments?" Franco asked, excited. "Why just me and Guillermo?"

"You're young, free, single guys," Rourke said. "You don't want to see the world?"

"You're assigning us overseas?" Franco asked, almost jumping from his chair.

She narrowed an eye on her friend's smirk when it came around to her, but it didn't linger, not on her gaze anyway. So she folded her arms, plumping her breasts, luring him, entrancing him. Try to keep that train of thought now, Boy Scout. If the meeting was important enough to sideline sex, a view of her boobs through her white shirt shouldn't distract him.

"Our London office needs a hub for Hope," Rourke said. "We may go international after the pilot period. You guys are it."

"We're it?"

Running her tongue along her upper lip, she wriggled in her chair like she was just getting more comfortable. She wasn't and he noticed.

"You're so forward thinking, sir," she pouted.

Too bad her body was far more interesting for him than her face. "You're playing with fire, Radley."

"I don't mind getting burned," she said, her voice breathy. Yes, she was screwing with him, and the others would probably know that, but it was just too tempting an opportunity to miss. "Not if it's in the company's best interest. Your best interest… sir."

"The company's interests don't always align with my priorities."

"Meaning?" she asked, innocent in her act.

"As your boss, I should remind you to wear underwear around the office. As a man… with access…"

"Whatever you need I'm here to deliver. I wouldn't want to make things hard for you, sir."

"Everyone's excused." His eyes found hers again and apparently the confused others weren't moving fast enough. "Dismissed! Get the hell out of here."

She didn't even turn around. "But I have more questions, Mr. Rourke." He stalked toward her. "You're so strong and handsome and—"

Grabbing her wrist, he yanked her to her feet. "You were right," he murmured, boosting her onto the table, still covered in paperwork and hard copies of the presentation. "For maybe the first time ever…" Wasn't it fun when he mocked her with her own words. "You are going to ruin me."

Parting her legs wider as she slid to the edge of the surface, she unbuttoned her shirt. "You can afford it."

"What happened to the bra?"

"It might be in my private restroom. Maybe." Tilting her chin up, she pretended to ponder. "I'm so careless with these things, I put them down and forget to pick them back up."

"You take off your clothes to pee?"

"No one said anything about peeing." Opening up her shirt, she bared herself to him. "If you're so worried about my bra, I guess you don't want to see these." Except she slanted back, lowering herself slowly until she lay on the table. "Should I put them away?"

Pressing his curved hands into her thighs, he forced them up, pushing her skirt higher. "I'm more interested in if no bra means…"

She smiled when his gaze darkened. Yep. No bra. No panties.

"Does this go against the company dress code?"

"Oh, yeah," he said, loosening his tie. "You'll have to be disciplined for sure."

"With us sharing an office, it's unclear who is actually in charge. I'll have to shake things up around here."

"You shake whatever you want, Babycakes."

Though her breasts quickly occupied his hands.

"Maybe you don't deserve the treat," she said, urging his hands away.

"I deserve it."

Every time he tried to touch her, she intercepted him until their hands were palm to palm, fingers interlaced.

"Where's my job in Europe?"

"You don't get a job in Europe. You have too many responsibilities here."

"To your cock?"

"Is there anything more important? It should be your primary concern."

"Can I ride Guillermo before he goes?"

He couldn't even keep a straight face. "That's inappropriate for management, Babycakes. You shouldn't screw the staff."

"I screw you," she said, using his hands as an anchor to pull herself up again.

"In every way possible."

Insinuating her hands into his boxers, she squeezed his cock, freeing it and stroking her thumb across its head. "You didn't get the no underwear memo?"

"I'll do better next time."

"This is becoming a habit, Boy Scout. I'm miles ahead of you. How much credit can I give you? I'll have to cut you off sometime."

Bowing close, he breathed against her lips. "But not today."

Disappearing in a crouch, he hooked her legs, parted her folds with his tongue and sucked her clit before licking and tickling it with the tip.

Shit. Did he have to be so good at that? Her fingers coiled in his hair, but they slipped free as she lay down again, savoring the entitled plunge of his tongue as it delved into her. Her nerves tingled, sending signals out that pleasure was right there and climax just over the horizon.

Before it came close, she anticipated it. Just the excitement of his stimulation and the delicate titillation of his teasing prickled the hair on the back of her neck.

"Xavie…" she gasped, her knees rising, her back arching. "Shit, yes, baby."

Some things were fun. Some were arousing. Xavien Rourke was the only man who could do both at once. Even as he aggravated and ridiculed her, he couldn't disrespect her. No. He could try. Often did. But he gave himself away in his attentiveness. At the house, dinner, the car, even the Hope system. It wasn't just the big things, the little things mattered too.

"Xavie," she said.

Her thighs closed around his head until he grabbed them with a bruising power to force them apart and come higher, changing his angle to slide his tongue up one crease, down another and into her.

Rubbing her clit, she played as he fucked her right to the edge and as she gasped—he snatched her hand away, right on the cusp of her climax.

"My toy."

Her eyes didn't open, but her lips curled. "My pussy."

"Not today," he murmured and hummed against her.

The sweet vibration carried her back to that point. Right there. Where it was just the tiniest step away. And—"Xavie," she called, her body bracing into the release that wrought a yelp from her throat.

Before she'd even taken a breath, he was inside her. Hammering fast, he was on a mission; one that didn't have to include her.

Except she liked it.

Liked that he was overcome and desperate. In need of his own climax. Aching to feel the same pleasure that wracked her trembling system. It was a lifeline, a necessity. Orgasm wasn't just for fun, not there, not in that minute.

Her eyes opened to his. Serious, focused, he wasn't playing. He wanted to reach the end, the finish line—

"Xavie!"

Another surge of hormones shot through her blood. She'd been so intent on him, so eager to see him crest the summit that her own tumble hit her off-guard.

It didn't matter. As she called out for him and her body clamped tight around his, he drove into her again, coming inside her, just the way she liked it.

He planted his hands on the table, panting, without freeing himself from her body. "Consider that your signing bonus."

Tucking her hands beneath the loose fabric of his open shirt, she stroked his torso. "Roxie rates Zairn out of ten."

"Oh, yeah? You talk about sex?"

"With Roxie?" she asked and grinned. "Yes, it's Roxie."

"In case there's any confusion, I don't want to talk about the sex lives of my oldest friends, men I consider my family, my brothers."

"Then you shouldn't have introduced us all," she said. "You only have yourself to blame."

"As is so often the case when it comes to you." Coming lower, he kissed her quick, and exhaled. "We'll have the house to ourselves tonight."

"Should we go check out Dyce's house? Make sure Zairn's people didn't leave a mess."

He brushed his nose across hers. "You want to do it in his bed?"

"In his house," she said with a semi-shrug. "It doesn't have to be his bed if that weirds you out."

"I'll tell him it was you."

"That I seduced you? He'll believe that. I'm irresistible."

"That it was your fantasy. That you forced me into it."

"Oh, and he'll believe that," she said, not

believing it herself. "He's met you, right? He knows no sentence exists with both your name and the phrase 'refuses sex.'"

"Other than the one you just said," he said and threw both arms around her. "Most women aren't as easy as you, Babycakes. He's used to me being more discerning."

"Discerning? Like Diva?" And as their eyes met, it hit her. "Alaina Havenash." The insanely gorgeous supermodel. "Your ex is Alaina Havenash."

"So?" he said like he wasn't happy to hear the name.

She couldn't blame him. "Sorry, I didn't—wow." Exhaling, she got her composure from him. "I didn't realize it until now." And he probably didn't want to talk about her at all, much less only minutes after he'd got off. "Now I get why you called her Diva."

"It's the guys' name for her," he said, backing off to fasten his pants.

"Don't go in a mood. What did I tell you about pouting?"

"I don't want to talk about Alaina," he said, almost warning her. "Whatever you want to know—"

"I know everything I need to know. I didn't know her name before, but I know her. You told me about her. When you were together, when you broke up. I don't want to talk about her." Extending an arm, she waited for him to put his hands in hers. "It's lucky you have me now."

Suspicion raised his chin an inch. "Oh, yeah?"

"Yep. You'll never have to worry about having your heart broken again."

"Babycakes, my heart is—"

"I won't let it happen," she said, cutting him off before his swagger could gain momentum. Laying a hand on each of his cheeks, she pulled him down until their eyes were just a few inches apart. "I won't let anyone treat you like that ever again."

His gaze bounced back and forth between her eyes. "Who says I'll let you step in?"

"I don't need your permission." Her fingers slid into his hair. "I'll be around, watching, always watching, and if she tries any of that shit, if any woman tries that shit, I'll kick her ass." He laughed. "It pays to have a best friend who didn't grow up with a silver spoon in her mouth. I'll look after you."

"Okay," he said, tucking her head down to kiss the top. "You do that, Rocky."

He could tease like she was kidding, but she wasn't. Throughout the relationship, the way the supermodel treated him took a toll. From the nuance of his voice at the time, she sensed it. Felt it. He was a guy who liked to act like everything rolled off, but he had feelings. Feelings she wouldn't let any woman play with ever again.

TWENTY-SEVEN

ONE WEEK QUICKLY became two. It was amazing how time flew by when she needed as many seconds as she could get. No doubt LA was a beautiful city with plentiful sights to see. The rack of leaflets in the hotel lobby suggested that anyway. Given her mission, she didn't see anything except the inside of her hotel and Crimson, LA.

Helena kept up and Mieux was a lifesaver. Johann and Myles stayed behind at Mosaic to continue the day-to-day running of Hope.

Roxie visited but she and Zairn were up to their eyeballs in press for the *Nothing to Hide* documentary. As predicted, it was causing a storm of interest. Every time she checked her phone or turned on the TV, there was some new soundbite or clip making the rounds.

In a stroke of luck, Jane was wedding planning and had a bunch of useful recommendations, both who to chase and who to avoid. Just knowing who to pursue saved her so much time.

In the habit of visiting the club, it was just

another trip there on the Saturday. Like any other day. But that was the day Huddle Hope would become real to the world.

Walking around just before the doors opened, the sparkling lights and the glittering champagne flutes changed everything about the moment. Planning was over. It was time for the main event.

In the kitchen, the to-do list seemed never-ending. "No," she said, waving her pen at one of the servers she'd auditioned that week. Yep, in LA, even menial work required an audition. "Those are not the welcome platters. They come after."

The kitchen staff was incredible. The chefs? Quick, efficient, and amazingly talented. The food? Better than she'd tasted anywhere else. Growing up hadn't been caviar and canapés, but this was her life now.

"Switch that one with that one," she said to another of the servers. "Move that over there."

Redirecting trays, the half-empty ones had to be closer to the kitchen, not the pass.

"And the work is done," his voice announced behind her just moments before his hand slid onto her waist to turn her around. "Looking hot, Radley. You wearing that just for me?"

The dress. The hair. The makeup. They happened around her while she scrambled with the last-minute necessities. Somehow, it had all come together.

"Not for you," she said, trying to extricate herself from his hold.

It tightened. He wasn't letting her get anywhere. "It's time to come and enjoy the party. And I haven't seen you for days. Did you forget?"

No, she hadn't. Keeping busy filled the time usually spent being aggravated by him.

"Do you know how much I've got done since chasing you away? I could be running all of Mosaic if you weren't standing in my way."

"Go to it, baby. I'm happy to be a kept man filling my days with porn and prank cyberattacks."

"I won't rise to it. I'm busy. And you're back to standing in my way."

"I'm standing in your way now because it's date time."

"Your date is busy," she said. "Working."

They hadn't discussed attending the event together or being each other's date. Talk wasn't necessary, it was just the plan.

"Stop working."

"There's alcohol," she said. "Lots and lots of alcohol. If you get drunk enough, it won't work anyway. You don't want to disappoint me."

His hands skimmed around to her lower back, pressing her against him. "It'll work right now."

"Right now, I'm busy."

"No, you're done," he said, plucking the pen and binder from her hands to toss them onto a nearby stainless-steel table.

"Rourke," she said, grabbing for her authority.

It was stolen again when he snagged her wrists to drape them around his neck.

"The party's started. The work is done, Radley. Everyone is out there waiting for you. The people want to see you."

Everyone was out there?

Blinking, her attention landed on the door beyond his upper arm. "Everybody's here?"

She'd seen the first few guests arrive when the doors opened and had shaken half a dozen hands. Then the lighting director had a question about additional power, diverting her focus.

"Yes," he said. "Everyone we care about. The party is in full swing. You did it." He laced their fingers together. "Come see what you've done."

It wouldn't hurt to take a peek for a few minutes. When he led her into the main nightclub, with its chandeliers and draped silk, she almost couldn't believe it was the same Crimson as before. They even had oak hardwood floors brought in and installed specifically for the event. A limitless budget made everything possible.

People smiled at them and nodded their way. Some appeared eager to chat, but Rourke tucked her hand into the crook of his elbow and ignored them.

"This is the part of the night when everybody tells you what a good job you've done and how impressed they are that it all came together so quickly," he said and stooped lower to rest his lips in her hair. "I'm not impressed. For the record. I think you could've done better. Much better. Parties like this are a dime a dozen."

"I know. I modeled it on your house parties. Your example was my framework."

"Ah, so that's why you weren't taking part?"

"You don't have to be here, you know," she said. "You've shown face. You've done your bit. This isn't your idea of fun. If you want to leave—"

"Why would I want to leave? If there's any chance of you falling on your face, I want to soak up every second."

After passing through the people at the edge of the dance floor, he swung a left and escorted her to the back of the room. They ascended to the slightly elevated seating area, teeming with familiar faces.

"Roux!" Roxie exclaimed, jumping up to climb over Zairn and give her a hug. "Where have you been? This is wonderful!"

"It is," Jane agreed. "It absolutely is. You used the caterer I recommended!"

"I did. Their samples were by far the best. You were right."

"So is this a preview of the wedding?" Roxie asked, sitting on Zairn rather than returning to her own place at his other side.

Zairn didn't twitch in objection. He combed Roxie's hair away from her shoulder to lay his lips against her.

Lilya was next to stand up and kiss her cheek. "You've done a really good thing." Stepping aside, she presented the man who'd sat at her side. "And this is Zach."

"Fiancé," he said, standing up to offer a polite cheek kiss.

"Kintyre," she said. "I've heard a lot about you."

"Oh, I didn't—" Jane flapped her hands. "I don't know where Knox is."

"Upstairs," Zairn said, brushing his lips back and forth on his fiancée's skin. "He'll be down in a minute."

"Why aren't we upstairs?" Rourke asked. "I don't like being with the minions. I told you that on the Kystmeister's birthday."

"Roxie's birthday was friends and family only, not the general public."

"Minions," he said. "How many figures were they worth?"

"You don't even care about money," she said, jabbing him with an elbow. "Stop looking at the negatives. This is a target rich environment. There's plenty of heirs and heiresses eager to take you out for a spin."

As he'd invited Franco to do with her.

He dug his chin into the top of her head. "I thought it wasn't going to work tonight."

"I'm sure you could find other ways to entertain new friends. You kind of know what you're doing with your mouth, but don't expect anyone else to be as good as I am at faking it."

Kintyre's eyes narrowed, switching from her to Rourke and back. "I can't tell if you're in love or homicidal."

"They're in love. We established that," Lilya said, pushing Zach back onto their curved couch to then sit next to him. "Friend love."

"Don't tell her," Rourke said. "She has big ideas. I'm using her for sex. I'll get bored soon."

"Oh, I can't wait for the day." She leaned back to pat his thigh, underlining her sarcasm. "Go make me a daiquiri."

"Ha," he laughed. "There are around five hundred bartenders here." Proving his point, he turned. "Hey!" A passing server stopped. "We need daiquiris up here, for everyone, strawberry."

For a second, the young guy stood dazed, like a deer in the headlights, then quickly nodded and ran off.

"That wasn't polite."

"When am I ever polite?" he asked, tossing his arms around her shoulders to hug her against him from behind. "Are we going to dance?"

"No, I like these shoes. I don't want you stomping all over them."

"Can mine be virgin?" Lilya asked. "I'm not drinking alcohol."

"Yeah, you forgot that, didn't you?" she said, digging her nails into one of his hands. "Now Lilya feels left out."

"She's not left out. She's drinking for two. Why not get the kid wasted? Then he might just slide on out."

"Oh!" Jane exclaimed like Rourke's jibe was serious. "It's much too early. Way, way too early. Premature babies can survive from twenty-two or twenty-three weeks, but it's super rare and often they have a lot of issues growing up."

"Medical issues?"

"Have you thought about that?" Jane asked. "Is it something you worry about?"

"About him being premature or having medical issues?" Kintyre asked. "If there's anything medically wrong with him, he'll get the best care available in the world."

"I'm actually excited," Roxie said. "I wasn't at first. I didn't really get it, but all the planning and scanning. The doctor appointments. It's fun. It's like Christmas is coming, but you already know what you're getting." Roxie laid her head on Zairn. "The best part about it is, we can give him back."

"Give him back?"

"Yeah, we get to play with him until it's not fun anymore and then we send him back to Jane."

"Back to Jane?" Kintyre asked.

Everyone laughed.

"Yeah, I don't think you're going to see much of your kid. Maybe you'll get to see him when he has babies. I'm sure he'll know who you are. Jane will show him photographs."

"Guess that's something."

"I'm sure Jane will be his favorite auntie," Roxie said. "But I'm godmother. I better get the best gifts at Christmas."

"I think we're supposed to give him gifts," Zairn said, kissing her shoulder again. "And advice. Teach him how to make good choices. Good, moral choices."

"Says the rehabilitated former playboy," Roxie stage whispered from the corner of her mouth. "The poor kid is doomed."

"We didn't think it through, did we?" Kintyre asked, putting an arm around Lilya to pull her closer. "Imagine the mouth he'll have on him when he's a teenager."

Roxie jumped. "Teenager? Oh, God, I'll have

him sassing you long before then. Roux will help round him out. Make sure he can see how fun it can be to poke and prod."

"Lola," Zairn warned. "This is a big responsibility."

"Oh, I'm only kidding," she said. "You think I want to turn their kid against them? Turn about is fair play. If we screw up their kid, imagine what they'll do to ours? Do you know how good they are at math?"

"Accounting? That's what scares you?" Kintyre asked. "I am so happy I know that."

"He's coming to the Halloween party this year as an actuary."

"Ha, ha, laugh it up," Roxie said, because everyone was. "I have a secret weapon."

"Secret weapon?"

"Jane would run circles around both of you," Roxie boasted.

"We're giving her a kid. What are you giving her?"

Roxie's smile fell. "Huh, checkmate."

But she could still rely on Jane because the beauty diverted the subject… sort of. "Knox and I were talking about babies," Jane said quietly, though she glittered with excitement.

"Having babies?" Lilya asked.

"He just won't be outdone on anything, will he?" Kintyre asked, grinning.

"Oh, I don't think he meant to—"

"Relax," Roxie said, reaching over the table to pat Jane's wrist. "Having babies is a great idea. Then the little ones can have playdates together." She slid from Zairn's lap, still touching Jane's wrist. "Z and I had a baby today."

Everyone gasped.

"It's not a baby, it's an embryo," Zairn said. "Not

the same thing."

"Depends on who you ask," Rourke muttered. She twisted around to show him a glare. "Back in your cage, Hilda. We're not getting into that tonight."

"Do you have a fertility problem?" Kintyre asked, seeming honestly concerned.

"You can use Radley's uterus if you need one. It's superfluous; she won't be using it."

"No, I will not. Are you eager to rent out every part of me or just the reproductive ones?"

"Any part I can make cash out of, I'm good."

"Yeah, 'cause you're so short of it."

"I don't make money out of you because I need it. I do it because I can."

"Haven't managed it yet."

"This looks like gold, right here," he said, twisting them both to the side to give her a quick glance at the bustling room.

"I should get back to—"

"Enjoy it," he said, squeezing her tight. "You won't get this group together again anytime soon."

"It's my—"

"It's nothing. Mieux is on it. She's in charge tonight."

"You promoted her over me?"

"Yeah, that's it. I'm exerting my superior power to give her a boost. Think she'll sleep with me?"

"She's smarter than that."

"What does that say about you?"

"That I'm kind to plants and animals."

"Which am I?"

"A little of both. You plant yourself on the couch like a stray beast and primate all over the place."

"Primate as a verb? That doesn't even make sense."

"Do you want children now?" Kintyre asked.

Oh, yeah, the embryos. "Our doctor is—"

"It's just in case I die or dry up," Roxie said. "Or if I dump Z and want to gouge him for child support."

"Never knew plastic specimen pots got you going, buddy," Rourke said. "The things I'm learning about people today. There really is a kink for everything."

"What a surprise you're grateful the conversation got back to sex."

"I love it when you make things about sex."

"Everything is about sex in your head."

"The specimen cup wasn't what got him off," Roxie said, stirring her drink with a fingertip. "It's amazing what money will let you get away with."

"You didn't," Jane gasped. "There in the…"

"We didn't do that. The point was to get it in the cup. If we did that, it would never have got there. It was weird, really weird."

"You get so used to them finishing inside you that giving it up feels—"

"Wrong," Roxie said, nodding. "I told him I'd be jealous, and I was right. Handing over his love seed is a strange process. I wonder how many women saw him in there and begged to have their husband's specimen switched with his."

"And now you have an excuse if any secret babies show up," Rourke said. "That is an excellent plan, my friend."

"Trust you to be impressed by cheating."

"Forty-five."

The jarring unfamiliar masculine voice carried over the music and its owner stopped beside them.

"Radley, meet Knox Collier."

The guy was so fucking hot. She tried to step back, but Rourke was still holding her. Square jaw, tan skin, his hair was LA beach boy dirty blond with darker hues lifting its charm.

"Fuck, he's expensive."

"He's not for sale, Rad. You think I got you an opening night bonus?"

"No, but I mean…" Leaning against Rourke's embrace, she used it for balance as she touched the frowning Knox's jaw. "Wow, he's the real deal. Hollywood elite."

"Sickening, isn't it?" Roxie asked. "His personality counterbalances all that hotness."

"Roxie," Jane whined.

"I'm kidding. You know I love him," Roxie said, picking up a canapé from the tray in the middle of their table. "Besides, Cam is adorable… and hotter. They were not made equal."

"Knox is adorable too."

The circular table had four short, curved benches around it. The side closest to them was open, allowing those at the table to observe the room. If she and Rourke weren't there anyway.

Knox passed behind Roxie and Zairn to sit by Jane. He swept her hair aside, and she turned to meet his waiting lips.

So sweet, these couples all together, happy. Eurgh, it was kind of sickening.

"Come on," she said, tugging on Rourke's forearms. "We should go schmooze."

He'd used the word, so couldn't mock her for it. Well, he could, but he groaned instead.

"I don't want to go schmooze people. Can't we stay here?"

"I don't know," she said, then appealed to the table, "how many of you have donated to Huddle Hope? Tell Rourke."

"All of us, Rourkey-Baby," Roxie said, pushing the tray toward Lilya. "Try the green one."

"Then these are not the people we need to

schmooze. I gave you a chance to escape, you didn't take it. Too bad that's over. Now it's time to get your schmoozing hat on, Boy Scout. Schmoozy-schmooze."

"You like that word, don't you?"

"I've had a couple of champagnes," she said, slapping her palm to his when he offered it. "Let's get this party started."

TWENTY-EIGHT

THEY DANCED, they drank, they schmoozed. Somehow, they ended up back at the elevated seating area, him in a huddle with the guys standing next to the women occupying the table.

Her feet hurt and her jaw was tired. If that was a measure of her night, there wasn't a person in the city who didn't know everything she did about Huddle Hope. Still, it didn't feel like a job, like a chore she wanted to get out of the way. Huddle Hope was important; it was her duty to make others see that.

For too long, complacency ruled. Disparaging the system was easy. Anyone could talk about how things needed to change and how someone had to try something because doing nothing failed them all. Huddle Hope was that something. If it didn't get off the ground or failed, it wouldn't be because she hadn't given it her all.

Slumping at the table by Roxie, she loved her friend for pushing a fresh cocktail over to her.

"Z and I are going back to New York."

"Oh no!" Straightening, she picked up the fruity drink to sip. "LA was bad enough, now you're crossing the continent?"

"Jane's coming," Roxie said. "We were talking to Merci and she really wants to meet you."

"I want to meet her too."

"Reid, her fiancé, he has all kinds of medical contacts in New York. And there's a woman you absolutely have to charm. Her support could be pivotal."

"That's great. Maybe we can ask some of their contacts to donate their time. Focus group them. Float our ideas and get their take. Johann will hate it, but I'd love to hear thoughts from outside our circle. And the more endorsements we collect, the better. Do you think they'd campaign for us? Maybe do some videos, something for the marketing packet? You know how these things can snowball if they have the right faces involved."

"Toria has a marketing background and our friend in Chicago owns a marketing company. She's jet-setting around the world right now, but she'll come back for this. Well, she'll come back if you convince the doctors in New York."

"Me? No. This can't be done over video call. What does that say about our commitment to Huddle Hope? No, it has to be done face to face, in a formal or informal setting fine, but we have to show reverence for what we're doing."

"I agree."

"Mosaic is officially working in tandem with Lola's Liberty on this. That gives you exactly the—"

"Not me," Roxie said. "You're going to do it."

"I can't. Web link—"

"In person. You're coming to New York with us."

She blinked. "I am?"

"Why not? There are a lot of deep pockets in New York. Get the docs on board, get together with Merci and Toria. All goes well, we'll bring Rainie in and set up another party, just like this one. We can have all kinds of fundraisers. Rich people love that shit. That view that they care about more than just themselves. And you have some Hollywood darlings on board now. Invite them and the Wall Street guys will eat it up. Money means acceptance, right? Might be worth doing the same in Boston. Lilya has all kinds of contacts up there. I told you we had a network."

And Rourke had been right about only needing to convince one person. Getting in front of Zairn was the best thing that happened to Huddle Hope. Other than Rourke noticing its potential, but she wouldn't give him explicit credit for that.

"But New York…"

"It's an amazing city, and that's coming from a Chicago girl. I wanted to hate it, but just couldn't."

"I can't afford—"

"It's on Mosaic's dime and you can stay with us too. Crimson is your home. There's plenty of space in Rouge HQ and so many people I want you to meet."

"You can stay in my apartment, if you want," Lilya said across the table. "If you want your own space."

Away from Crimson people? Roxie was full on with her friends, but it wasn't the people that held her back. What was holding her back? New York offered amazing opportunities.

"Whatever makes you happy, honey," Roxie said. "We'll look after you either way."

New York. Hmm, it deserved at least some thought.

Before she could reach any conclusions, Mieux hurried over and dipped to whisper. "Diva's here."

Diva? Who was she talking about with—no. Her

mouth opened in a gasp that clenched her guts. Diva. Rourke's ex. Alaina Havenash. No fucking way.

"What?" she barked, her head snapping around. "Where? Who invited her?"

"No one," Mieux said, clearly nervous. "She's not on the list, but…"

"She'll expect to get in anyway."

They didn't call her Diva for no reason. And why shouldn't she get in? As far as any employee was concerned, Alaina Havenash was a beautiful woman with grace and allure. She'd never met the woman, but already knew better.

"Okay, thank you. I'll handle it."

Mieux nodded once and scurried off. Diva was one responsibility she had to take care of herself.

"What's going on?" Roxie asked, drawing closer.

First thing was first. "Keep an eye on him," she said, gesturing Rourke's way with her head, so as not to draw his attention. "Do not let him leave this table until you see me again."

"Okay," Roxie said, confused, her brow descended.

Her friend sensed her worry, but there wasn't time to explain. Leaving the table, she headed outside. Fast. If the model got in and people saw her, word would get to Rourke. He'd never just let it go. He'd end up face to face with his ex and that would ruin his whole night.

And there the beauty was. Trust a model to eat up all those lenses trained on her.

The gorgeous, incredible Alaina stood on the red carpet in front of the Huddle Hope backdrop. Flashes cascaded over and around her; dozens of hungry paparazzi gobbled up the chance to get as many photographs as they could.

It was publicity, sure, but not the kind she

wanted associated with the event. Diva was one personality Huddle Hope did not need in their arsenal.

She got the attention of the security guard at the other side of the display. Widening her eyes and tipping her head to the side, she gave him the signal to cross the carpet, catching Diva on the way.

The model's own guard was stopped by another from getting too close. Perfect. Just what she needed. Jane's security recommendation paid dividends. They were earning their fee and then some.

At the edge of the carpet, in the shadow by the entrance, she walked right up close to the beauty. Her heels gave her a boost, but not enough to counter the supermodel in her own heels. Still, she stood tall.

"You weren't invited," she said, her lips hardly moving from her smile.

They might be in shadow, but the press was still right there. If they wanted a story, any face off would be a scandal they'd seize. A photograph or whisper of any confrontation could change the story of the night.

"I don't need an invitation," Diva said. "Everyone wants me at their event."

The arrogance might be well-placed in other environments. It wasn't welcome at Crimson. Not that night.

Without blinking, she locked their eyes. "I don't want you here and I don't want your money." Still, she kept her smile high. "I will let you walk through the front door, providing you walk straight out the back. No canapés, no champagne. Your ass leaves via the alley."

Diva laughed, tossing her hair from her shoulder. "I don't know who you think you are—"

"You think I'll let you fuck with him again?" she asked, her eyes hardening as her smile faded. "You walked out of his life when he should've run from yours. I won't let it happen again."

The model might not have expected something personal, but the man they had in common was not up for debate. Alaina Havenash had her chance with Rourke and had screwed it up by screwing him up. Friendship meant more than business, altruistic or not.

"Xavien? You don't know what you're talking about. You have no right to bring up my personal life."

When Diva tried to step around her, she shifted into her path. "I don't give a shit what you think you know. Your personal life means nothing to me, providing you stay out of his. If you try to weasel your way back in, then it's very important to me. Very. Important."

"Are you his latest fling? They never last, sweetie. He won't stay with you. You can't give him what he needs."

"Because you couldn't give him what he needs?" Surprise flashed on the model's face. "He was lucky to get away from you in one piece. You're a trauma no man deserves to endure."

"You don't know what you're talking about. If he hears you've talked to me this way, you'll lose your job, your home, and anything else I ask him to take from you."

"Let me worry about that while you make your undramatic exit."

"Where is he? Let's ask him. Hmm? Ask him who he'd rather have at his party. Me or…" Diva did the superiority thing well. "He'll choose me over you. You're no one. You don't know him, and you don't know me."

"I know Huddle Hope has put him back in the headlines. He's hip, right now, for you and your shallow friends, that's exposure you want a piece of." She moved in closer. "And I am telling you, it is not happening."

"Move out of my way."

"You want to do this?" she asked, her voice

dropping in volume and tone. "Those pap flashes mean nothing to me. Do you want the whole world to see you get your ass handed to you on the red carpet? Because nothing would make me happier than to take you down. Choose. Back door or on your ass right here. How would you like to leave this party, Babycakes?"

"If you put your hands on me, I'll have you arrested."

"If you try to set foot in the party, I'll have security escort you to the cops. You're not getting in here. I'd take jail over watching you mangle him again. Does Diva want to keep her dignity or to lose a fucking eye? Imagine what that would do for your career."

Her faux gasp only provoked the model's frown. She shouldn't gloat, but it felt good to win. Alaina Havenash was welcome everywhere. Except anywhere Rourke was, it would stay that way so long as she had anything to say about it.

TWENTY-NINE

AND THAT WAS THAT. Done and dusted. Proof that no job was beneath her. If something needed to be done, she'd get it done.

With the trash taken out, she returned to the party. Drinking it in, the atmosphere was high. Not a bad night after all.

Someone stole her hand and whipped her around. She collided with a body and—

"Hotshot," she said.

Guiding her hands to his chest, he wrapped his arms around her and moved like they were dancing. "Roxie's being weird."

Probably by delaying him somehow. Now it was her turn to distract him. "You know, there's an actual dance floor," she said. "Right in front of the band over there. It's a new concept."

"Figured you went looking to bust someone's balls."

"Why would I do that when yours are so conveniently close all the time?"

"So you didn't go looking to assert your

authority?"

He hadn't noticed. No way. If he had heard about her face off with his ex, he'd have ribbed her about it. She knew him too well. And this didn't constitute a thorough ribbing.

"You trust Mieux. I trust Mieux," she said and relaxed against him, but stopped to look up. "Why don't you offer her a permanent position? Steal her from Brooker."

"You like her, hire her."

"I have to offer her more money."

"Never makes a difference," he chanted. "Tuck your head under mine like you do when we're asleep."

When they were asleep, she could get higher. At least this tall person wasn't wearing heels.

"What do you mean it doesn't make a difference?" she asked, laying her head on his chest. "Have you tried?"

"A bunch of times. We all have. She works all over and doesn't like to be tied down."

"That I can identify with. We can find a way, we have to. She's too good to lose."

"Hot too, if you're thinking…"

On a sigh, she closed her eyes. "You'll grow up one day, Peter Pan."

"Don't bet on it, Tinkerbell."

"Did you know about Roxie and Zairn's fertility thing?"

"No," he said. "Don't usually talk to my friends about their girlfriends' uteruses or them coming in a cup."

"It's kind of romantic, isn't it?"

"Coming in a cup? If I'd known that was your thing—"

"That they would go to those lengths for each other. That or it's super creepy and one of them plans to off the other."

"Took Z this long to find Rox, I'd say she's safe. Him, on the other hand…"

"They're suited. It just works. You don't have to look into it, they sink into each other… I feel icky talking about this."

"Love and romance?"

"It's easier to think those things don't exist. I can't imagine anything worse than being gooey eyed over someone."

"They keep the gooey eyed thing to a minimum, but there's no denying he's sunk. Poor guy. The prenup better be up to par or the Kyst-meister will take him for everything."

"She must be sure she wants kids. To do something like that. If they split up, that's one other thing to fight over. Why do you think they did it? Do they want kids now?"

He tightened his hold. "This is a conversation you should have with Rox. Baby talk scares away the boners."

"Jane and Knox seem like an unlikely pair," she said, ignoring his quip. "She's so sweet and… high-strung. I don't mean that as an insult, she obviously cares." About everything. "But he's a cool customer. Aloof."

"He's a Collier. Collier's get what they want, he has nothing to be stressed about. What worries does a guy like him have?"

"Good point," she said, sliding her hands lower. "He really has the world on a string."

"Caspian, the oldest brother, he's the powerhouse behind the brand these days. Behind the scenes anyway, doubt he's left the office at all in the last three years."

Hadn't she heard something about a trio? "Are

they the only brothers?"

"Cam is the youngest."

Lifting her head, she raised her gaze to his. "The 'lifestyle' guy? What does that mean?"

"Cam gave it all up. Had no interest in the media monarchy life. His father and grandfather wanted him to go all in, just like Caspian. Knox has always been in, but he's less possessed by it. He works for the company, but values friends and family too. He works to live; Caspian lives to work."

"And Cam?"

"He's a law unto himself."

"Does he live in California?"

"No," Rourke said on a snicker. "God, no. If he did, Thena, their mom, would never leave him alone. She's a dynamic woman, tenacious. You'd like her."

"Was that a compliment?"

He sneered like he loathed the thought. "Shit, no. I'm saying you could learn a thing or two from a woman who steps up when needed."

"Okay, good to know I can forget to step up any time you want your cock sucked, if that's what you think of me."

Ducking forward, he buried his lips in her hair. "Except the problem is, you love it. You can't help yourself."

"And I can't wait to prove you wrong. It'll take a lot of persuading—"

"You love that too."

"Seeing you beg?" she asked, cocky in her glow. "Yes, I do. That's exactly where you should be, on your knees, admitting your inferiority."

"This is a good joke; I like this one. Almost sounds like you believe it."

Something occurred to her. "You think that's Jane and Knox's deal? The sub, dom thing?"

"So not where my head was with that conversation, but maybe. Again, not something I discuss with my friends."

She didn't believe him. "You don't talk about sex with your friends? Ever? Guys talk about sex all the time. What makes you the exception?"

"I prefer doing it than talking about it," he said, checking his watch. "This conversation's stretching my limit."

"Doing it with friends rather than talking about it with them?"

"Certain friends," he said, bending his knees to squeeze her ass. "Want to find a corner somewhere?"

"So we can not talk about it?"

"Exactly," he said and winked. "I've got access to the VIP pods upstairs."

"Isn't this our party? We're supposed to be hosting."

"Even the hosts deserve a break." Pulling her closer, he pressed the hard length of his cock against her. "Live dangerously."

"I thought talk of babies killed the boners."

"We'll talk about something else," he said, whirling her around to pull her against him as he cut their way through the crowd.

She should've known sex was his motive the minute he put his arms around her. He hadn't left his friend huddle of man talk to dance with her. Guy was horny. Another good reason to kick Diva out. If he'd been in the mood and his ex got too close…

They went into a stairwell and up into the deserted VIP area. The ghostly room held whispers of conversations and the notes of forgotten music coming from down the stairs, turning it into a haunted treasure.

Rourke didn't linger and opened a glass door to push her inside just a second before the glass went black.

"Do we need it off?" she asked.

"Your dress? No, I can work around it."

She loosened the zipper to let it fall to the floor. "I didn't mean that... I meant the glass."

Backing toward the couch in the room decorated like a modern lounge, she stepped out of her shoes and freed her hair.

"Told you the exhibitionist thing did it for you."

"If you're afraid..." He touched his watch again and the glass became clear. "Good boy." She cast aside her bra as he lost his jacket and tie. By the time their bodies met, only his pants were in the way. Sliding the leather from its buckle, she freed him from the fabric. "Are you scared we'll get caught?"

"Yes," he said. With one harsh push, he sent her down to the couch. "Distract me. Prove your worth."

Sitting with her, he kissed her shoulder, her neck, easing her onto her back to find his place between her legs.

The softness of his styled locks warmed her splayed fingers. He made his way down her body, kissing and teasing every inch. Every tingling, savoring cell of her skin wanted this, him, his mouth and hands, his kiss, his touch.

And then he spoiled her clit. "Xavie," she exhaled.

In the frantic pace of the previous week, there hadn't been time to stop and enjoy each other. Even in the nights, when she dreamed of him, she didn't call or ask him to visit. If she'd wanted sex that bad, she could've found a server or musician to seduce. But they wouldn't have matched up to the innate way Rourke pleasured her body.

It was weird that she didn't have to tell him, didn't have to ask. Somehow, he just knew how she liked to be kissed. His body read hers, letting nature take over, shedding anything contrived to just be in the moment and do what felt good.

His finger slid into her, one, then two as his tongue worked to arouse her to the edge of climax.

"Mmm," she purred, her body undulating against his tongue's caress. "Good boy." Definitely good. Until the moment he surged up, abandoning her pussy to kiss her lips. "That didn't mean stop."

He thrust into her, pushing a gasp out of her at the unexpected intrusion.

"How's that?" he asked, moving inside her. "That good?"

She smiled. Her eyes were barely open, and she couldn't feel anything except him, but… "Yes," she murmured, rising and falling against him. "So much better."

Sneaking away was an incredible idea. All the stress and concern about the party, and unexpected guests, melted away with every advance. One or both of them had signaled the other, he'd just picked up on it before her. They'd gone too long without enjoying each other. And what a perfect moment to make up for lost time.

THIRTY

"THIS IS A DISASTER!"

Facedown in bed, it took her a second to place the voice. Leon. Mm, the fabric smelled of Rourke. Must be his pillow.

"It's not a disaster." That was Rourke's voice. "Knox's people are working on it. I'm pissed I missed the drama. Where was I?"

"How the fuck do I know?" Leon exclaimed. "This will be a PR nightmare."

"No, it won't. Why do you think I'm friends with the Colliers? We can spin this if it gets out."

"If?"

"Yo! Radley!" Rourke shouted. "The cops are looking for you!" She smiled without opening her eyes. "Get up!"

"She's here?" Leon asked.

Someone tugged the sheets down to uncover her back. "Lazy witch is still in bed. I did all the work last night, why do you get to sleep in?"

With all the time in the world, she rolled onto her

back. Leon screeched and spun away.

"I threw the party," she said, stretching her back. "What's wrong with him?"

"Your tits offend him."

"Why?" she asked, dropping her chin almost to her chest to check them out. "You left stubble burn everywhere again." And more than a few bruises. "How is this discreet?"

"Who gives a fuck about discreet? You just flashed Leon. That's sexual harassment. You're the harasser. Another lawsuit I'll have to settle out of court. Your tits are fucking expensive, and not in the good way."

"You didn't mind my boobs last night," she said, pulling herself onto her hands and knees to crawl toward him. "And this is our private bedroom. What did he think he'd see?"

"*My* private bedroom," Rourke said. "Cock, maybe."

She rose high on her knees at the end of the bed. "Did I interrupt? I can tag out if you and Leon need the bed."

"You are tagging out because the cops are here."

"So? I'm over twenty-one, handsome. I promise."

"That's good to know. But they want you, not me."

"Are you over twenty-one?"

"Last time I checked," he said. "Wanna role play?"

"With the cops or age play?" she asked.

"Either. Both. We should get rid of the real ones first." He looked at Leon, who still faced away. "Did we check they are real cops? She probably ordered herself strippers."

"Why do I need strippers when Roxie already

invited me to her bachelorette party? A guaranteed six-pack feast. Want to bet that will be a night to remember?"

"If you get there," Rourke said. "Know why the cops want you?"

"I'm hot. I'm in demand."

"These guys want to put you in the slammer."

"Am I playing a bad girl? Are you directing a porno? Hollywood's gone to your head."

"No, this is something to do with you threatening my ex-girlfriend." Her smile dropped as his curled. "You think I wouldn't find out?" His eyes stayed on hers. "Leon. Scram."

The guy did as told.

"I don't care that you found out," she said, pushing him aside to climb off the bed. "Where are these cops? I'll talk to them."

"Naked?"

She glanced down, but put her hands on her hips, thrusting her shoulders back. "Yeah, maybe I'll direct my own porno."

"My people are dealing with it. They just want to lay eyes on you."

"Okay." She turned to eat up more of the room. "Naked makes me memorable."

He hurried over to snag her wrist and pulled her to him. "Slow it down." The pause dragged. "You didn't have to."

"I didn't have to what?"

"Scare her away. Threaten her with violence."

"I'm sorry, since when do I need your permission for anything?" she asked, angry and offended. "I did what I did for me. Because I wanted to. It's nothing to do with you."

"Nothing to do with me, really?" he asked, deadpan. "You just so happened to railroad my ex-girlfriend out of a party you didn't invite her to? She just showed up? For no reason? And you were pissed for you?"

"I didn't want to hear it, to witness it. Last night was about Huddle Hope and I need your attention. I don't want you getting distracted by supermodel putang."

"Oh, my focus."

"Yes, your focus. I don't know if you remember what it was like to be with her, but you weren't the most together. You were distracted. Always tense. Always on edge."

"I wasn't distracted. I couldn't shout at her," he said. "You got the heat because you could handle it."

"You twisted yourself into knots for her. And you are not that guy. Every demand she made, you made it happen, even when it was totally unreasonable. Impossible. The business suffered. You suffered."

"I took care of it. I took care of her."

"And who took care of you?" she asked. "You deserve to be who you are, not who she wanted you to be. It's okay to be over. It's okay to quit when something is sapping the life out of you."

Maybe she was biased against the leech, but beauty wasn't enough for Rourke. He'd always need more than a pretty face.

"You," he said, catching a section of her hair between his first two fingers to tuck it behind her ear. "You took care of me, Radley."

And she wouldn't shy from that responsibility. From that honor.

"That's all I did last night," she said, softening. "We're good, aren't we? Life is good." He nodded. "So why do we need her?"

"You do things like that without telling me, I can't protect you. I don't give a shit about her hurt feelings or that she wanted to cause a scene. I mind you went behind my back.”

“No, you don't. Because it's exactly what you would've done if someone showed up to hurt me. What was it you said? I don't apologize for who I am or the decisions I make. If it feels good, it's allowed. And it felt good to get between you. She wanted to use you. And I won't let anyone do that. Not anyone but me.”

“And if the cops take you away for it, who looks out for me then?”

“If I go inside, I'm taking you with me,” she said. “They wouldn't be able to handle both of us.”

“Because of all the sex or all the arguing?”

“Alternative is you go into the corrections business. Build me my own prison.”

“That would look a lot like my bedroom and your mouth sewn shut.”

“You have uses for my mouth,” she said, cupping his cock through his pants.

“Good point. We'll take your vocal cords or something. Keep you quiet.” Sly delight crept onto his face. “Ultimate fantasy.”

“If you'll build my mother her own hospital, you'll build me my own prison.”

“A lot of building going on for a woman who lives in my house.”

New York. Had no one told him? She hadn't.

“Rourke,” Leon's voice came from the doorway where he stood facing out. “This detective—”

“She's naked already. Send him in here.” Despite the order, he went to grab her a robe from the closet. “All else fails, Rad, flash him. I'll stand up in court and confirm he grabbed your boob.”

“Excellent defense strategy, baby.”

“Perjury,” he said, slinging an arm around her shoulders to lead her out past Leon. “Nothing I won't do for you, Babycakes.”

"How do you know he won't grab my boob?”

"You're right! Maybe we can trade. No charges for a little DP. There's two of them, right, Leon? This is shaping up to be a good day. I love LA!”

"LA hates us!” Jane exclaimed as they entered the living room.

Roxie was there too, though she seemed to be having a ball. "This is so typical,” her friend said. "You should've stayed with us at the house last night. We might have missed all the fun.”

Rourke was in a fancy hotel suite. Fancier than the room she'd been in all week. Roxie, Jane, and Lilya had gone back to their house with their guys after the party.

She'd stayed late, until the last guest left, and Rourke had been with her all the way.

"Where are the cops?”

"The Zs have them in the hall,” Lilya said. "Zach and Zairn.”

"We have experience,” Roxie said, opening her arms to drop onto the middle of the couch. "A lot of experience with law enforcement in LA. At least it wasn't me getting arrested this time.”

"You got arrested in LA?”

"Twice so far,” Roxie said, showing the peace sign. "Zairn enjoys bailing me out. It's foreplay.”

"And there was the time you went missing,” Jane said. "Had all of us stressed out.”

"That stress got you laid, Little Miss,” Roxie said, pulling Jane onto the couch with her.

"Not that night!”

"I don't get enough credit for getting you and Knox together,” Roxie said, finger combing the length of Jane's hair down her back. "You're so pretty.”

"I never heard how you and Kintyre met,” she

said to Lilya.

The expectant mom was eating toast from somewhere. "He was naked, commandeered me to his plot. From there, I guess it was inevitable."

And she was none the wiser.

"Lola!"

Came a call at the same time the door swung shut.

"Yes, my love?"

"We're getting the hell out of LA. Leaving LA and never coming back." He and Kintyre appeared and nodded in greeting at Rourke. "What is with you and this city?"

"This one wasn't me. But I do miss New York. Should we stop in Chicago on the way back home?"

"If we stop in Chicago, we'll never leave again. Though your dad wanted to talk investment opportunities."

"You are not investing money in my family. Not in my sister's boyfriend or my dad."

"Actually, he wanted to invest with me."

"Stop taking money from my dad!"

"I didn't take the wedding money. We talked about it in private. And I have a guy who can double his yield. Triple it."

"Since when were you a shady shyster?"

"We pay Dunlap to be our shady shyster," he said. "You mean a grifter."

"I mean a scammer. You're scamming my father."

"By marrying his daughter and ensuring he'll have grandchildren?"

"You're too friendly with my dad," Roxie said, suspicious. "You talk all the time." Her friend gestured around. "Look at all these people, all these guy friends you have. Take their money. Call them. Talk to them."

"They're busy. I talk to your father because he calls and I enjoy it."

Roxie blinked, almost aghast. "You enjoy conversations with my dad?"

"More than I enjoy this."

"You're right," Roxie said and leaped up. "Let's go back to New York. One out, all out."

"We're staying here," Kintyre said and looked at Lilya. "Are we staying here?"

"For now. Roux might stay in our New York place."

"Not like we're using it," Kintyre said.

"Why would she be staying at your place?" Rourke asked.

"Yeah, I told her to stay with us," Roxie said. "Rouge HQ is where it's happening. And we have a club in the building. Alcohol. Hot guys. Backstage passes."

"Memories in that club," Zairn said. "Backstage."

The moment his eyes met Roxie's, they both smiled, obviously remembering the same moment.

"We should mount a commemorative plaque," her blonde friend said.

Zairn's drawl was smooth. "Mounted something."

Rourke grabbed her shoulder to haul her backwards, drawing her away from the others to hustle her back into the bedroom.

"New York?" he said the moment the door closed. "You're going to New York?"

"Reid has medical contacts. If we pitch Hope to them and get them on board, our credibility will grow. We need it to grow. Now we have the momentum and the support. We're going to gather pace. This is going to work. I know it is."

He skimmed a fingertip down her jaw. "New

York is a big step."

"You want to come with me? If we're both there—"

"Someone needs to steer the ship," he said. "You're going to eat New York up."

And it was such a relief he wasn't making a big deal of it. The last thing she wanted was for anyone to believe she was trying to take anything away from Mosaic.

"If I'm allowed to leave California."

"Why wouldn't you—the cops? One thing we rich have is lawyers. Don't worry about the law. I'll deal with that."

But could she warn him against contacting his ex? Yes, actually, she could. Hadn't he said she wasn't allowed to hold back?

"If I get even a whisper that you've talked to Diva or seen her…"

He laughed and wrapped a fist around the finger she raised. "Yes, Mom."

"And I will hear. I am now friends with the women who sleep with your best friends. You did that and can't take it back. Roxie will tell me."

"And Jane can't keep a secret… or so everyone thought before Knox."

"I can't get a read on him. We haven't spent much time in each other's company."

"Oh, if you think he's an enigma, you'll love Matteo Reid."

With so much to look forward to, there wouldn't be time to look back. Would there?

"Fuck!"

The exclamation rattled through the walls from the other room.

"That's not good," Rourke said. "When Knox Collier is unhappy, the rest of us should watch out."

THIRTY-ONE

TAKING HER HAND, Rourke led her into the living room again as Zairn turned on the TV.

"…quite a surprising revelation." A woman in a cocktail dress stood on set with a glitzy banner flashing on the screens behind her. Zairn and Roxie's names faded up with a picture of them at the side, like people wouldn't know who they were.

"Has it been confirmed?" the presenter said. "No, but we have several eyewitnesses…"

Damn. Did this mean Diva had leaked their conversation to the press? Wasn't Knox supposed to be keeping a lid on it?

"And there is footage of a black town car pulling into the alley behind the clinic at the same time these witnesses claim to have seen the couple. We can only assume they're expecting. A surprise given their breakup not so long ago when Roxanne, excuse me, Roxanna, claimed Zairn wanted her 'barefoot and pregnant' and that is a quote. Has the beauty changed her mind for love… or money?"

"Nice. Never miss a chance to bring up the gold digging," Roxie said. "It's not money, it's the sex! Do you have any idea how much experience my Casanova has?"

"This reproductive clinic is one of the best in the country for all kinds of reproductive and fertility needs. I can't imagine they're having fertility issues. If Roxie was so against having children, it can only be an accidental pregnancy."

"This is fun," Roxie said. "It's been a while since we've been in the news."

Yeah, like a whole ten seconds.

Zairn muted the TV. "Do we care?"

"No," Roxie said, opening a hand to him.

He came to take it and sat at her side. "I'm sorry about this." His fingers went into her hair as they curled around the side of her head. "I'm sorry they're invading our privacy again."

"This is our life. I know this is our life. I've told you to stop apologizing. Who cares if they know we were there? Won't that be the evidence you need if the kid asks about its mother? Now you have proof!"

"The kid asks? Are you dying?" Jane asked, full of panic. "Why are we sitting around here? What do you have? We should be at a hospital!" The innocence switched to Zairn. "Why don't you have a team of doctors for her? Don't you love her? Don't you want her to live?"

"If I made the rules, she'd have a team for everything she could ever need. Including a designated charger. But she's not dying. At least, she assures me she's not."

"I'm not deliberately dying," Roxie said. "So the world knows we went to a clinic and thinks I'm pregnant. At least they're saying it's your baby. In six months, when Lilya's pushing out her kid, and I don't even have a bump, they'll get a clue they were wrong. They move on from these things quickly."

"It's the documentary," Kintyre said. "You're hot right now. The paps are watching everywhere you go."

"Oh, we know that. Believe me. It's a damper on my sex life. Now we have to do it at home all the time, and I love having sex in the car." She pushed out her lower lip in dramatic misery. "I can't walk ten feet without someone flashing in my face, and not the good flashing."

Roux smiled. "I don't know if I would be so calm."

"You're never having kids," Rourke interjected. "What are you talking about?"

"She might want kids," Jane said. "People change their minds all the time. Some people think one thing until they're in a situation and then they change their minds."

"Jane wants everyone to have kids," Roxie said, stroking her friend's leg.

"I don't want to have kids," Jane said, drawing everyone's attention. "I don't."

"Says the woman who picked out names before she hit puberty."

"It's about the situation. I don't want kids now, but I want them later."

Situation? Like who you're with? "You don't want kids now because you're with Knox?" she asked.

What kind of father would the Collier be?

Roxie sat back, out of Jane's view, shaking her head like maybe she'd hit a nerve.

"No, because I want to do it right."

"And Knox is doing it wrong?" Rourke asked on a snicker. "Don't worry, dude, I'll draw you a diagram and explain it real slow."

"Who are you kidding?" she asked. "You don't

do anything slow, two-pump chump."

"Yet you get yours every time. I'm irresistible, baby."

"Knox is an amazing lover. The best lover I have ever had," Jane said, raising a defiant chin. "I wouldn't change anything, not a single thing about how we make love. And we've talked about it." About sex or babies? "Yes, we had a sticky moment, and I hurt his feelings. I'll always be sorry about that."

"Blossom, you don't owe anyone anything."

"But we are, aren't we?" Jane asked, her eyes round in innocence. "You said we would have babies one day. Is that still true?"

"Anything you want, Blossom, you get. You know that, baby."

"And if it happens by accident…"

"Nothing happens by accident," Roxie said.

"Oh, yes, it does," Lilya said, a hand on her bump as she went to Kintyre's side to put his on it too. "This kid wasn't planned, he's a sucker punch."

"Good name choice," Rourke said, earning himself a sharp elbow in the ribs.

"Just because we didn't plan him doesn't mean we don't want him." Lilya wasn't offended, she was adamant. "He knew it was the right time and who he wanted his daddy to be. Babies pick their parents, not the other way around."

"Now there's an existential discussion," Rourke said, laying an arm across her shoulders. "Whether we're religious, whether there's a higher power, does karma exist? Are we all on a pre-destined path? Is the future fate or free will? Do we choose, or are we blindly following a path we have no control over?"

"Blindly following a path we have no control over?" she repeated the words. "Yes, I am blindly following a path I have no control over. That's not my fault. It's yours."

"You blame me for everything."

"Only things that are your fault. I had no free will when you made this real world."

"I owned that decision then. I own it now."

"I don't think you're fate. You're arrogant. You have manipulated and contorted everything these past few weeks. We wouldn't be here if it wasn't for your choices."

"You stayed," he said. "I offered you a contract in California. You could've said no."

"And ruin my career?"

"Your career is what you make it. If you didn't want Mosaic and Huddle Hope, and everything that was on offer, you would've turned and ran to find another way. Roux Radley does not need anyone's permission for anything. Might be why she screws up so much."

"I don't screw up," she said, pushing away from his arm to put a few inches between them. "Unless you call falling into bed with you a screw up. Yeah, that maybe was a mistake."

"Haven't we just decided that sometimes the mistakes, the accidents, the unforeseen consequences actually become a blessing we didn't expect?"

"This means the press will camp outside."

That didn't worry Roxie. "No one has anything to hide."

"Except Roux's brush with Diva."

"The cops will leak that anyway; we knew that would happen. Knox can only do so much, and we've got the routine down. They report it, we no comment, and then we change the subject with something juicier."

"You're a pro," Zairn said, beaming with pride.

"Do I ever let these things upset me? It was these things that brought us together. What we are is not their business. They can think what they like, believe what they like, make up whatever they like. Providing you and I know the truth, providing we're on the same page, that's all I care about. You. Us."

"So we're no commenting?"

"Call Salad, he'll figure it out."

"And New York?"

"We have a schedule in place. There's no point putting it off. We'll be asked about it one way or the other."

"Will the Diva thing cause problems?" Roux asked. "If you need me to take responsibility—"

"You did nothing wrong." Roxie didn't let her finish. "No one thinks she did anything wrong, do they?"

The pointed look her friend landed on Rourke spoke for itself.

"Hey, I'm just a bystander," he said, tugging her hair like they were in the schoolyard. "I'm not surprised she got territorial. I told her I'd fuck her either way, but she just can't stand other women wanting me."

"Oh, ha, ha, ha," she mock laughed. "Think of the fortune I'm saving you in hookers. They are the only other ones who'll sleep with you, right?"

"It's getting hot in here again," Lilya said, bobbing her brows at Roxie.

"When the Diva story hits, we'll tell the truth," the nouveau-blonde said.

"The truth?" Zairn asked. "We don't usually do that."

"Trying on a new hat today, Casanova. Does it suit me? The truth diverts the story. Yes, Roux stopped Diva getting into the event and hustled her out before she could get comfortable, but people are more interested in our sex life and your love seed."

"You like saying that."

"I do like saying that." Roxie grinned at her fiancé. "Does anyone have a problem with the plan?"

Zairn raised a hand, then laid his arm across Roxie's legs. "I do. Why am I paying Salad when you do this so well, Lola?"

"I couldn't do it full time, especially with us reserving the mornings for future planning."

A single burst of laughter came from Zairn. "From now on, that's what I'm putting on our calendars."

"Works for me. I have nothing better to do with my mornings, except gold digging. Obviously."

"Will Diva talk to the press?"

"And make herself out to be the innocent victim?"

"Bet on it. Diva laps this shit up," Knox said. "But we can control who leads with the story and who buries it. We're having dinner at the house tonight, Blossom."

"We are?" Jane sat poker straight. "Why didn't you tell me?"

"I just did."

"No! Earlier! Why didn't you tell me before?"

"Because I just decided," he said, typing into his phone.

Zairn squeezed his fiancée's leg. "What about New York?"

"We'll go tomorrow," Roxie said. "That gives Roux a chance to go back to Mosaic and grab what she needs. We'll chopper you down from there."

Chopper her down. This really was a different life.

"What about the others? Helena, Myles, and Johann. Should I bring them?"

"Your team aren't needed for the pitch." Rourke told it straight. "Leave them at Mosaic for the routine stuff. You sell it in New York and come back to find out what you're selling."

"They might not like that."

"I put you in charge." Rourke was stern. "Yours is the face people want to see. This is your job. To head Huddle Hope. To be in charge. You have the ear of the money, that makes you the most valuable. We can replace others."

To get to the top like Rourke and his friends had, being ruthless was a necessity. Sentiment wouldn't get them far.

She'd say that she didn't want to leave anyone behind, but Franco and Guillermo had grabbed opportunities to move on up the ladder in other locations. Huddle Hope meant something to her. Did it mean the same to the others? Maybe this was just a step on the ladder for them too.

"Okay, but I need Mieux."

"The woman doesn't like to sit still for more than five minutes anyway," Zairn said. "She'll be happy to jump states."

"She's always welcome at CollCom," Knox said, smirking at Zairn.

"Hey, we've all tried it. We've tried to pin her down and she won't have it. She's a wanderer."

Rourke had told her the same thing.

"Brooker is lucky to have her. Have you ever sent her to Cam?"

"No," Knox said. "Because I know he'll love her and want to keep her, and she never lets any of us keep her. Then whoever I send next will pale by comparison."

"You don't want to set standards too high," Roxie said. "That's the same criteria I used for my love life. Don't aim too high. Take what you can get. Sevens need love too."

Zairn squeezed her knee again. "Take what you can get anytime, Lola."

A phone rang and Kintyre retrieved it from his

inner pocket. "This should be interesting," he said, flashing the screen at Lilya.

Stroking her bump, Lilya shrugged and explained as he answered. "Reeve Crosby."

"He'll want another exclusive."

"He can want all he wants. It's not happening."

These people pulled together for a common purpose, not because they had to, but because they were family. Maybe not by blood, but in every way that really mattered. And they'd accepted her into their fold. It was an honor. One she didn't take for granted.

THIRTY-TWO

NEW YORK, New York. Already it had been an adventure. Roxie's Crimson tour featured tales and antics of the Crimson crew. Each location meant a new story and, wow, the woman could weave a yarn. Definitely wasn't the standard tour.

It ended in her apartment. Yes, hers. Turned out Zairn had apartments in the building for his closest employees and friends.

She hadn't checked the whole place out. Under time pressure, Roxie's whirlwind, hand-waving explanation of where everything was happened fast. Then her friend disappeared to meet Zairn with the waiting press.

Flopping onto the couch face-first, her arm hung from the edge. Wishing there was someone to bring her wine, she couldn't move and didn't want to. What an exhausting day.

Rourke hadn't seen her off. He'd been busy with Leon and a couple of other guys in the office as she bid farewell to her Hope colleagues. Mieux was the only one who came with her. She needed a change and didn't like to be tied down. Much like her own sister.

On the floor, a few inches from her dangling hand, her purse flashed and made a noise she'd never heard before. Her purse didn't usually flash. Her phone was the only thing in there that might ding that way.

Raising her heavy arm, she dropped it into the purse to rummage around until she found the device. She dug it out and shifted onto her side to check the screen. The whole thing was blacked out with a big red circle in the middle bearing the letter 'X.' Still, it flashed and sounded again. A big red button. Hmm, no prizes for guessing who was responsible for the hijack.

She pressed the circle and spoke before he could. "Still stalking me?"

"Radley!" he said, like he was calling to her at a party. "Miss me yet? Don't answer that. I know you miss me. I heard there was crying and wailing on the plane."

"Uh huh, in your dreams maybe. I'd fire whoever told you that."

"It was Mieux."

"Another thing I don't believe. She's smarter than to share secrets with the likes of you, blabbermouth."

"Vagabond."

"Asshole."

"Don't mind if I do," he said, a smile in his voice.

"Not on your life," she said. "Exit only. You know what happens when you try to get on at an off-ramp?"

"Santa puts you on the naughty list?"

"I remove your ability to penetrate anything ever again. How does that sound, Hotshot?"

"Like a felony."

"Two minutes in a courtroom with you and any judge will take my side. Just like Mieux. She knows the score. I'm the one handing out the schedule and to-do list."

"I'm the one handing out the paychecks. Yours and hers."

"Oh, there's no way you pay me enough for what I do for you. And Brooker pays Mieux. The agency. If you don't settle your account with them, that's your problem, not Mieux's. Roxie likes Mieux too and views of her streams are hitting record high numbers. We'll avail ourselves of that megaphone if you start screwing women over."

"I will screw a woman over anything she chooses, the couch, the desk, the patio table, the upstairs banister. You remember that night?" Oh, he was infuriating, but fuck, he turned her on. "What happens to Huddle Hope if you decimate Mosaic for sport?"

"Mosaic wouldn't go down over a single unpaid contract. But we don't need Mosaic. We're partnered with Lola's Liberty and right now, we're their only beneficiary. We're the only contract they have. Their focus is ours. I feel good about our chances. Johann doesn't like you. He'd be happy to say goodbye to you."

"Johann doesn't like you either."

Fair point. One she couldn't argue with because the doctor butted heads with everyone.

"Franco called me," she said. "While I was in the air. He gave me a video tour of his London pad. Very nice. He invited me to visit in person. I'll need a few vacation days, weeks, maybe. It'll be better to see it up close, personal, you know? Right in there, all the way."

"If you leave the country, they might not let you back in. Scratch that, they won't let you back in. Good luck fighting Homeland on that one. I told you I work with the DOD, didn't I? I know people." He sighed. "The loyal employee is too busy anyway. He has to make a good impression on his new coworkers."

Rolling to her back, she pushed her hair from her forehead. "It didn't escape my notice that the two men you sent overseas were the same two who wanted to shtup me, or I wanted to shtup."

"Gotta pick up that game, Radley. You want it, you've gotta make it happen or it passes you by. And you know me, there's no point in playing with you if you don't see me winning. I like the glory. I bask in the glory. Thank you for noticing."

"Playing with me? You're not winning. You don't know what to do with yourself without me. Are you all sad and lonely, baby?"

"No, I figured you'd need a pick me up. Being so far away from my cock can't be easy on you."

"And you thought hearing your voice would help? Wrong again, Hotshot. It only reminds me you're not here and I really need someone to bring me—"

Her door opened. No knock or call. It just opened, and a server came in with wine on a tray.

The guy laid it out in front of her, filled the glass, then disappeared without a word.

"You were saying?"

"I'm not impressed," she said. "Have you been watching me this whole time? You've probably hacked security."

"I don't need to hack it. We all have access to each other's security," he said. "Though I wouldn't mind a video. There's no camera in the apartment I can access until you open up your laptop, so…"

"Maybe later," she said, stretching as she sat up. "I have wine."

"Want to find a booth?"

She smiled, tucking her feet under her. "Feeling nostalgic?" she asked, and the smile faded. That was a lifetime ago. "Are you home? In your lair?"

"Yeah." He paused. "The walls echo without you

inside them."

And how would she feel that night without him inside her? "Been a while since I've slept alone."

Discomfort prickled, though it was out of place. In New York, her career would fly, especially with Roxie and Zairn's support. This should be a happy time, an exciting time. She'd never been a homebody, never yearned for home. Maybe because she moved to a new apartment so often. New York was exhilarating, but it didn't feel like home. Not that it should after less than a day.

But there was something missing. It missed something. That reality hit her the moment she stepped off the private jet. No amount of pampering and high life could alter or better what she needed most.

"Who says you're sleeping alone?" he asked, his voice a low rumble. "We don't have restrictions anymore, Babycakes. That means you and I don't ever have to hang up."

Sounded good to her.

Being in the new city was for a good cause. She didn't want Rourke to think that she couldn't hack it on her own.

"New York is incredible," she said. "Roxie's been amazing."

"Her girls are important to her. Don't ask why. With the latitude Zairn gives her, the Kyst-meister could have her own army of personal shoppers."

"Not every woman gets her kicks with a credit card."

"Yeah, I know how you get your kicks," he said. "What are you wearing?"

Just like old times again. "That's your trivial?"

"Nothing trivial about it. That information is valuable and if you won't turn on your camera…"

It wasn't that she didn't want to turn on her

camera. If she turned on hers, he'd have to reciprocate.

"Is that a good idea? You already miss me so much; won't it break your heart to see what you can't have?"

"I can have it any time I want it, babe," he said, ignoring her mocking pout. "Your pussy's just waiting for me. I choose not to get on a plane."

"Because you don't want to embarrass yourself. Who needs you? There's a nightclub here in the building. Lots of drunk guys, easy prey. And Roxie's friend Toria knows all the best dating hotspots, where to find the best guys."

"The best guys are here in California. I'm surprised Toria travels so far for a decent date."

"California is okay. If you're loaded and pretty."

"I am," he boasted.

Closing her eyes, she absorbed the intonation of his voice. The seconds ticked by. His breathing synced with hers and she soaked in every moment.

"Tell me something real, Xavie."

"All day I was spacing out," he admitted. "Staring at your desk. Which is stupid because it's been your desk for thirty seconds. You are coming back, right? Otherwise I wasted a heap on the remodel."

"If I don't find some richer, sexier guy with a bigger cock, then yeah, I'm coming back."

"When?"

She smiled because the raw need in that single word told her more than she'd get from a thousand cameras.

"I want your hands on me," she whispered. "I took for granted how you touch me."

The texture of his skin, his warmth, his need. At the time, it was no big deal because it was right there for both of them to enjoy at their leisure.

"We should find a booth."

"We should," she said, getting up.

Roxie said her things were in her bedroom. Sure enough, she found her suitcase and her laptop. She slipped it out to turn it on. Putting the call on speakerphone, she tossed it to the bed.

"Doesn't sound like you want to."

"I want to do something else," she said, stripping. "Put the camera on. Impress me, Hotshot." Loosening her hair, she shook her fingers through it and lay down on the bed, adjusting the angle of the computer as it came to life. "I hate that you do that." That was a flat lie, as her grin attested. It powered up and the camera immediately came on. "I don't miss you. It's late and you're cheaper than escort services."

From the broad view of him in the darkness, she could tell he was using a camera mounted above his wall of screens.

"This is more like it," he said.

"Closer, Xavie." Why should he get such an intimate view of her when hers was from such a distance? "I don't want to be so far from you."

"Shouldn't have got on the plane then, should you? Still pissed I made this real world?"

A flash changed the picture from the distant camera to what she assumed was his tablet. Right there in his lap, where she wished she could be.

"Shut up and get your cock out," she said, licking her fingertips and lowering them to her clit. "Tuck me in, Xavie."

THIRTY-THREE

"ROUX RADLEY, meet Freya Dere," Roxie said, gesturing between them. "You want to get on her good side. She's worth more than the pope."

The elegant woman smiled at Roxie. "I am not richer than the pope."

"Your heart is bigger; we can at least agree on that."

The three of them sat at a small dining table in a dedicated room of Roxie and Zairn's Crimson apartment.

"My grandfather may be richer than the pontiff," Freya said. "That is entirely possible."

Roxie poured coffee from a French press. "Freya is the woman to know when it comes to health causes in this city. In the world, probably."

"My specialty is children's health. I'm not sure how I can help with your cause. It's mental health?"

"Huddle Hope will eventually branch into different specialties. The plan is to get a working model going by the end of the year. We'll start with some test cases, screened by a specialist team.”

“It’s encouraging to know you’re not running into this all guns blazing. When I heard this was under Mosaic, I half expected it to be up and going already. It isn’t like Rourke to sit on his hands. He must have settled down.”

“Settled down?” she asked. “He can barely sit still for five minutes.”

“Roux keeps a steady hand on this,” Roxie said. “Hope is her baby.”

“I can understand that. We care about what we care about.”

“We do.”

“I’d have to see numbers and projections before injecting any cash. And it would be preferable if you had a niche for often neglected children’s mental health. Though childhood trauma carrying into adulthood gets lesser time.” She looked at Roxie. “I suppose coming to me is as much about contacts as it is about money.”

“You got me,” Roxie said, holding up her hands in surrender and distributing the cups.

“You want me to talk to my grandfather?”

“Of everyone who has signed up to support this, you’re more on the ground, at the grass roots of what’s needed. We don’t want to be lofty, puffed-up mustache twirlers. We want to know that what we’re doing isn’t missing the mark. No one knows that better than those dealing with clients like this every day.”

Hearing Roxie’s own passion for the project fired her determination. They were on this; it was happening, and she wasn’t the only one at the helm. When she went back to California, they’d have transcontinental cover. Next, it would be the world.

“It’s true that what I do is more hands on,” Freya said, “as much as it can be. I take what I do seriously.”

“What is that exactly?” she asked, figuring it

wouldn't hurt to have some background. "Are you a doctor? A therapist?"

"No. No. Nothing like that. In my work, I fund a scheme that helps families pay medical bills. Their children's medical bills."

"It's more than that," Roxie said. "You spoil them."

"It could be the way I was brought up, but spoiling means something different to me. I enjoy what I do and enjoy spending time with the kids and their families. It has to be about more than money. Too many arrogant wealthy types toss a billion dollars at something and call it philanthropy."

"Freya gets to know the families she helps. She goes to their homes, cooks for them, spends time with them."

"It's important," Freya said. "Caring isn't paying money. It's paying attention."

"I like that," she said, picking up her cup. "We should put that on bumper stickers."

When Freya smiled, the open sincerity poured from her. "The problem is, it's not something that can be taught. It can be faked, but not taught."

"Not the way you do it," Roxie said.

"How do you know Reid?"

Freya and Roxie made eye contact. "How do I know Reid?" the former asked.

Okay, what was she missing? "Roxie said that Reid and Merci—sorry, I thought you were friends."

Roxie laughed. "They're more than that. Freya used to date K2."

"K2," Freya said, enjoying the moniker. "I haven't heard Loch called by that name in a while."

"The man's a mountain."

Freya nodded. "True."

"And he's the second K in the group. Kintyre

and Kinloch were too much for them to wrap their prepubescent and adolescent brains around. So K2 he is." Roxie leaned a little her way. "They were childhood sweethearts. Freya and K2."

"Until his family figured out I wouldn't be the model daughter-in-law." After a brief pause, the altruist shook her head. "It wasn't like that when we were young, our families were close, but there's five years between us. I guess you could say we grew up together in a lot of ways."

"Both of their families are loaded. They were sort of betrothed."

"We weren't betrothed. That sounds so… archaic."

"I've never met him," she said. "I've heard he's not the most personable."

"His family put a lot of pressure on him. His parents brought two multibillion multinational companies together, and he's an only child. The only chance they had to maintain their empire. It messed with his head. And he never quite knows who to trust. Who had his best interests at heart?"

"That's why he loved you," Roxie said. "You were you, unapologetically. That's what Z says."

"I understood the pressure. Not to the same degree, but my grandfather needed a crutch after we lost my dad, and I was it. Our families just dealt with their situations differently. His mom was most supportive of him being him. Some say her encouragement of his talents and interests outside the company broke up his parents' marriage. Something else that put pressure on him. He's a man who belongs everywhere and nowhere."

"Did he mean you? Is this what Rourke meant when he told me I could use K2's name and he wouldn't care? Did he mean I could use it with you and you'd help us?"

"Loch, K2, cares about things in a different way. One thing he never cared about was status. Still doesn't, even now. Sycophants circle. Everyone wants to be his friend, to know him, to be connected to him. It exhausts him. He couldn't care less about reputation or who's who."

"Is that why he's selling? To get away from the brownnosers and the pressure?" Roxie asked. "The guys know it didn't mean the same to him, but to give it all away…"

"You only live once. I used to tell him that always. Life can be taken any second and when you're alone, you need to love whatever you have left. Life has to be real or there's no point living it at all."

Profound and the woman wasn't blowing smoke. She was right, it couldn't be faked. Freya Dere was the real deal. Genuine in her words and actions, that honesty came from every part of her. From her gaze to her posture and the sincerity of her words. Freya would be a gold star ally, if they could convince her to come aboard.

"Damn, listening to you talk… How are you so wise?"

Roxie laughed. "I know, right?"

"Please, don't. My work is my focus. In every other area, I fail miserably. I talk about this with authority because it's the only thing I know."

"Are you married?"

"No," she said, showing her bare ring finger. "No husband. No kids."

"Have you and K2 been broken up long?"

"Oh, years. It's been…" The woman raised her chin. "We went our separate ways, and he got with the perfect woman."

"You'd think the guys would learn from each other's mistakes."

"Hallie wasn't a mistake. She embraced

everything his parents wanted her to embrace. Everything they wanted him to embrace," Freya said on a sigh. "I suppose we should learn from our friends' mistakes. Not that I have any friends. Not any grown-up ones."

"You have grown-up friends," Roxie said. "You have me and Merci. We come with a whole troupe of girlfriends." Their hostess took Freya's hand but addressed her. "Freya's so crazy rich, and so soft-hearted, that everyone takes advantage of her… until her grandfather runs them out of town. Why don't you get back with K2? He's single."

And the gossip was too tempting to pass up. "What happened to Hallie?"

"He learned his lesson," Roxie said. "His parents loved her."

"They laid his future out before him."

"And it wasn't the one he wanted."

So he did something about it. She could appreciate that clarity. "Sometimes these things come out of nowhere. Like an epiphany. I didn't know I wanted to build something like Huddle Hope until the See It Through opportunity came up. From there it was obvious, it came to me that we can make a difference. Someone needs to try."

"I couldn't agree more," Freya said. "Money only goes so far. That's why I make a point of engaging with as many families as I can. They mean more to me than paying the bills. Some of them, they make space for me. The generosity of people is overwhelming. Often those with less are more giving than those with the most." She smiled at Roxie. "Though not all. Zairn would give his last for you. I'm so happy he found love. After everything he's been through…"

"I'm not going anywhere. I'm Lola for life. And I will find love for all my girls, one way or another."

"Men complicate things. I'm terrible at reading them and get tongue-tied." The sophisticated beauty seemed too elegant to be anything less than composed. "K2, as it turns out, is not a good barometer of all men. If my track record with the opposite sex is any gauge of my future, I'll be single for life."

"That's why we have our work," she said. "All in the name of a good cause."

"I heard you and Rourke were hot and heavy," Freya said. "Aren't you an item?"

"They're a something."

"We do what we want." Was the shrug too glib? "We don't put up a fight. Why should we? We're consenting adults who do what feels good. The world would be a saner place if we all followed our instincts."

"K2 would agree. Xavien's either got you well trained or he's found his perfect match. His matter-of-fact view of the world is enviable. The way his brain works, that linear process… He's too smart for his own good."

"It's got him where he is."

"It has."

"He likes to rule people. To get under their skin and stir them up."

"Or shake them up."

"Roux is tenacious. She handles him better than anyone else. You should see them together, it's fascinating theater."

"With him it's a tragedy, not a comedy," she said. "He spouts some amount of crap. I just put him in his place. Other people are afraid to stand up to him."

"I'm not afraid," Roxie said. "Arguing turns him on. Probably why my guy tells me not to respond."

"It does turn him on."

"Turns you on too," Roxie said with sly delight in her gaze. "You two are hot together. Super hot. I watch you spar for five minutes and tie Zairn to the bed for a week. You shouldn't see them together, Freya. You'll grab the nearest guy." Roxie angled her head. "Maybe that's why my Casanova has stuck so close these past few weeks."

"He sticks close because he loves you," Freya said. "The documentary is incredible. It's a guilty pleasure. It's voyeuristic."

Roxie pointed at her. "That's what watching Roux and Rourke is like."

She didn't want to roll her eyes, but talking about her sex life while the male lead was on the opposite coast frustrated her already tingling libido.

"It's not my fault he's good at it."

"You know, I feel your pain on that," Roxie said. "Even when I want to be pissed at Z, if he turns it on, I'm toast."

"Rub it in, why don't you?" Freya asked with a smile on her face. "I'm the only one sitting here not getting any."

"Z said you were dating some detective."

"That's over. Oh, so, over."

"On to bigger and better things," Roxie said. "Come to the club tonight. The Ruby Room, cocktails, dirty dancers if you want them."

The smile on Freya's face became a laugh. "You are irrepressible, Ms. Kyst."

"Is that a yes?"

"That's a why the hell not."

"Excellent!" Roxie exclaimed. "Party time!"

THIRTY-FOUR

HOTSHOT: You should be working. You shouldn't have time to message me.

FIREFLY: I am working. Unlike you, I can do two things at once.

HOTSHOT: So can I. Sitting at my desk here while wondering what you're wearing.

FIREFLY: Clothes.

HOTSHOT: Funny, I never picture you like that.

FIREFLY: Because you're ruled by your reptile brain.

HOTSHOT: Is that it? I thought I was horny.

FIREFLY: You're that too. You're always that.

HOTSHOT: MAYBE BECAUSE SOMEONE FELL ASLEEP EARLY LAST NIGHT. ONE ROUND ENOUGH FOR YOU NOW? YOU'RE SLOWING DOWN, RADLEY. GOTTA KEEP UP.

FIREFLY: I GOT MINE TWICE. NOT MY FAULT YOU TOOK TOO LONG TO GET UP TO SPEED THE SECOND TIME.

HOTSHOT: THIS IS EXACTLY WHY WE SHOULDN'T HAVE A CONTINENT BETWEEN US. ANYTIME YOU FALL ASLEEP HERE, I JUST HAVE SEX WITH YOU ANYWAY.

FIREFLY: YOU'VE GOT TO STOP WITH ALL THE SENTIMENTAL MUSHINESS, HOTSHOT, YOU'LL MAKE ME BLUSH.

HOTSHOT: I'D MAKE YOU DO MORE THAN THAT IF YOU WERE HERE NOW. TAKE OFF YOUR CLOTHES, I'M SWITCHING TO VIDEO.

FIREFLY: I'M ON A VIDEO CALL WITH SOMEONE ELSE. SUPPOSED TO BE ANYWAY. DON'T THINK YOUR SIT SHORTLIST WOULD APPRECIATE A SHOW.

HOTSHOT: YOU'RE IN THAT SIT THING WITH LEON?

FIREFLY: I'M NOT REALLY IN IT. I'M JUST IN IT. I'M NOT DOING ANYTHING. I DID AN INTRO AND LEON'S BEEN TALKING SINCE. I'M JUST ART ON THE WALL.

HOTSHOT: EVERYONE APPRECIATES NAKED ART.

FIREFLY: MIGHT LIVEN THINGS UP. I'LL GIVE IT ANOTHER FIVE MINUTES THEN "LOSE MY CONNECTION."

HOTSHOT: SHOULD YOU BE TELLING THE BOSS THAT?

FIREFLY: IS THE BOSS HERE? OH! I GET IT. YOU STILL THINK YOU'RE IN CHARGE. HA. FUNNY.

HOTSHOT: I AM IN CHARGE.

FIREFLY: YEAH, AND I'M CELIBATE.

Except she kind of was while Rourke was so far away.

"Ms. Radley!"

Yanked from her conversation, the expectant faces on the screen were all aimed at her. "Yes, sorry."

"If you're busy with something else…"

"Not at all," she said, trying on a modest smile. That was personable, right? No one would know she'd been talking about sex with the man kidding himself that he was in charge. "I'm sorry, was there a question?"

"You're running Huddle Hope," one of the fresh, eager faces asked. They were all grouped together in rows. From her angle, it wasn't immediately obvious which one had spoken. "You pitched it for SIT and now you're running your own department. Your own company within Mosaic."

None of these statements were questions. "I am working hard to bring it to fruition, yes. Me and my team."

"How did you do it?" That voice was female, different from the first. "How did you convince Mr. Rourke to go all in on your idea? Was your pitch amazing?"

"Everyone here pitched well or they wouldn't be here." Was that an obvious diversion? "Your focus has to be your idea. See it as a reality, as a possibility, or you'll never give it the full attention it deserves. Is there anyone here who doesn't believe in their idea?"

Mumbles in the negative trickled then cascaded around the room. Only one of these teams would be successful. Giving it their all would be the only hope of moving on in the process.

"Huddle Hope is the exception," Leon said. "Mr. Rourke has his own interests, his own passions. When a chance to fulfill one of those passions arises, he grabs on with both hands."

A laugh sneaked from her lips. When everyone was on her again, she cleared her throat and straightened her smile. "Yes, absolutely, he's a both hands kinda guy."

What he grabbed varied. Mostly, it was her ass. Sometimes her breasts or her hair, but mostly her ass.

"Do you think that's a possibility for the rest of us?" the same female voice asked. "That maybe if we show him we're committed that he'll give us our own divisions?"

"Mr. Rourke doesn't—"

"Doesn't what?" Rourke asked.

On a collective gasp, everyone fixated on something she couldn't see. The something was obviously their boss.

"I didn't realize you were joining us," Leon said.

"Just wandering by," Rourke said and came into shot, though he walked past, giving her only the rearview. Not bad. "So this is our hope for the future?"

"Would you like to meet everyone?" Leon asked.

"No, I don't care. Only one of them makes it through anyway, right? I don't need to know the failures."

"We were talking about Huddle Hope," the woman said. Only when the speaker squirmed and rose a little higher did she figure out which woman was talking. Young. Blonde. Probably perky. "With Ms. Radley."

Only when the others looked did he feign interest and glance over his shoulder.

"I wasn't lying," she said.

"No, I see you. Why are you spinning your wheels in here when you could be pedaling Huddle Hope?"

"Because someone got me involved. Someone wanted the work off his desk and onto someone else's."

"And this is the result," Rourke said, scanning the new faces. "Interesting. I'm sure all of you will excel. Or not. If you don't, it's not my fault, I didn't pick you."

"Mr—"

"I'm going to need the room," Rourke said, startling everyone, including her.

"You need—"

"Yeah, everyone out, come on." He clapped his hands and gestured to the door. "Everyone leave the room. Now."

The newbies scrambled to gather their things and filter out.

Leon went to Rourke. "Do you need us to—"

"I don't need you to do anything except leave," Rourke said. "All of you means all of you."

He stepped back and Leon chilled, his eyes moving over her as he went out after the others.

Eventually, the door closed.

"That was rude," she said when he touched his watch and the transparent walls became black.

Light flickered on. "I got a call from that place you liked for your mom."

And that was another surprise. "I thought you cleared them out for sex."

"We can do sex in a minute. It's the third one, the fourth one maybe, I don't know. The one with the pool."

"It was a water feature, and they said their

waiting list was astronomical."

"Not anymore. It's done. We're in."

And that narrowed her eyes. "What did you do?"

His lopsided grin was fooling no one. "I did what I do and made it happen."

"You're not the only rich guy around. The waiting list probably includes a lot of wealthy names. We can't be the only people interested. So, I ask again, what did you do?"

He shrugged. "I'm updating their security." The next sentence came out in a rushed mumble. "And building them a new wing." His volume rose again. "You're in, baby. We're in. Show some gratitude, take off your shirt."

"A new wing?" She couldn't believe it. "What does that mean? What will that cost? What if my mom hates it and wants to move after a week?"

"Money is money, it's not what's most important. If she doesn't like it, we'll move her to somewhere she does like. Still a good thing. Their waiting list numbers will drop because they'll get more people into the new wing. It benefits everyone, not just us. You've really got a hard on for this charity stuff, Radley."

"I didn't ask you to—you're seriously building them a new wing?"

"Not with my own bare hands. It'll take some time for the planning to go through. I've already lined up an architect and we get first dibs on choosing a room for your mom in the new place once it's up and running."

"First dibs."

"So now's the time to tell me if you were just being polite. If you don't want this, we'll back out. The contracts aren't signed. I wanted your take on it first."

"I thought you always knew best."

"I do. Just want to see if you better understand that after learning I've done this good thing. Why is your shirt still on?"

They were a team. A duo. A force to be reckoned with. He came across as standoffish or even snobbish to people who didn't know him. When he did things like this, took steps without needing her go, he was far from withdrawn.

"You were rude to the SIT people."

"They'll get over it."

"You didn't make a good first impression."

"Good. They'll come to you and Leon if they need anything. I'll never remember who they are anyway. Take interest in anyone?"

"I was too busy answering your messages. You're a distraction. You should find something else to do with your time."

"I did, and then she moved to New York."

She tsked. "I did not *move* to New York. I'm coming back."

"Still haven't told me when."

"I don't know yet. Rox introduced me to Freya Dere."

"Hey! Frey! How's she doing?"

"Amazing, she's an amazing woman. I don't know that I understand your K2 friend for dumping her."

"It was mutual," he said. "His family didn't make it easy for them to be together and her grandfather wasn't wild about the family putting pressure on her."

"If they loved each other, they would've made it work."

"Yeah," he said. "They did love each other. Still do, I'd bet. But it's not that kind of love anymore; it's not sex and sparks."

"They're friends?"

Which might make sense, except she and Rourke were friends too, and they were all about the sex and the sparks.

"I'll send you into the forest with K2. He'll explain it. I don't know. He's odd anyway, he'd rather commune with nature than chase pussy. He's a crazy guy."

"You don't chase pussy, you just claim the nearest one when the urge takes you."

"Instinct, Babycakes. We're still cavemen at heart. When we want it, we've got to do whatever it takes to get it."

"Whatever it takes? Within the confines of the law."

"Another reason you have to come home," he said. "I don't have to worry about gray areas when your pussy is always available. It is available now too, if I could be bothered getting on a plane."

What a hardship, a private plane, every whim catered for, and he still implied it was effort.

"You haven't stopped taking advantage of my pussy, even with the country between us. Zairn gave me an apartment." Which he knew. "We'd have the place to ourselves."

"I gave you an apartment here. What's wrong with that?"

"Well, your apartments are more like upscale dorm rooms. Zairn gave me a view over Central Park."

"The difference between me and Zairn is, he has his pussy with him and doesn't need yours. You don't need a view here because the drapes can stay closed. You'd be on your back for a week as soon as you got here."

"Only a week? You losing interest?"

"If I was losing interest, I wouldn't be telling you to take your shirt off. Take it off."

"I'm sitting in an office on Roxie's floor in Rouge HQ. I don't think her people would like to watch us having sex."

"We do it in my office."

"Yeah, which you own. You want to explain that to Zairn?"

"I can or…"

He took his phone out and a second later, the surrounding walls went dark.

"How did you do that?" she asked as her lights flickered on.

"I told you we have access. Now, shirt."

"You are going to hell," she said, but started to unbutton. "Is the door locked?"

"Does it matter? You don't care if people know."

"When we're together, but what the hell kind of people have video sex in the middle of the day and in the office?"

Come to think of it, what kind of people did do that? Even while wondering, she opened her shirt.

"People with their priorities straight. Now I know what you meant about being too far away. Distance is a bad thing when it comes to your tits."

"Is this a trade?" she asked, rolling her chair from the table closer to the wall-mounted camera. "I give you a show and you build a wing for my mom?"

"If that's what gets you off," he said, discarding his jacket and grabbing a chair to turn it her way. "Is that what we're doing? Big, bad boss man. Yeah, you want your mom to be safe and close and have the best care available? I want your fingers in your pussy now. Take off your panties."

Going full nude in the office could give someone a real shock. She still didn't know if he'd locked the door. Adrenaline shimmered through her as she gathered up her skirt, taking her butt from the chair just enough to wriggle out of her panties.

"I'm having fun already."

She tossed her underwear toward the camera and he laughed.

"Mine for yours, Boy Scout. Tie off, shirt open, and I want your cock out of your pants."

"Does it have to be in that order?" His deliberately uncomfortable movement curled her lips. The last on the list was begging priority. "Fuck, I want you," he mumbled, unbuckling his belt to free his dick before he got to taking off his tie and loosening a few buttons. "Let me see it, Radley."

"I didn't read this section of my contract," she said, sliding her butt to the edge of her seat, parting her legs further to let her fingers slip through her folds. "Is this standard operating procedure?"

"For us, yes," he said. "I've been thinking about it all day. Your pussy fucking haunts me."

"It is possessed."

His fist tightened around his shaft, working slowly, matching the pace of her fingertips tormenting her clit.

"Yeah, by me. Fuck, baby. I want to be inside. I should be inside—"

"Every minute," she whispered, raising her hips.

Her head went back, and her lips dried, in need of his. "You want me on top, want me riding you hard, gasping, desperate for you?"

"You got me, baby. Fuck, you got me. Right fucking here. You ride fucking hard, but you know I'll put you on your back, slam into you, fuck you hard, empty my balls into that sweet, tight cunt."

"Oh, naughty, Boy Scout. Playing makes you bad."

"You're bad," he said.

The need in his voice was obvious, but her own eyes closed, losing herself in the fantasy like he was really there. Like everything they said was true and happening to her in that vivid moment.

"You do it. You make me bad. All your demands. The way you need to be inside me."

"You make me want you, make me need you. Fuck. Being inside you is the only place I want to be. The way your pussy squeezes my cock. Shit, baby. That noise, that gasp, it's like you're calling to me."

Moving with her own fingers, she sped up, picturing them together. Just like he said. Picturing being beneath him, feeling him everywhere. The heat of their desperate bodies, the panting, sweating, breathing, needing.

"Xavie," she pulled the word in on a breath.

"That's it. Fuck, yeah."

The clench of his teeth, she could hear it in his tone.

How he needed her. How he wanted her.

"Xavie, I—"

A burst of pleasure exploded in her gut, pulling her muscles tight, squeezing like he was there, yet she was empty. Damn, being with him felt good, until it reminded her of the distance between them.

"Shit."

His exclamation was ground out from deep in his throat. She hadn't thought about how he'd finish, where he'd finish, until the haze cleared from her eyes to show him wrapping up some Kleenex.

"This is romantic," she said, pushing her skirt back down.

"You don't have to miss it."

She could have it if she got on a plane. "There's still work to do. I'll be home soon."

"Be good, Radley."

"Not if there's a chance to be bad."

And the line disconnected.

She sighed. Did he need more time to clean up,

or was that all he wanted? Maybe his climax reminded him as it reminded her. They weren't close enough to be everything they had to be. Before him, she had Hotshot, but it wasn't like this. Becoming real world, a part of each other's lives, the draw grew. She didn't just want to be near him. Her core was empty, her gut light. It just didn't feel right. Thank God they wouldn't have to feel like this forever.

THIRTY-FIVE

"MEN ARE COMPLETE idiots," Roxie said, coming into her apartment on Sunday.

"I agree with you." Why was that relevant to the moment? "What did Zairn do now?"

"It's not my guy, it's your guy. He's an idiot."

Another point she wouldn't refute. "I'd ask what he did this time, but I'm not sure I want to know." As she closed the door and turned, the look of confusion on Roxie's face stalled her. "What?"

"There's a party downstairs. For you." Was that the time? "All those contacts we promised to woo for Hope."

"Shit, I'm sorry," she said. "I got caught up in— can you give me a half hour?"

"I thought that's why you were… You didn't hear about Rourke? He didn't call you?"

"Call me about what?" she asked on a laugh. "If he's being idiotic, he won't call me. No, actually, he will because he never thinks he's being idiotic. It's up to me to clue him in."

Roxie was wary. "Okay. Then a half hour it is. Have you tried Gin and It yet? I'll mix some while you get ready."

Except now she was intrigued. "What did Rourke do?"

"This party has to happen tonight if you want me and Zairn there. We're flying across the ocean tomorrow."

How could she forget? She wasn't ducking out on her responsibilities but wouldn't relax and have a good time without knowing what her jerk of a friend had done.

"You have to tell me now. I'll get ready straight after. How can I call and mock him if I don't have the insider information?"

Her blonde friend seemed reluctant, apologetic even. "He thinks he's doing the right thing. It's a man thing. They always want to fix everything. Have you noticed that? Sometimes we just want to talk, want to vent and they take it as some call to arms. The Zs and Knox are all guilty of it. I'm betting Rourkey-Baby is too. You protected him, so he wants to protect you."

And that changed the hue of things. "Protect me from what?"

"She threatened Huddle Hope, and he knows how important it is. To you. There's no way he'd jeopardize something that means so much to you."

Going closer, this was no longer funny. "She who?"

"Her influence isn't the same as ours, but maybe there would be enough… overseas and—"

"Diva," she said, getting there fast. The jerkoff. Her worst fear for him realized, yet anger overcame the insult. "I told him not to see her."

Roxie just sighed. "He's doing what he thinks is right. You can't fault him for that."

Oh, yes, she could. "I'll kill him."

Without another word to Roxie, she swiped her phone from the table she'd been working on and marched into the bedroom to close the door and dial.

"Babycakes, I—"

"Don't you dare," she snapped, pacing like the devil was on her heels. "You're seeing her?" Silence. "Damnit, Rourke. What did I say?"

"You said, 'it's exactly what you would've done if someone showed up to hurt me.' If someone's threatening to hurt you, it's my job to get in front of you."

Why did he insist on being deliberately infuriating? By far, his worst trait. Despite her pacing, frustration still burned within her. This was stupidity. Sheer, ridiculous stupidity. Far worse than he usually displayed, and that was saying something.

"She's doing this on purpose." Her speed picked up. "It's not about me. It's about you. Getting you back. Being in your life. Manipulating you."

"You don't think I know that?" he hissed. "But I don't give a shit. If she spreads lies and whispers in enough ears about you, negatively about you, Huddle Hope could suffer."

"So this is a business decision?"

"I don't answer to you and don't need your permission to do anything. You said that too, and you were right. It's my right to keep my free will."

"And this is what you choose to do with it? To date your ex-girlfriend?"

"It's dinner, not a date."

"Dinner is a date, jackass. Are you going to sleep with her?" More silence. "Shit, Rourke, this is insane, you know that! You're smarter than this."

Even the pleading in her voice couldn't shake him. "I'm smart enough to know that Hope is the real deal. We've worked too hard, you've worked too hard, to throw it away over one meal."

"This doesn't stop at one meal. As soon as she has you, as soon as you agree to one demand, she'll have a list of two hundred more. This doesn't stop with one dinner. Or is it the sex you've signed up for that's driving this? You looking to get laid?"

"If I was looking to get laid, I'd get on a plane."

"Not to here you wouldn't, because if you do this, there won't be anymore easy access for you."

He snickered. "Baby, you can't—"

"I'm not kidding, Rourke." Her sincerity cut his obvious tease short. "No. Doing this is a mistake. Seeing her is a mistake. Opening yourself to that hurt again is a mistake."

"I should just let her drag your name through the mud?"

"Who cares about my name? I'm a nobody. If we have to put Roxie at the head of Hope—"

"I already told you that's not an option."

"It is. I'd rather that than see you kowtowed by Diva because of me. I can work in the background, behind the scenes."

"You need to be up front."

"Why?" she asked. "Why are you hellbent on—"

"I'm the fucking boss, okay? What I say goes and I'm telling you I want you at the forefront of Huddle Hope. No backchat. I make the damn rules."

Pulling rank? She wasn't the only one not kidding around. "Then go to her." Her chest hurt. "Persuade her. Wine her, dine her, screw her, but know that's the end of this, us, whatever it is." She exhaled an unamused laugh and stopped walking. "And you thought you misjudged this when all along it was me. I got this wrong."

"Radley—"

"No, I won't do it. I won't watch you be broken by a woman who almost took your soul the last time. I don't regret what I did at the fundraiser. If I have to quit my job to take responsibility, that's exactly what I'll do. If you go to her now and she sinks her teeth in, you'll resent me for the rest of your life."

And she couldn't wait around while their friendship, which had once held so much value, was reduced to ashes. Diva would do it. *"He'll choose me over you."* Diva, it turned out, was right. She'd been so damn cocky, so damn sure that it was her right to speak for him, to protect him, when she should have stepped aside.

What had her actions caused? His pain. And friends didn't do that to each other.

"Don't blow this up into something it's not," he said. "I'll have dinner with her, we'll talk—"

"Have sex."

"Is that what's juiced your snatch? There is no way I'll have sex with her. I don't want to have sex with her."

"Until you're sitting in your lair with alcohol, reminiscing, and she leans in…"

"No sex, Radley. She was never allowed to hang out in the lair. Not that she'd have wanted to. Entertaining was her thing; she'd always rather be downstairs surrounded by a hundred people than alone with me in my sweats."

"Another reason you shouldn't be doing this. Is that why you throw those parties? Because she wanted them? It's like learned behavior. Stockholm Syndrome." The guy was actually traumatized. "If you know you're incompatible, why open the door again?"

"This is not me opening the door. This is one night. I'm not getting back with her. You don't mean that much to me."

"Stop, this is not funny. You want to joke, and

you want me to quip back so we can fall into us. Except us never was an us if you'd do something like this without talking to me."

"We've both acted on our own before. This is what we are. What we do. We protect each other."

"I got in front of Diva to protect you and it cost me nothing. You get in front of Diva now and she'll never let go. You'll lose everything, who you are, what you love, what you value in life. I can't watch it happen."

"No one's asking you to watch anything. You're in New York."

"But you will call me after, the next day, a week later, and you'll want to tell me what happened. I'll want to know, because I always want to know, but I can't do that to myself. God, it makes me feel sick just imagining it."

Them together in the moonlight. Alone. Intimate. A smile. A touch. And all because she'd got mouthy. She could've handled Diva better, been more personable or calmer, less confrontational. Damn her mood. It got riled so easily and that was a button she needed to ease off more often.

"There's no point fighting about it. It's done. It's happening."

"Tonight?" she asked. "Are you taking her out or eating in?"

"Whichever she prefers."

Of course. "Because she makes the rules." It would be funny if it wasn't so tragic. "She's going to hurt you."

"But she won't hurt you. I accept those odds."

"It doesn't have to be me or you. Stay home. Alone. Please. I'll come home."

"Good. I expect you on a plane within the hour."

Usually, being held to ransom would fire her fury, now it aroused her hope. "And you won't see her?"

"I'll see her, but it'll be done by the time you're back."

"No. You don't go from her to me. Never. I won't be able to do it. You know I can see through the bullshit, right? You'll smile and talk about it like it's no big deal, but I know your voice. I don't even have to see you to know that it will take a toll on you. And you already know that. You don't need me to tell you. Don't do this, Rourke."

"It's done. We made plans."

"Cancel them. Cancel on her."

"Because that will help the situation," he said with sarcasm. "Canceling now will make things worse."

"Things can't get any worse." If she wasn't on the phone, she'd throw up her arms. "This is worse. The worst."

"Trust me, Radley. I know what I'm doing. I know how to handle her."

"Handling her comes with a cost, financial and personal."

"We can argue about this all night, it won't change anything."

"Your mind's made up?"

"Yeah."

"Okay," she said, swallowing to moisten her throat. "Then you won't need me to come home. I'll stay here in New York."

"Permanently?"

"Permanently."

"There's no need to be so damn dramatic, Rad. I'll call you tonight after—"

"Not after anything, I don't want to hear it." Squeezing her eyes closed, she fought to silence her mental narration on how that conversation would go. "There's nothing you can say that will change my mind either. I can't listen to you talk about her again. I can't."

"Okay."

"You want to give this up for her? If our friendship is over, there's no need for you to go through with this dinner. It won't be your place to protect me anymore."

"Then I guess there's nothing stopping me from fucking her."

"I guess not."

"Is that where we're at? An ultimatum?"

She hadn't thought of it that way, but it seemed accurate. "Her or me?"

If he needed it in simple terms, it couldn't get plainer.

"We don't do ultimatums."

"Apparently we do now," she said. "You put the language to it, not me."

"To show you how crazy this is! Shit, baby, nothing has changed since—"

"It has. I misjudged this." She'd thought she held sway with him. Apparently, that was an illusion. "Have your dinner with her, but if you do, we're done."

And her efforts to protect him had been in vain.

"Great, this is really great, Radley. Thanks. Thank you very fucking much."

The line died and she sucked in a breath. Were they done or was that just a fight?

A light knock at the door drew her attention as Roxie poked her head into the room. "You need booze?"

Her feeble smile wasn't genuine, but it was appreciative. "More of it than you have in the building."

Because with no prospect of Rourke calling later, or ever again, she needed to lose herself in something.

THIRTY-SIX

NEW YORK WAS great. She loved New York. It could be home forever, couldn't it? Maybe not. Restricting contact with Rourke meant avoiding him. While they were on opposite sides of the country, that was easy. But could they ever really be done if she lived and hung out with his closest friends?

"Should I quit?"

Mieux looked up from her laptop. Sitting at opposite sides of her desk in Rouge HQ, they'd been working independently for a while.

Until she broke the silence.

"Should you—what? No!"

"I'm mad," she said. Slamming her laptop closed, she shot to her feet. "He's an idiot. I mean completely ridiculous, but that's his right. Right?" Mieux managed a loose nod. She wandered toward the transparent glass wall, then turned to stroll back. "If he wants to be an idiot, then it's my right to exclude us from each other's lives. But if I do, I can't keep working for him." She stopped, appealing again to the assistant. "Do you know how difficult it is not to pick up that phone and dial him now? We'd come across each other in person, eventually, if I keep working for Huddle."

"Don't you have his number?"

"Have what?"

"His phone number."

"Yeah. So?"

"So it doesn't matter if you work for Huddle or not, you could call him anytime."

True. Unless he changed his number. Maybe she should change hers. Get a clean break. Roxie told her something about Zairn blocking her number once, though for a different reason.

Blocking him wouldn't change anything. If Rourke wanted to find her, he would. He'd just hack her computer or her Huddle account. That killed any chance of going back to her old job, if it was even still there.

But Huddle Hope.

She exhaled.

Damnit.

Did she think him getting back with his ex was a good idea? No.

Their friendship wasn't about laying down ultimatums and rules. No friendship should come with restrictions like that.

Fuck. She'd have to apologize and that would not be fun.

Her phone rang.

Damn, was he psychic?

Must be he could sense her shame and annoyance. Probably sent out a unique kind of bat signal to his spidey sense. And, yes, she knew those didn't go together.

"Do you want me to answer it?" Mieux asked.

That would be the coward's way out. And she'd never been a chicken.

"No, I got it," she whined and dragged her feet back to the desk. Except when she picked up the phone, it wasn't Rourke's name on the display. She answered fast. "Mom?"

"Ms. Radley, I'm a nurse from your mother's residential home. There's been an incident."

"An incident? What does that mean? What happened?"

Shit. This wasn't exactly a shock; she'd had calls like it before. But her heart always sped up a little as trepidation crossed her shoulders.

"Your mother had an episode. She's been skipping meds and—"

"I thought you were supposed to watch that."

"She has a new therapist—" the woman sputtered. "In her mania, with her low mood. It's not a good combination."

"What did she do?" she asked, rubbing her forehead. "We'll pay for any damages." We? She. "Please don't lock her up again, she gets—"

"No, Mrs. Radley, I'm sorry. Your mom is in the hospital."

Her hand fell. "The hospital?"

"She locked herself in one of our therapy rooms, cut herself, she's okay, we think she's okay, but she lost a lot of blood. Security had to break through the reinforced—"

"I'll be there as soon as I can," she said, glad her apartment was in the building. Clothes she didn't care about, but her cards, her ID, she'd need them to fly. "I'm across the country right now. It will take me a few hours."

"Your sister is a contact too, but we couldn't get hold of her."

"I'll try." Though her sister could go weeks without turning on her phone. Most of their communication was via email. "She's not the easiest to get hold of. I have to get in the elevator. I'll call from the airport."

She hung up and used her time in the elevator to search for flights.

Her mom needed her and she was far away. That was never supposed to happen. It was on her to be around, to be available. There she was prioritizing Huddle Hope, harping on about the importance of responsibility while neglecting her own family.

It couldn't happen again. Her mom needed her support, the support of family. That's what counted more than anything else.

THIRTY-SEVEN

I, ROUX RADLEY, take full responsibility for the incident that occurred in LA at the Huddle Hope event held in Crimson Los Angeles last weekend.

Yes, it is true that I barred Alaina Havenash from festivities. As we did not invite her to the event, we had to maintain structure and discipline in who was granted admittance. It was not as simple as letting any famous face attend. We handpicked the invitees for their connections to the medical and mental health communities, to charitable work and/or their personal connection to the cause.

To my knowledge, Alaina Havenash has no such connections. Hence why she was not invited in the first place.

Invitees were people we believed could be valuable Huddle Hope members. To help further our reach and expand our horizons.

The event intended to raise awareness and funds, but it was also to show deference to the importance of the cause. We do not pretend to know every aspect of the issue and are happy to take guidance or see others get on board.

I apologize for any upset or inconvenience, but the integrity of Huddle Hope was at the forefront of my actions.

The cause is not about photo ops, it's about caring. Understanding the sheer gravity of the mountain we have to climb is utmost. We need people with us willing to pull for the long-haul.

Huddle Hope needs endurance runners. Who said what to who or how things went down is irrelevant in my opinion. Getting bogged down in these trivialities marginalizes the focus. Our petty grievances should not take precedence over Huddle Hope's aims and intention to help as many people as possible with real, honest to goodness distress and pain.

Once again, I apologize and hope this in no way tarnishes the reputation of the cause so near and dear to my heart.

This will be my final word on the matter. Thank you for taking the time to read this statement.

Time in the air gave her a chance to regroup. Worrying about her mom got her nowhere. With the hospital details saved in her notes, she'd go there first, before anywhere else. But she had to fly across the continent first.

Rourke.

With Roxie and Zairn out of the country, she'd had no update about what happened with Diva the previous night. The ultimatum, just the word, curled her lip. If their friendship was over, she had nothing left to lose. Protecting him from what Diva could put him through would be her last act as his best friend.

If he wanted nothing more to do with her, why shouldn't she set the record straight?

In the airplane bathroom, her cellphone droned in her ear.

The ringing stopped. "Roxie?"

"Why are you whispering?" her friend asked in a similar hush.

"I need Knox Collier's phone number and I need no one to know I asked."

"No one like Rourke?"

"Or Zairn. Anyone. I don't want a debate; I just want to do this."

"Do what?"

"Protect him."

Roxie exhaled. "You're as bad as each other, you know that?"

"I do. Will Knox help me?"

"Of course he will, because Rourke would never forgive him if he denied you anything."

"Thank you."

"Talk slow, but be firm and sure with Knox," Roxie said as her phone pinged, signaling the shared contact. "And, Roux, if he hesitates, just tell him you'll make sure your humiliation eclipses Rourke's."

She squinted. "What does that mean?"

"It doesn't matter," Roxie said on a whisper of a laugh. "He'll know what it means and who it's from. Good luck."

They hung up, and she stared at her phone for a second. Firm but sure? That was definitely in her repertoire. If nothing else, fixing this, taking responsibility for her actions, took away Rourke's ability to blame and resent her as time went on.

If he wanted Diva, he could have her, but it wouldn't be on her head. Not if she could help it.

Calling Knox's number, it rang fifty times before anyone answered. Okay, maybe that was an exaggeration, but it felt like a million.

"Who is this?" came his sharp response on answering.

"Is that any way to answer the phone?"

He exhaled a semi-growl. "Roxie gave you this number?"

Despite the tense situation and what she was heading into, a smile seemed inevitable. "She did, but only because I don't have access to Rourkey-Baby's phone right now."

"God, it's like she's multiplying," he grumbled under his breath.

"Would it be better if I said Jane gave me the number?"

"Better? No, because that would be a lie."

"Yeah, but I'm for role play."

"Roux," he said. "Radley."

"Got it in one. Good job!"

"This bullshit with Diva has—"

"That's why I called you. I've written a statement."

"Good for you. Why do I care?"

This guy didn't shoot the shit. She could respect that. "Because I'd like someone to take notice of it. Someone to publish it. Air it. Whatever."

"You want me to go behind his back?"

"You and I both know him dating Diva is a recipe for disaster. Whatever happens, it will not end well."

"If you could do anything about it—"

"I am doing something about it." Someone knocked on the door behind her, so she twisted to toss a word their way. "Occupied!"

"Where are you?"

"On a plane," she said, reversing to lean on the sink. "Back to my statement."

"What does it say?"

"Give me your email and I'll send it to you. Put this out and he has no excuse. Diva can be as mad at him as she likes, I'll be the bad guy. I'm happy to be the bad guy if it gets her hooks out of him. You don't want your friend to be extorted and blackmailed like this, do you?"

"No. You'd all do much better if you followed Jane's example."

Jane would never put Knox in a vulnerable position. "You're biased." And she loved that. "Jane is a sweetheart. Beautiful, smart—"

"You don't have to sell me on my own girlfriend," he said as her phone chirped. "There. My email. Send it to me."

"And you'll get it out there."

"I don't know until I read it."

"You can't tell him about this either. If you tell him, he'll stop you, and we can't let him. If anyone has to fall on their sword here, it's me. And I'm doing it willingly. You're not forcing me into—"

"I forgot you even existed until you used Roxie's name for Rourke. I couldn't care less about your reputation."

But he cared about Rourke's. "Good," she said. "Read it, put it out. At the very least, you'll make sure my humiliation eclipses Rourke's."

He muttered something that sounded suspiciously like a curse word. "And who said trusting the women on the inside would change our dynamic?"

"Is that a yes?"

"Fine," he said, breathing out again. "But I am not interested in the drama."

Odd given his family's line of work.

Sassing him wouldn't help her case, so she went with agreeable. A novelty. "Nope, no drama for you. Thank you, Knox."

"Thank me by not calling unless Rourke's life is in danger."

She laughed. "You'll be the last guy I call whenever there's drama. Promise."

The line went dead and her eyes closed. One drama down. One more to go… for the day, so far anyway.

THIRTY-EIGHT

FLIGHT OVER, SHE got into the slowest cab in the city. Okay, yeah, maybe it just felt that way, but seriously? What was taking so long?

By the time he stopped, she didn't need to hear the fare. She'd been watching every cent tick up. Tossing a bunch of bills at him, she heaved her hold-all onto her shoulder, along with her purse and laptop. Shit. She hadn't been thinking straight. Did she need her laptop? Right then, all she needed was to get into the hospital. To see her mom.

Running into the closest door, she didn't slow and lurched over the admin desk under her own momentum.

"I need…" Out of breath, her chest tightened. "My mom was brought here from a—"

"Radley."

Somehow, the word cut through all the background noise. She turned toward it and there he was, standing just ten feet away.

Rourke.

Her hands opened; her shoulders dropped. As every muscle loosened, her bags fell to the floor on either side of her. Nothing else existed. There he was. Right there.

She took one step, then another, until she was less than a foot away.

"You're pissed about the—"

"Shut up," she exhaled and grabbed his collar, yanking his mouth down to hers.

He'd come. There. For her. Not for anyone else. Because she couldn't be there soon enough. Her guilt at the distance had pained her, caused her actual pain. The shame, the guilt… Just like that, it was all gone.

His hands squeezed her waist before continuing around to her back until she was in his embrace, tipped back, absorbing the growing heat of his kiss.

Laying a hand on his chest, she eased him back an inch. "You came here."

"You were in New York."

"When? How long have you been here?"

"Since this morning. When I got the call."

Her eyes closed as relief escaped her lips. "Thank God."

"You're not mad?" She could only smile and kiss him again. This time, he tore his lips from hers. "I didn't think you'd want me here."

"Why?" she asked, stroking his cheek. "I was so far and I—"

"I know. She's getting the best care in the private wing and don't give me shit about—"

"I'm sorry." Her apology provoked his frown. "We don't do ultimatums, we don't. And you have the right to love whoever you love. Real and permanent, right?"

Except he didn't seem so sure and drew out his response. "Right."

"Can you take me to see her? We can work us out later, but—"

"You want to see her," he said, holding her at his side until she got her balance again. "Yes, you can see her."

"Let me get my—" except when she turned, there was already a young man holding her things.

Rourke's hand slid around her jaw to bring her focus to his. "You've got nothing to worry about, you hear me?" Intense in a way that wasn't arousal; his certainty touched her clarity. "I'll always take care of you."

And he meant it. She didn't need him to say it, not really. Yes, she'd doubted it in the confusion of Diva, not him, but them. Like she'd come to her senses, it seemed he'd figured it out too. This wasn't a typical friendship. They were soulmates, in the platonic sense of the word. Meant to be, to rely on each other, not for marriage and kids, but for forever.

Roxie and the other girls wouldn't understand it. She wasn't sure she did either. The sex was fun. Amazing. But they'd survive without it. The only thing they wouldn't survive without was each other.

His hand stayed in hers on the ascent and trek to the private wing. A security guard had to buzz them in.

A uniformed nurse hurried over as they approached the central nurses' station.

"Ms. Radley, your mother is doing very well. Her vitals are strong. She's showing excellent recovery. We do plan to keep her in for observation over the next few days. Mr. Rourke has given his permission and promised to cover all expenses.

"We're also bringing in a private psychiatric nurse to be with her twenty-four hours while a dedicated team assesses all of her needs. We'll ensure everything is taken care of."

Hiding her smile, she turned her eyes up to his. "Show off." He just winked. "Can I see her?"

"Your mother?" the nurse asked. "Yes."

"Is she awake?"

The nurse walked backward, gesturing for them to follow. "Yes, well, she's in and out. Don't be distressed to see—"

"The restraints, I know," she said. "I've been through this before."

Her mother would calm down again. They would find a level. Until the next time anyway.

"She's just in here," the nurse said and opened a door for them.

The curtain was pulled around the bed. But she was in there. Her mom.

Just like every other time, she inhaled and held the breath. This time there was no panic. She wasn't even afraid. The calm had everything to do with the man holding her hand. Without looking at him, she raised his knuckles to her lips and brushed them back and forth a few times before kissing them. They'd been at no risk of losing each other. They were each other's default. Forgetting that, even for a second, was idiotic.

"Thank you," she said to the nurse. "Can you give us a minute?"

The nurse nodded and scurried off.

When she tried to go inside, Rourke held back. "I'll give you privacy."

"Yeah, you will," she said, without letting go, "while you're at my side. You don't get to wriggle out of it." He didn't resist again, and they went in together, stopping at the bottom corner of the curtain. "Mom?"

Pushing the curtain back, the sight on the other side didn't surprise her. Slightly reclined, the sheets over her mother's lap hid her hands.

"Roux."

And she was awake. Thank God. One of these times, her mom wouldn't wake up. Whether it was by her own hand or age, her mother would be gone one day. They weren't close. A patchwork of people made up their family. Related by blood, but with little in common.

Going over to sit on the bed, she finger combed her mom's hair from her face. "How are you feeling, Ma?"

"Your boyfriend is very generous."

"Yes, he is," she said and glanced back. "I don't need to introduce you, do I?"

"No, he and I are old friends now."

"Now that's a meeting I'm sorry I missed."

"Xavien said you are working in New York."

"I was, yes."

"New York," her mom said, her chin going to the side as she beamed. "That's the big city, honey. You've made it."

"Thank you, yes. And what about you?" she asked, pushing aside the covers to unfasten the restraint on her bandaged arm. "Why, Momma? Why do you hurt yourself like this?"

Her mother frowned. "We're a number in that place. No one cares. They would've let me die if that assessor person hadn't been there."

"Assessor?"

"For their accreditation," Rourke said, sliding a hand onto her shoulder from behind.

"Rourke, your friend, he says I don't have to go back there."

Twisting, she looked at him over her shoulder for an explanation.

"Didn't we already pick a place closer to us?" he asked.

"Yes, but…"

Fuck. She couldn't swear, her mom didn't like it.

In a manic phase, her mom could make a sailor blush, but when she was coming down again, anything could set her off again.

His brows rose. "But…?"

Sucking her teeth, she surrendered in a whisper. "We have to talk about boundaries."

His expression sharpened. "Have you been talking to Z?"

"I'm getting tired," her mom said, her eyes closing.

"We'll let you sleep, okay?"

"No, stay," her mom said, grabbing for her. "Stay until I'm asleep."

"Okay," she said, bringing her mom's hand to her cheek. "We'll stay. We're here."

THIRTY-NINE

"YOU DIDN'T HAVE to stay," she said as they stepped into the elevator after her mom was asleep. "I appreciate you did, but you didn't have to."

"Oh, whatever, Radley," he said, tossing an arm around her shoulders, using her as an anchor as he swayed over to hit the button. "Why'd you want to talk about boundaries? Where'd I overstep?"

"You didn't overstep anywhere. There is no overstep between us."

"Right, that's what I thought. So what's the problem?"

"You shouldn't do things that make me want to rip your clothes off when you're in faithful mode." Wow, and she'd thought their dynamic wouldn't change? Didn't most of what he said turn her on? "Maybe we should draw up a flowchart. That kiss earlier was probably over the line."

Maybe. Could be. If Diva found out, but lies weren't a sound foundation for a relationship.

"Faithful mode?" Confusion colored his words.

"Who's in faithful mode?"

"Your relationship with Diva might be new, but she's an ex. That means it's basically serious from the get-go. Oh, why am I still educating you, caveman?"

"Why am I with Diva?"

"Screwing a woman like Diva, an ex like Diva, slots you in as boyfriend. Fully committed and faithful boyfriend. Maybe I'll find myself a boy toy. If I have to do all this educating anyway, I might as well have young and eager, right?"

The doors opened and she went to exit, except his hand landed on the frame, blocking her in.

"Diva came to the door last night. I told her to throw anything she wanted at us, we're rock solid and so long as I've got you in my corner, nothing else matters to me more." She blinked. "Then you went and sent out your crazy statement. What the hell do you have on Knox that you got him to—Roxie. It was Roxie, right?" She said nothing. "Diva is not back in my life or my bed, and no, we don't do ultimatums, but so long as we're playing at absolutes, here's one you have to get through your thick skull…" Stooping, his fierce, sure, definite gaze locked onto hers. "The answer to that question will always be you. I pick you. You pick me. We don't do ultimatums because when you're one of the options, I'll always pick you."

He'd always pick her.

Just like she'd always pick him.

That was the trade. The deal. The contract.

Taking her hand, he pulled her out of the elevator and through corridors. They would always pick each other. Whether it ruined him or not. Her or not. He'd always pick her. That wasn't a default position. That was a concrete, no confusion, completely unapologetic stance.

Nothing she could do would ever prompt him to

turn his back. What did that mean? They went out a side door and down a path toward a row of cars parked by a curb.

What did it mean? It meant more than default, friendship, or soulmates. He'd come all this way for her, for her mother. That was how much she meant to him. They were family. Forever family. And he'd given up sex with a supermodel knowing it would upset her.

Shit.

Her eyes widened as it hit her, though she still traipsed along behind him. Would a friend drop everything and run to the mother of another friend?

He'd dropped everything this Labor Day and— Labor Day.

She yanked his hand to stop him. "It's Labor Day."

"So? The car's just over here."

But when he tried to move again, she held him back. "Labor Day when you have a dinner in Washington D.C. You told me that at the conference, way back when, you asked if I wanted to go."

"We're on the wrong side of the country. I think we'll miss dinner now," he said. "I'm sure the President will have a space in his schedule next month if you want to throw on a fancy frock."

Another tug on her arm and they went down the sidewalk.

The President? As in *the* President? Shit. He'd given up dinner at the White House to come babysit her ailing mother. She almost laughed because it was just so… wow.

Lights on a car flashed and he reached to open her door. "Wait," she said, stepping between him and the door before he could open it. "You should say it."

"I should say what?"

Was he really going to stand there and deny it?

She almost felt sorry for him.

"It's nothing to be ashamed of. I should've been stricter with you. I was too kind. Too soft. It was inevitable, I suppose. Just get it off your chest."

"Get what off my chest?"

Inhaling, the breath came out in a brief sigh. "You're in love with me."

"What? Yeah, I love you—"

"No, you fell in love with me. The soppy, sappy way. You're in love with me."

Though he was frowning, he didn't linger. "So what if I am? You're in love with me too."

And as much as she wanted to object, as her parting lips attested, there was nothing to say except, "Huh."

Damn him for being right. They could deny it, but they weren't the denying types. They were who they were and felt what they felt. Neither required an apology.

"What do we do about it?"

"I don't know," she said. "Why would I know?"

"The sappy stuff's a woman's thing. What do we do?"

Being in charge didn't daunt her. She could tease him about being afraid, but this seemed like a logic problem that they had to solve fast.

She opened her hands then brought them together. "We get married. Here, today, do whatever we need to do to make it legal."

"Right. That's what people in love do. The legit thing... Is there like a waiting period?"

She groaned. "Then we stay a day, whatever, we get it done. No muss, no fuss. We do it fast, no party or foo-foo dress, just ink on a page. We're not doing rings or formal announcements; we're just completing the paperwork."

"Cool." Reaching around her, he eased her aside

to open her door then started around the car. Dead center at the hood, he stopped. "There's sex though, right? With the marriage thing."

Holding the top of the door, she rolled her eyes. "Yes, there's sex."

"I don't want some dried-up nag as a wife. Sex is a deal-breaker."

"We'll still have sex. Nothing changes. Everything stays the way it is. Marriage just gives us the right to make medical decisions for each other and I get all your money if you die."

"You'll run it into the ground."

"Mosaic? Oh, definitely. That's what you'll get for dying on me."

When he got walking again, she sat in the car and closed the door as he did the same on his side.

He started the engine. "What about kids?"

"No kids."

"No kids, okay." He tipped his head to make eye contact. "You think marriage is an outdated construct designed to subjugate women. Meant to make them inferior to their husband."

"And you think it's a tired tradition forced on men to drag them down with the weight of a family when really they should be free."

"But we're going to do it anyway?"

"Yep."

"Okay. You're not taking my name."

"Of course I am," she said and grinned. "Only because I want to be Roux Radley-Rourke."

A short, playful laugh left his lips. "Oh, yeah, take my name for sure." For a few seconds, their eyes danced. So simple and straightforward, forever was one thing they could agree on. "Roux Radley-Rourke..." he came over all serious. "I do love you."

She touched his cheek. "I know, baby. How

could you not?"

"Even though you're wrong so regularly. I'll help you work on that."

She smiled. "I love you too." She exhaled faux resignation. "Despite your proclivity for being an arrogant jackass twenty-four seven."

"See, wrong, just like that. Let's face it, no other guy could keep you in line. You need a firm hand, Babycakes."

"And you need an ego check. I'm only doing this to humor you."

"I'm only doing it to subjugate you."

"Forever means forever," she said. "Regardless of your ridiculous ideas. It will take a lifetime to manipulate you into becoming a decent member of society."

"Just decent?"

"I don't have a lot to work with."

He kissed her palm. "We need to renegotiate our original contract."

"Original terms stand."

"Agreed. This official thing is for tax purposes only. The friendship comes first." When his voice went stern like that, she shivered. "Radley?" She nodded. "Good." He gave her back her hand and as she fastened her seatbelt, he put the car in gear. Then nothing happened for a few seconds. "No one has to know about this, right?"

"God, no," she said, strapping herself in. "I'm not telling anyone you're the best I could do."

"Good, that makes it easier to screw around. Married doesn't mean exclusive."

"Are you kidding? I'm already interviewing pool boys."

"I need to get a young, sexy assistant," he said, drawing a breath in through his teeth. "A blonde, I think.

At least a D-cup."

"Good luck with that. We share an office."

"I'll take business trips with her. And you love doing it at the office. Maybe we can share her."

"Maybe."

He winked and got to driving. "Bet it's better when there's a chance of the wife catching you at it."

With a smile, she shook her head. "Oh, Boy Scout, you don't even know how sunk you are."

"I know it, baby," he said, retrieving her hand to put it on the stick shift again. "You never did open your box."

Her present? No, she'd forgotten all about it. "What's inside?"

He flashed her a smile. "Just wait 'til we get home."

EXTENDED
EPILOGUE

ONE

OH, LIKE SHE'D just let that lie. "You have to tell me."

He snickered away to himself in his smugness. "No, I don't."

"We could be up here with my mom for a few days."

"And?"

"And I want to know now."

"I want head."

Another restrained groan. Always with the quick quip. Someone needed to smack this guy upside his head.

"This is serious," she said.

"So am I. Oral for me, answer for you."

"Rourke," she challenged his smirk and prodded him in the ribs. "I'm your wife."

"To-be," he said, raising his arm to give her better access for her poking. "My wife-to-be is impatient."

"Impatient enough to break something important like—" except as she looked around and opened the glovebox, it hit her. "This is a rental." A classy clean one, but a rental nonetheless. She plucked the agreement from the glovebox. "A rental?"

"Yeah, so?"

"So you love driving. Why didn't you bring one of your fancy fast cars?"

"When someone from your family is in a hospital, you haul ass. You get there as fast as you can." Fuck. Fuck. Fuck. How was she supposed to be mad at him now? "Where's the Grand in this town?"

"The Grand hotel?"

"Yeah, the Grand hotel. Where else?" She typed an address into the onboard satnav. "That's not a—"

"It's my apartment."

"Damn, you have an apartment in town. Cool. Free digs."

"Not free to me, I still pay the mortgage."

"Even better, I can freeload."

"It's the first place I ever bought." In her attempt to put down roots. "I did work on that place."

"Marriage is working for me already. You got ID?"

"Yeah, for?"

"Might as well stop at wherever we have to sign up for the paperwork."

"I think there's a waiting period."

"There isn't in California but if we're not planning to be back there any time soon, check the rules here. We're doing it this week. Before I come to my senses or anyone finds out."

"Okay," she said, opening her fingers to take his between them. He glanced her way and winked. Reluctantly, she let go to start reading up on her phone. "You've never been married before, right?"

"No. Once and only once. You're lucky I'm doing this much for you."

"Oh, my hero."

"That's right, Radley. Your alpha."

"If it makes you happy to think that, honey, good for you."

"We're going to be good at this. Marriage. I can tell already."

"A blessing or a curse. Only time will tell."

"It's easy. I'm the husband, I make the money. You're the wife, you make the babies."

"We're not having babies."

"Right," he said. "I'm the husband, I…" He frowned. "Wait, this doesn't seem like a fair division of labor."

"How about I'm the wife, I keep my bikini line trimmed for you."

He side-nodded once. "It's a start."

She went back to looking up things on her phone. "The place is closed until tomorrow."

"Wake someone up, Babycakes, we have cash."

"You can't buy your way around the law," she said, putting her phone back in her purse. "They probably weren't open today anyway. And there's a three-day waiting period. We'll get up and go tomorrow."

"Get up? Like we have work?"

"You can be in the office if you want to be, you ever hear of video calls?"

"You ever hear of morning sex?"

The day had begun on a different coast. With the adrenaline wearing off, tiredness was starting to catch up to her. "We'll have to get up to visit Mom anyway."

"Mom, right. Up early, get the license tomorrow, married on Friday?"

Now they had a plan. For the rest of the week anyway.

"Have you spoken to the facility in California?" she asked. "Are they even ready to accept Mom?"

"One of their people is arriving tomorrow. They

were going to come today, but I told them to put it off for twenty-four hours. I didn't want her overwhelmed."

No one gave him credit for how considerate he could be. Her included.

"Freya envies the way you think," she said, complimenting him by proxy. "She envies your brain."

"Yeah, she always did. They all did." The swagger on his expression was all front. "You've got yourself a catch, Rad."

"Yes, I did, maybe I should shave my legs at least once every couple of weeks for you too. Just to show my dedication and gratitude."

"Stubble, mmm. You know how to get me going, Babycakes."

Goddamnit, she'd missed him. "We need a timeout."

"What did we do wrong? We like being bad."

Except when anything went, there really weren't any rules to break.

"No," she said on an exhale of a laugh. "In a timeout we can say anything we want to say, and it can never be repeated or used against us. By us."

"You're going to tell me you love me, right? Man, I knew it was your life's mission to tie a guy down."

"And you claimed it was your life's mission to never be tied down. Which of us is really the loser right now?"

"Say what you want to say in your timeout. Go on."

Did she trust him? Oh, he'd taunt, but he'd get his share too. "I want us to travel together."

"Travel where? Bali?"

"You're obsessed with Bali. No. Wherever we have to be. Wherever we have to go."

"You missed me this week?" he badgered. "It's okay, we're in our timeout, you can say it."

"Sometimes it's like dating a thirteen-year-old."

"Which you would only know if you had experience dating a thirteen-year-old."

"I do have experience," she said, earning herself a double take. "I used to be thirteen. Didn't you?"

"Okay, where does the timeout begin and end because—"

"Some people have normal conversations without riling and mocking each other."

"Sounds boring."

Anywhere he wasn't was boring.

"No more parties at the house unless they have a function or a reason. And we only invite people we know. Scratch that, people we like."

"Could put a lot of the help out of work," he said.

"Just change the address a little. Dyce is never home, would he know?"

He laughed. "Send a party to his house? I like it. Good call, Radley." He drummed his fingertips on her thigh. "Can't wait 'til he comes home to that. We should send strippers."

"Okay, you're soon to be a married man."

"Doesn't mean no strippers. My old lady's laid-back."

"Your old lady…" she said, leaning closer, "believes in equality. Have all the strippers you want, rubbing themselves all over you. Just know I'll be oiling up my own naked guys the next night, paying for them with your dollars."

"Every man's got to earn a living."

"Glad you think so, baby," she said and patted his shoulder. He took a corner and her hand slid higher until her fingers met his hair. "You know what the hardest part of not being with you is?" His backward nod requested the answer without words. "It's forgetting not everyone is like us. The girls, they think I'm being evasive, I think it winds them up, but… I love being with you. Just being around you. Just… you."

Rather than tease, he reached over to squeeze her thigh. "Not everyone is like us, which is why we don't take this for granted. We never make it more difficult than it has to be. Being with you is easy. Loving you is easy. It's just reality. It's not complicated and I love that. I love you. I say I love you and the next second we make the logical choice of marriage. I'd never be with anyone else. Never do that with anyone else. It's the way it has to work. It has to be that clear cut for me. I didn't think it ever would be and didn't think I wanted it until…"

He glanced her way and their eyes met. On the road, in traffic, she couldn't mount him right there, but it wasn't just sex plaguing her. Hope, adoration, need, desire, he was her everything.

"Okay," she said, closing her eyes and shaking off the moment. "Timeout over. Play on."

"Next round's going to be a doozy. Just you wait."

TWO

SHE UNLOCKED HER apartment and opened the door. He scooped both arms around her shoulders from behind as they entered.

"The famous Radley den. Many a man has fallen here. Oh, no, shit," he said, tightening his embrace. "Men don't come back here, do they?"

"I think you're a man," she said, arching back.

His mouth came lower. "I'll submit to inspection."

She nudged him and eased out of his arms. "Marrying you is a kindness to every other woman out there if that's your idea of a pickup line."

"I just show them my bank balance, don't have to say a word."

"Your bank balance is my bank balance," she said, going to check what alcohol she might have left in the cabinets.

"This place isn't bad," he said, strolling deeper into the apartment, checking the place out.

One long room separated by her bookshelves.

Her desk on the wall by the bedroom door on the right, dining, living room on the left.

"What did you expect?"

"A hovel. Isn't that what spinsters live in? Do you have cats and a caldron stashed somewhere around here?"

"Insulting the woman you intend to marry is one thing. Implying no one would have her insults you. Am I the best you could do, Boy Scout?" Pushing aside the empty cookie jar, she triumphed and grabbed the bottle behind. "Ah ha!"

"What's that?"

"My emergency rum stash," she said, taking off the cap to swig from it.

"Did you really finish these floors yourself? And plaster the walls?"

Something had gone in besides their irritation of each other. Why did he remember every little thing ever? Man, she loved and loathed that about him.

"I filled in little gaps, papered and painted the walls," she said, slipping off her shoes and putting down the bottle to toss her jacket off too. "We poor people have to make our own way in the world, pampered prince."

"Can't mock me for that if you're about to take half my net worth."

"I'll take gross, taxes and expenses come from your half."

After another drink, she got out of her pants and shirt.

"We doing naked dinner tonight? What are we having?"

"Maybe each other," she said, snagging her bottle to round the counter and join him near the desk. "There's nothing in the cabinets to eat." In her defense, she hadn't known they were going to be there. "You'll have to do your provide thing, hunter."

"I'm betting a sushi place around here delivers."

"There's an amazing sushi place a few blocks into town."

"Do they deliver?"

Another swig or two later, she put the bottle on the desk. "I don't know, they're too expensive. I've never eaten there."

"Watch me provide, little woman," he said, retrieving his phone.

The moment it was out of his pocket, she pushed his jacket from his arms and started working on opening his shirt.

When he had a bunch of sushi places listed on his· screen, he turned it to her, and she tapped the one she'd mentioned. As he placed their order, she kissed his chest, trailing her fingertips up and down his torso, feeling, tasting, needing.

Hearing him rhyme off her address stalled her, until she remembered typing it into the car's navigation system. Man, she'd have to keep an eye on that astuteness of his.

"There's a ten-k tip in it for you, if you get it here in twenty minutes," he said into the phone, which she then relieved him of to add…

"Make it thirty. He has some business to deal with first."

Hanging up, she leaned aside to put his phone on the desk.

Snatching her wrist, he yanked her against him. "Business? Business like where's the bedroom?"

She shook her head and twined his arms around her, holding them there as she retreated. "We don't end our night in the bedroom."

"We don't?"

Not there anyway. Continuing on, she took them

to the center of the couch and shoved him and his smugness down.

"Lay down and shut up," she said, going to grab the remote from next to the TV to turn it on.

Raising his legs to the couch, he braced his arms to stay semi-upright. "What are we watching?"

Cuing up the movie was clue enough, though she'd bet he anticipated the choice.

"Nothing," she said, starting the movie and casting the remote aside. "All those times I wished I could shut you up." Skimming one knee across his abdomen, it sank into the couch between his hip and the backrest. "Now you get to do something with that mouth."

That wasn't quoting the movie.

Sliding down until he was lying beneath her, he made short work of freeing her from her bra. "This where you talk to me?"

If he wanted to play, they'd play, but she hadn't dealt all the cards yet. Sinking down, touching her lips to his, she lingered, waiting, giving him a chance to decide. Did he want to mock her or fuck her?

That signal was clear when he snatched a handful of her hair to angle her head and force their mouths closer. A kiss. The beginning in the middle near the end of their single lives. Marriage. It wasn't something she'd craved or expected. Yet with Rourke, it made sense. It just was.

"Xavie," she whispered, trying to take her mouth back.

But he wasn't done and rolled to his side, managing to squash her between him and the back of the couch. "How many times you dream about this?" The deep murmur of his voice closed in around her, holding her as tight as his body. "When we were on Huddle, watching movies…"

"I didn't think we'd ever know each other in real life. This was never supposed to—timeout." Twice in one day, hopefully it wasn't a sign of things to come. "You turned me on, I denied it then, most of the time but, I don't know how I ever lived without you."

The slant of his lips was less smug than normal, and he tucked her hair away from her eyes. "I wanted to meet you. I wanted you. But I had no idea it would be this. No idea you were... We shouldn't have lived without each other, and we won't ever again."

They'd both see to that. Marriage would see to that. Walking away wouldn't be so easy when they had an official signed contract tying them to each other.

"That sounds like a challenge. You want me to run?"

"You tried that in New York, how'd it work out?"

Fair point. "New York is an amazing city," she said to be greeted by a crooked brow. "Okay, yes, it would've been better if we were there together."

"That's the rule now, right?"

"Depends."

"On?"

"If you can scratch my itch before the sushi gets here." Because she needed something else first, something more urgent, and only he could give it. "Timeout over."

"I know how you feel about sushi."

Trying her best to move against him, it wasn't easy to do much arousing while pinned in a corner. "Did you miss me, Hotshot?"

"I haven't decided. I'll tell you after the ink is dry and I've subjugated you."

"Are you afraid, Boy Scout? Worried I might see your vulnerable underbelly?"

"Problem is, around you, that's all I am."

"Stop it," she said, trying her best to push at his body with hers.

"Stop what?"

"Shit, how didn't we see it?" Was there ever a chance they hadn't been meant to be? "You're trying to romance me with that gooey shit. My guy doesn't do mushy." Pushing hard against her, he was thinking dominance, it was in his eyes, but she could only smile. "You want me bad, don't you? Say it. Tell me."

"Not a fucking chance," he said, swooping down to plant his mouth on hers.

Taunting was par for the course, but fuck, it was more now they had forever. Together, they could handle anything.

THREE

LATER, AFTER SEX and sushi, they lay spooned on the couch, her in front of him, the rum bottle on the floor beneath them. *Die Hard* some number or other played, but she wasn't watching. The sensation of his heartbeat on her back matched the rise and fall of his chest. It captivated her. Consumed her. Gave her such peace.

Could be he was asleep. They hadn't said anything for a while. But with the movie on, she'd bet he was paying at least a little attention.

Xavien Rourke. Hotshot. Forever. Like no one else ever forever. Why wasn't she worried? Hesitant? Scared? The truth was, she'd never been more at peace. Just like he'd said about ultimatums, it wasn't even a question. She didn't have to wonder. Xavien Rourke was the half of her she'd never known was missing. The only person, object, presence she needed to make sense of the world.

"What if we did get pregnant," she said, resting her hands on his forearms. "If I did want to have a baby."

"Hmm," he said like he might've been dozing, then cleared his throat. "Then have the kid, won't make any difference to me. Raising kids is women's work." He kissed her head. "Whatever makes you happy, Babycakes."

And then because she liked to look at an issue from all angles. "What if I wanted to abort it? If we got pregnant and I didn't want to have it."

In the silence, she couldn't see his face or hear his voice. Her avenues for reading him were too limited. After he had way more time to process than he needed, she shifted onto her back to look at him.

First thing he did was kiss her forehead. "You want to give it up, give it up."

"Really?"

All the times he said chauvinistic bullcrap, she assumed him playing a misogynistic dick was just a role. A comedic, ridiculous role. But they were in it now, headed for forever with vows and contracts, the full deal. The politics could matter one day.

"Yeah."

"Rourke, are you—"

"Pro-life, pro-choice, I'm pro whatever the situation requires. Do I think women, or couples, should use abortion as a form of birth control? No, I don't. It disgusts me actually. But do I think abortion should be freely available to all? Yes. You know why? Because it's not up to one person to tell another person what they can and can't, should and shouldn't, do with their body. I'm free sanity, free speech, and free do whatever the fuck you want providing it's not hurting anyone else. Allowing a woman the right to choose is the way I'm sure I get to keep my rights to my body. Creating laws against that is a damn slippery slope and who says stop? I should be allowed to choose or refuse surgery, amputation, a vasectomy, any and all medical care. I should be allowed to decide if I shave my head or tattoo my body.

"You should be allowed to share your body with anyone you choose because it's none of my damn business what you do in the privacy of your own home. Maintaining your rights, maintains mine. Just because it's not a choice I'd make doesn't mean it's one that shouldn't be available to others. Choice. Without choice, there's no freedom and that's something everyone should fight for. Autonomy over our bodies is the most fundamental of human rights. What's more basic than that?"

And if she wasn't already sort of engaged to him, she'd have dragged him down the aisle after that speech. "You're pro-choice," she said, sort of in a tease, but in wonder too.

"I'm pro-Radley," he said and kissed her forehead again. "I'm pro-Radley-Rourke. Under no circumstances should you be making decisions about our imaginary child's future alone. I would be pissed if you went behind my back with something like that, with anything."

"Sometimes women feel they can't discuss these things with their judgmental husbands," she said, squeezing her fingers between his. "But I could talk to my best friend about it. I can talk to him about anything."

"Is he hot?"

"He likes to think so. And if you're going to be my husband, I think it's a little bit your business who I do in the privacy of my own home. What if we double book?"

"The more the merrier. We double book they can screw each other while we debate who booked first."

"Okay," she said. "But you know that ends with us fucking it out."

"Only way we'll ever solve an argument is fucking it out."

"Thank God we're on the same page about that." But when he bowed to kiss her forehead again, she shifted back a few inches. "What do you want?"

"Wouldn't say no to a blowjob."

"Kids," she said almost groaning at him. "Do you want kids?"

"I've got more than a few buddies lined up for the aisle," he said. "Their women are baby crazy; we'll have enough kids in our lives one way or the other."

"That doesn't answer the question. Do you want kids of your own?"

"You don't want kids and I want you."

"Still not an answer."

When he tried to kiss her head again, she withdrew further until it was easier just to find her feet and get up.

"Radley—"

"Do you want babies?"

"This is a non winner for me."

"What does that mean?"

"I say I want kids, you'll jump back into your cave and hide. I say I don't and if you decide you do one day, same outcome."

"Since when have we had to agree on anything? And what are you talking about my cave?"

"You hid behind the screen," he said, sitting up in the middle of the couch. "We've been here six hours and you haven't shown me the bedroom. I'm getting a dicey message, Radley."

And as her lips tried to twist, she subdued them and held up her hands. "You want to see the bedroom?" She raised an arm. "Knock yourself out, Hotshot."

"I don't care about the bedroom."

"You just said—"

"It's the symbolism."

"Oh, the symbolism?"

"Yeah," he said, pouncing to the front of the couch. "You were in my private space within ten minutes of being in my house."

"Oh my God," she said to herself and unbuttoned the shirt she wore, his shirt. "You want to be in my private space."

"Sex? That's your argument."

"You love it when I make things about sex," she said, climbing onto him, forcing him to lay against the backrest. "Now…" Laying her hands on his cheeks, she kissed the line between his brows. "Grab my boobs."

"What?"

"Just do it." And he didn't need to be told again. When she was firm in his fondling hold, she arched deeper into the caress. "Do they feel like Diva's?"

His scowl deepened as his hands stilled. "Are you kidding me?"

"I am not one of your delicate supermodels," she said, getting her face closer to his. "You and I will spend the rest of our lives coming at things from opposite angles. We're contrary people and love to disagree."

"Having kids is not some bullshit foreplay fight."

"No. But my needs are not more important than yours. Diva taught you different and I want you to forget all of that. We are equals. Completely. Which means if you want kids, it's the circle of friendship. If you want something, it's our job to figure it out. If I want something, it's our job to figure it out. If you want to have children, they don't have to grow in my body. We can adopt or find a surrogate. If you had a child, now, from your past, it wouldn't change how I feel about you. This is not all or nothing, Boy Scout. It doesn't have to be one of us happy at the expense of the other. So if you want kids, let's talk about it. I'm the first to admit, I don't know everything. Maybe I do want kids, it's just never been a reality, never been a possibility."

His deadpan yet arrogant expression betrayed he didn't believe her. "You, in your life, would never admit you don't know everything."

And her sincerity gave way to a laugh. "I know more than you. All day long."

Grabbing her ass, he squeezed hard, shoving his erection up against her. "I don't want kids today or tomorrow, that's as much as I'm sure of."

"Always the forward planner."

She whooped as he surged to his feet, lifting her with him. "I'm planning my way into your bedroom."

"Our bedroom," she said and kissed him quick. "It doesn't have a bar."

Technically, neither did his. The bar was in his secret lair.

"Long as it has free pussy access, we're good."

Good. Yes, they were. They couldn't be more different or more exactly the same. It shouldn't work, but it did. The world didn't understand it. Who the hell cared about the world?

FOUR

"WE'LL BE BACK later today, Leon," she said to speakerphone, tossing an empty rum bottle into the open trash bag next to her.

"The SIT candidates are growing restless and we're running out of time-wasting tasks."

Those left at Mosaic had been vamping all week. No, it wasn't fair, and yes, sex had been high on her and Rourke's priority list, but it wasn't like abandoning their colleagues was frivolous.

Her mom was recovering in hospital and would be released to their care later. Rourke had a jet waiting to take them home where they planned to settle her mom into her new facility.

"We'll be back later today," she said again, opening the icebox to empty it. Everything they'd accumulated in the last five days would have to go. "I swear it. We'll come to the office before we go home." Though it would likely be late. "If you're still around, we'll make a plan."

"According to Rourke's schedule, he's in LA

tomorrow."

"He is?" she asked, pausing in her clear out. Tipping her head back, she hollered, "Hotshot!"

Only a couple of seconds went by before, "You holler at me like that, I think—hey, love the outfit."

It consisted of panties and nothing else. She'd showered first, so should probably be ready. But he came around the breakfast bar dressed, fastening his watch onto his wrist.

She nodded at the connected phone on the counter. "Tell Leon we'll be back later."

Idiot was preoccupied by the tits he'd played with all week and didn't even look at the device.

"We'll be back later," he said, picking up her wrists to twine her arms around his waist. "We've got time."

"Why are you in LA tomorrow?"

"I'm not in LA—is it Saturday tomorrow?"

Yes. Shouldn't he know that given the day's agenda? "Yes."

"Kintyre."

"What about him?"

"We're having dinner with him and Lilya."

Worry drew her upper body back from his. "Is something wrong?"

"Double date."

Right, uh huh, sure. "I thought we weren't telling people."

His eyes widened in innocence. "I said nothing."

"But you're planning to."

"Did I say that?"

"You don't care about double dates. You don't even care about single dates. You care about getting your hole."

"First time I've heard you complain about it."

"Then you haven't been listening," she said,

wriggling out of his arms. "What's the point in talking about something if you're just going to do whatever you want anyway?"

He opened his hands at his sides. "I said nothing."

His new favorite phrase.

"Why dinner?"

"Why not?" he asked. "Rox is in New York. Jane is in New York. You've gone through all this shit with your mom and I'm not the most sympathetic guy. Lilya's right there, why not talk about it with friends?"

Who also happened to be two of the most caring people she'd ever met in her whole life.

As much as she didn't want to, she exhaled in surrender. "Fine. Dinner. We'll have to settle my mom tonight, so we'll be in the neighborhood. That means we can meet Leon."

"For what?"

"The SIT candidates have been twiddling their thumbs all week."

"They need direction," Leon piped up. "And need to be observed by all decision makers. Interviews must take place in front of the entire panel."

"Radley gets a sense for these things. You do your thing, follow the program, make your own decisions, but tell Radley nothing. Don't report to her. When we're back, she'll meet with every team individually and draw her own conclusions. No one will say no to that."

The candidates wouldn't say no to anything if they wanted the gig.

"They have been especially interested in Ms. Radley," Leon conceded.

"Because I'm gorgeous and admirable?"

"Because you sailed through and skipped all the steps. You have the ear of the king."

Good thing they weren't on video call.

She stepped closer to slide her hand down Rourke's fly, stroking him through his slacks. "I have a lot more of him than that, Leon."

Rourke's laugh wasn't far from his words. "Okay, decision made. Go away, Leon. Leave me and my woman be." He stabbed at the phone to disconnect the call. "We're getting married today."

"I remember," she said, opening the last cabinet to see nothing but dry goods. They should keep, they'd be back eventually. Unless… "Are we selling this place? How often would we visit?"

"It's your call. I cleared the mortgage when you were in the shower yesterday."

Of course he did. "Without asking me?"

"What do you care? It's just money. I didn't transfer ownership."

"You actually called my bank to—"

"I called my guy, it's done."

Why did it seem he had a guy for everything?

"It might not be a bad thing to have a private space to escape to."

In spite of dealing with her mother's issues, the week hadn't been all bad. She and Rourke had time to just be together. Though it might surprise many, they hadn't actually come to blows.

"Are we getting married in Vegas?" he asked, interrupting her pondering.

"What?"

"The get-up," he said, eyeing her body again. "Figure anything goes in Vegas, not so sure about around here. Am I overdressed? Is it underwear only? Damn, I wish I'd got the memo."

"My dress is in the closet," she said. "I didn't want to get it dirty. Wearing white to clean the kitchen is asking for trouble."

"White? You're wearing white?"

And that was exactly the reaction she expected.

Thus, she grinned. "Brides wear white. What's wrong with following tradition?"

"Virgin brides and you don't give a shit about tradition. You're not even an hour old virgin, we did it before you got in the shower. You've been virginal for what? Maybe forty minutes."

"It's something. And it'll be at least two hours by the time we get there. Are you calling me loose? Cheap? Slutty?"

"Now you're just reciting my list of reasons to marry you. Stay as you are, I love it. I do. Just put a coat on, let's get married before you get arrested."

"After's okay?"

He gestured around the apartment. "After, if you're in the slammer, I get all this."

"Because you're so in need of a place to stay. You're using me for my apartment."

"I've got to get something out of the deal. The sex is getting old."

"Old? Is it? Then you won't mind if we spend all night in the office."

"Yeah, what was that about? Agreeing to spend our wedding night with Leon. Something you're not telling me?"

Huh, she hadn't thought of it that way. Wedding night.

She slapped a hand onto his chest to pat him a couple of times. "Hope you've got some moves left to impress me, Hotshot. I'd hate to have to tell the girls you flopped on our first big night of commitment."

Funny thinking of it that way. They'd never spoken of being exclusive, of being boyfriend, girlfriend. Never spoken about fidelity or not being with others or living together, not as a discussion with reasoned choices and sensible thought processes.

They were going from fuck buddies—at a push, friends with benefits—to man and wife.

"I'm going to wash my hands and put my dress on. Take out the trash. We won't be back here after."

His brows rose. "Take out the trash? Seriously?"

"It's a dirty husband job."

"I will be all kinds of dirty husband for you all day long, don't know what that has to do with trash."

In a final word, she prodded his chest before flouncing off. "It's a husband's duty."

"I don't even take the trash out in my own house," he called after her.

"There's a door at the end of the hall, says 'trash' on it, you can't miss it. Even you can't screw this up, Hotshot."

"Maybe I should call someone to pick it up. Now I get why the other guys travel with assistants."

"Call your fictional D-cup blonde, maybe she'll break a nail for you."

He grumbled, but when she glanced back from the bedroom doorway, he was stooped tying the garbage bag.

He'd welcomed her into his world, now he was getting a taste of hers.

FIVE

WEDDING. Marriage.

Formal labels that didn't quite fit their relationship.

Yet they did help her and Rourke figure out where the hell they were supposed to be in the courthouse. Choosing to do this thing in front of a judge was more them than any other option.

As they stood there, ready to get it done, said judge asked an interesting question.

"Have you written your own vows?"

Vows. Huh.

"Vows?" Rourke asked, sucking his lips and bobbing his brows at her. "Uh… yeah. We've done that. Are they compulsory?"

"We don't have to," she said. "We don't have to say anything. Filing the paperwork is what's important."

"No, hey, we can do this," he said, admiring the plunge of her cowl neck dress for the fiftieth time.

Her soon-to-be husband was only trying to rile her, probably the judge too, he'd noticed a couple of times himself. Maybe it helped that Rourke knew there was no bra underneath. Maybe he was thinking about the kitchen and Leon's call.

"It's—"

"No. Vows. We can do vows." Rather than take her hands or caress her face as other men in his position might, he landed his hands on her shoulders and bent his knees to stoop closer to her level. "I choose you. Simple as that. It's us. That's it. You and me. Over everything and everyone else. There's nothing without you, Radley."

"Damnit," she murmured.

She couldn't swoon but did bite the inside corner of her lip. Even in simplicity the guy went one better.

He returned to full height, his hands falling loose at his sides. "Your turn."

"Vows," she muttered under her breath. "You're an arrogant asshole who—" She paused to make eye contact with the judge, "am I allowed to curse?" The judge looked at the guy to his left, who shrugged. Obviously it wasn't a frequent request. "Okay, I'll call him a jerk instead. You're an arrogant jerk, but you're my arrogant jerk and you will always be my arrogant jerk. Love it or loathe it, happy or sad, there's nothing without you, Xavie."

He scooped a hand around the back of her head and pulled her close to kiss her hairline. Yes, they were unconventional, but at least they wouldn't be forgotten in a hurry.

The rings part was out because they wouldn't be wearing them, so the judge went straight to, "you may kiss the bride."

Except Rourke had just done that.

She turned toward the paperwork when Rourke grabbed her wrist to yank her back, swooping her down in a dramatic dip to plant his mouth on hers. Idiot. Anything for a kiss. Over the top. Flashy. Bold.

Ridiculous and melodramatic. But she swooned all over again. He'd found the perfect kiss that suited them for such a moment.

When he brought her back to her feet, she smacked his chest but laughed at him. "You wrinkled my dress."

"I'll do worse to it later," he said and smacked her ass. "Another vow. Now where do I sign my name? We've come all this way, no point falling at the final hurdle."

After what was probably the quickest wedding in history, they tumbled into the back of a limo bound for the hospital where her mom waited.

Sitting side by side, silence reigned. Rourke opened his hand, offering his flat palm like he had on the bench the day they met. She slapped hers onto it, twining their fingers together as his knuckles fell to his leg.

"How do you feel?"

"You mean do I feel different?" she asked. "Now that I'm your ball and chain? Not as different as I thought I would."

"We should grab Mom and go home."

"Damn, that's right, my mom will be on the plane."

"Why? What were you thinking?" he asked.

"Nothing that smile hopes," she said though it wasn't at all true. "Okay, the truth is, I only married you to join the mile high club. Can we annul this quickly?"

"You know you don't have to be married to have sex, right? We'll do it on the way to LA."

"In a helicopter?"

"Hey, you said try new things or surprise me or something whatever."

And it worked for him that her curiosity was working. "Do you think anyone ever did it in a helicopter?"

"Someone somewhere at some time, probably. It would be easier if it was on the ground."

"Well, obviously," she said. "We've got land, we can hire one."

"I love how our marriage is going so far. Start as we mean to go on. Prioritizing sex over everything else, over family, over friends, business…"

She kicked off her shoes. "We could do it now, get it out of the way."

"Cool."

He leaned forward to take off his jacket and she undid a couple of his shirt buttons, not that it was necessary. As she wriggled out of her panties, he opened his fly, and she leaped on to straddle him.

Just as flesh met flesh, she tensed. "Wait," she said, grabbing his shoulders. "Are we allowed to do this?"

"More allowed than we were this morning, living in sin. Worst is we don't get our deposit back, but we're not the first two people to screw in the back of a rented limo. I can loop Zairn in on speakerphone if you need him to talk you through the logistics. He's always at it, if you believe the stories."

"My mom will be in here with her nurse person soon. Isn't the first time supposed to be special?"

He snorted and with cause, since when did they care about special? "The wife thing's really gone to your head. Our first time was at home."

She shoved his shoulder. "Our first time as a married couple. You're ruining the mood."

"You brought up your mom!"

"Fine, let's just stop talking. No talking. Forget about it."

Instead of climbing off his lap, like he might have anticipated, she snatched his cock and speared herself to his hilt.

"Shit, Rad," he said, grabbing her hips.

She rocked. "Isn't this what you wanted?"

He smiled and skimmed his hands up over her breasts to ease down the spaghetti straps of her dress. No bra bonus. He remembered. And that bonus got her moving up and down.

Fondling her breasts, he seemed so happy, so content. "I'm still thinking about your mom."

Her momentum died in an instant. "Seriously?"

"I'm kidding," he said, all innocence. "I'm kidding, Rad." Squeezing her, he bowed to kiss each of her breasts. "Why would I think of your mom? That would be wrong. So wrong. Your sister on the other hand—"

"Okay, you know what? Now we are forgetting it."

Before she could get up, he strengthened his hold and thrust up, working her from beneath. "You remember? I choose you? I saw, that got you."

"It was corny."

"Nah, you loved it. You love that mushy shit. Just like every other princess out there."

Grabbing the open edges of his shirt in each fist to pull tight, she decided his mouth needed to be occupied. Their hips moved, rolling and undulating against each other as the depth of their kiss ebbed and flowed.

Being in love with him was so much easier when he wasn't talking. He'd probably say exactly the same about her. The longer their kiss, the faster their movement until their mouths simply rested on each other, lips to skin, need to want, lust to forever.

"Xavie," she whimpered his name, tilting her pelvis to increase the friction on her clit as she raced closer to the summit they both sought.

In his own urgency, he pumped harder, faster,

until propelling himself up one more time, he shoved her over the peak, grabbing hold at the last second to go right along with her.

She paused. Her tight muscles needed time to relax against him until she rested her head on his shoulder, burying her face in the side of his neck.

"Not a bad start," he panted, kissing her hair.

"Not bad at all."

SIX

LA.

Funny that not so long ago, it seemed like a distant, foreign land. Not in geography maybe, but in lifestyle choice. Now she left the private chopper to enter the chauffeur driven car only to down the champagne poured by her billionaire husband.

Business as usual.

Getting anywhere in LA took an age. That was why sticking to the same circuit was a good idea, but they had to get to the house first. Hours and hours passed in the car. Okay, maybe not hours, but it was a long time.

She drummed her fingers on the seat. "We should have sex."

"Just for something to do?" Rourke asked, typing into his phone, smirk at full tilt. "Am I a piece of meat to you?"

"A piece of meat and your wallet, yeah. Is there more to you than that?"

"Don't you have Hope copy to write or something?"

"Oh, yeah, right, I'm the one they'd call to welcome people to our program. Here it is! What you've all been waiting for…" she announced like a ringmaster then went deadpan, "like it or lump it."

"Well, honey, that's why we hire people to tweak these things. I love it. As your husband, it's my duty to love everything that comes out of your mouth."

"No, you love everything you put into my mouth," she said, patting his groin. "This takes much longer, I'll be asking you to put it in there just for something to pass the time."

"Uh…" Rourke said, shifting in his seat to shout forward. "If you could take the scenic route—"

"Ignore him," she said, grabbing his arm to pull him back. "The faster we can get there, the better, sir."

She hit the button to raise the privacy screen just before her husband coiled an arm around her to pull her back against him.

"Everything's going good, Babycakes, don't stress out. Your mom loves her new place. SIT is at the office waiting for you, Hope is taking flight. We had an excellent wedding night. Why are you so tense?"

"Because we just spent the last week shirking our responsibilities, staying up late, making out—"

"I preferred the fucking."

"No one doubts what you prefer, Mr. Meatstick."

"Another name for Kintyre to throw in the hopper for the baby," he said, but she didn't appreciate the joke. "So what? You want to go back to the making out or it's taken your momentum? You're all about the momentum, Babycakes."

"We need a vacation. Like regular vacations. We'll get the SIT stuff and Hope under control then it's you and me on the beach."

"Pacific or Atlantic? I can give you either."

"You mean your friends can. Why don't we have an island? Are we inferior to them? Shit, and you said Dyce was single too, I knew I should've met him."

"That guy will be uncle to our never-come-to-pass kids."

"The alternative is Zairn, won't he be an uncle too?"

"As it is, Radley, we do own our own slice of heaven on the Crimson Isle, we ponied up for the Huddle Hut."

She wrinkled her nose. "Doesn't exactly sound flashy."

"How flashy you need? Naked sunbathing does me."

"Okay, but I'm bringing my pool boy. The vacation can wait until I've hired and broken him in. And I want to check out Dyce's island too. Then I'll decide if we're having an affair."

"Of course. Now where are we on the…"

The car slowed to turn onto a driveway. Aww, their destination.

"Guess oral has to wait," she said, climbing out of the car to head up the path to the front door.

Lilya and Kintyre welcomed them in with hugs, kisses, and… Knox.

"What are you doing here?" Rourke asked his friend who appeared from the kitchen.

"I thought Jane was in New York."

"Don't remind me," Knox said and shook his friend's hand in greeting.

It surprised her that he ducked to kiss her cheek, especially given their last conversation. Maybe it was just a façade, their public face in front of others. The guy didn't like her much.

"Are you having an affair with Knox too?" Rourke asked her. "That how you got him to publish your craziness?"

"I would if he wasn't so dedicated to Jane. Woman's got him good."

"Yes, she does," Knox said, a frown lowering his brow as his attention drifted toward a muted, wall-mounted TV.

"Does anyone want to—"

"Amour," Kintyre said, putting an arm around Lilya to switch her angle so she could see the TV too.

The volume came on. Someone must have found the remote.

A hot guy, very hot, approached a podium as flashes went all around. "My child is missing," he said. "Abducted. And whatever it takes, I will get my baby back."

"Kids?" Rourke asked, appealing to Kintyre. "Since when has Jamison Dawes had kids?"

"Oh my God," Lilya gasped, searching the middle distance. "It's impossible for anyone who doesn't have children to understand. There's nothing more important than our family. Kids! He has kids!" Her focus snapped to Kintyre. "This is why he backed out for us." Her hand rose to her belly. "He gave up the Gramercy deal for our baby because his own children… I have to call Roxie. We have to get up there."

Lilya rushed out of the room with Kintyre on her heels. Knox was already on the phone, walking out to the patio.

"You know him? Jamison Dawes?" she asked Rourke. "He's your friend."

"Acquaintance," he said. "But he did a solid for Lilya not long back. Gauge will want in on this too."

"Because…?"

"They clash a lot, him and Jamison. They're in the same trade and go after the same meat."

"They don't like each other? I don't think this

Dawes wants enemies around him now."

"Babycakes," he said, squeezing her shoulder. "There's a thin line between friends and enemies. Of everyone out there, I'd think you'd know that best."

But this was in a different league. The man had lost his child. The child had been stolen away. Another reason not to have kids. Even without her own, it was clear their vulnerability consumed their parents.

Sliding her arms around her new husband, she closed her eyes as he held her. Only one thing in her life came first. One man. No one would ever take him from her, of that she was absolutely certain. There was nothing without them.

Read more from the Roxiverse in
Nothing to This Prequel:
One Wild Night...

Thank you for reading this tale!
If you can, please take the time to review.

~

Ask your local library for more Scarlett Finn
novels!

~

For all things Scarlett Finn
check out:

www.scarlettfinn.com

Next in the Roxiverse:

SCARLETT FINN